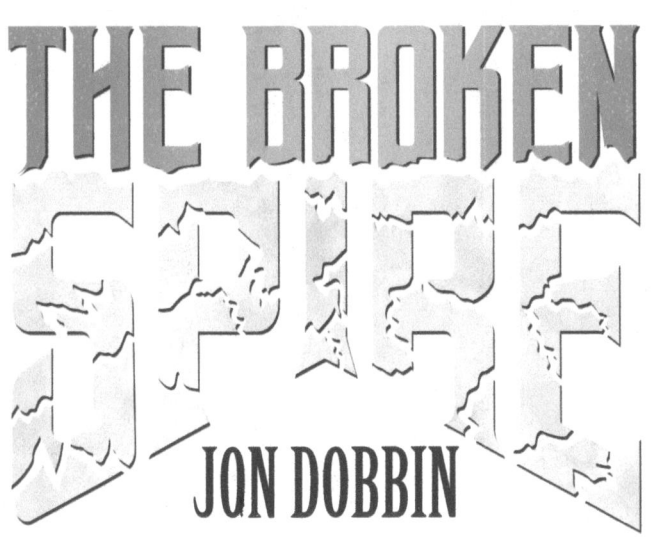

THE BROKEN SPIRE

JON DOBBIN

THE BROKEN SPIRE

JON DOBBIN

ENGEN
BOOKS

Published in Canada by Engen Books, St. John's, NL.

Library and Archives Canada Cataloguing in Publication

Title: The broken spire / Jon Dobbin.
Names: Dobbin, Jon, 1982- author.
Identifiers: Canadiana (print) 20200368869 | Canadiana (ebook) 20200368907 |
ISBN 9781989473856
   (softcover) | ISBN 9781989473849 (PDF)
Classification: LCC PS8607.O215 B76 2020 | DDC C813/.6—dc23

Distributed by:
Engen Books
www.engenbooks.com
submissions@engenbooks.com

First mass market paperback printing: December 2020

Cover Image: Mandi Coates
Cover Design: Jon Mercer

For my parents
thanks for nurturing my imagination
and for teaching me to seek out my dreams.

PART ONE
CHAPTER ONE

Edric's first memory was not of walking, nor was it of his mother's face, or the feeling of his father's rough, stubbled chin as he rubbed his small hands over it. Edric's first memory was of the castle. Not the castle as he would come to know it, but the castle that he remembered as a cloud floating high above him.

It had started as a celebration; the entire town had gathered there, surrounding the glittering, black rock. There had been music and cheering and singing. The castle had come — it was a good omen. They sang an old harvesting song as they carried him from town. Edric laughed the whole way, it was as if he were a prince or a king. It wasn't until the crowd had started to peter out that Edric noticed something was amiss.

"When are we going home?" Edric had asked around a stifled yawn, rubbing at his eyes. It was only his father and mother left then, and the sun had started its slow descent from the sky. Edric's parents sat him down. His mother was crying, and his father just nodded his head. Edric asked them what was wrong, asked them what had happened, but they wouldn't say. Instead they placed the cold iron shackles around his wrists and left him, chained to the rock, sitting on his knees and staring at the sky.

He had been chained to that grassy hill for three days, mostly alone. His father would come to check on him sometimes and would bring him food and water.

"Please, Daddy," Edric would cry and strain his arms at the chain's length to reach for his father. "I'm sorry, Daddy. Please let me come home, I won't do it anymore." Though he didn't know what he had done.

His father, a tall, thin man with dark, hooded eyes, refused to say anything in return. Instead, he would just stare down on Edric for a scarce few minutes before he would leave, taking what Edric hadn't finished eating with him.

Edric only had the clouds to keep him company during those three long days. The clouds and the ever-looming castle. He watched the clouds and tried to decide what they looked like most. Often, he decided that they looked like animals, and to Edric that meant dogs, goats, and chickens.

The nights were the worst, chained to that grassy hill and surrounded by an outlying forest. Animal noises crept in around him with the dark, and he only felt safe when the pale moonlight fell directly on him: his child's mind building up the fantasy that nothing dangerous could break through the shield made of light and stars. When an animal did come investigate, it was nothing that meant him harm. A thin brown fox; some chittering squirrels; and even an owl that gave him an unsettling look. He thanked the gods that the bears known to travel the forest didn't happen upon him. On his second night there, he thought that he heard a wolf howl, somewhere in the distance, and shuddered.

At times, Edric thought he saw his father standing at the edge of the forest, his slender form hiding just at the edge of the tree's branches. Edric thought he could see the moon reflect off his father's wet eyes and illuminate his drawn face and scarecrow-like grey hair.

What he hated the most about those nights was that he was unable to see the clouds: not knowing what shape they had taken, if they had changed with a gust of wind, had divided or multiplied. It was at night when Edric was alone, truly alone for the first time in his life. The stars were too large a number to count, the animals that would visit would run from his sounds and movements, and the trees and grass just waved in the breeze, a nonchalant avoidance of his presence.

It was that second night when things changed. His father had just left, and the sun was setting in the distance. Even so, it was a huge orb that had darkened to a hideous blood red as it sank below the ground. The sky was a dark violet hue, the castle a bleary shade in the distance, but Edric knew that the stars would shine through soon to keep their silent vigil. Again, he saw the moonlit reflection of his father's eyes in the distance, and despite the hurt, the betrayal, he wanted to run to him. Edric pulled and tugged at his bindings, but the iron cuffs did their duty and bit deeply into his soft flesh. The warmth of his own blood ran down his wrists and hands as he sobbed into the jagged, black, crystal-like rock that served as his pillow. He cried himself asleep.

When he woke the dark night had fully set in, but there was a glow. Not the pale glow of the moon and stars that he had become accustomed to, but a purple light that leaked around him, dull and throbbing. Edric stood, his chains clanking as he reached the end of their length. Tears that had been suspended on his eyelids and lashes now fell cold on his cheeks as he looked down on the rock and saw it wink at the moonlit sky. Silence pervaded in the few minutes the light lasted; even the animals had ceased their chattering. As the light died, Edric thought he saw something move within the light: large worms that squirmed within that were reaching out to him.

On the third day, the day after the purple glow, the castle arrived. His little mouth gaped as he took in the tower, the turrets, and the huge cone shaped chunk of earth that still clung to the castle's foundation. At the time, Edric had wondered if a piece of dirt or rock might fall from the larger body of earth. If so, would the castle's foundations know or care?

The golden flags and banners flapped with motion and wind. Edric smiled, thinking that they were the castle's wings; they kept it afloat. If only it were true that the castle propelled itself with the flapping of flags and banners, or even by enormous wings. But no, how it really flew was much more troubling.

CHAPTER TWO

"Come child," Leandra's father beckoned her with his large hand. He was kneeling on the stone floor at the very edge of the courtyard, his girth massed there like an ape; like a gorilla she'd only read about in Obelius' books.

"I want to show you something." He beckoned again, a broad smile on his face. He had a warm smile, a smile that made her feel better when she was sad. Now it excited her. What fun were they going to have?

She ran to him, crossing the courtyard in bounds, and jumped into his arms. He twirled her around, short bucks of laughter coming from his belly as he did. Leandra squeezed her eyes tight and felt the crisp air as it danced through her hair.

"Where are we going, Daddy? What are we going to do?" His hand enveloped hers, creating a shelter around it to keep it safe from the outside. They walked down corridors of the castle she hadn't been before. They were dark and smelled like dust or something worse. She crinkled her nose.

"My princess," his voice was loud, booming, but he was happy; playful. Leandra giggled. "We are going to attend a ceremony, of sorts. It's something all rulers, or future rulers, should see." His eyes dipped towards her and she giggled more.

"But where are we going, Daddy? It smells funny," Leandra said, holding her nose and sticking her tongue out.

The king laughed and nodded. "It does a bit, doesn't it?"

Her father brought her to a long stairway. There were no windows and the stairs were lit by the flickering orange glow of torchlight. It was still dark. Too dark. She gripped her father's hand tight, wrapping her slender arms around it.

He looked down at her with a soft smile. "There, there. I'll be with you the whole way."

He moved down the stairs and Leandra, begrudgingly, followed.

They stopped at the flickering light. Leandra's father paused at the bottom of the stairs before cresting the long hallway, staring about; expectant. Leandra crept around her father's massive legs and stared into the open hallway, the orange light faded to black the further it went, until she saw only darkness. She shivered.

"Daddy," she said, trying to tug her father back to the stairs, but he couldn't be moved.

She felt something warm on her neck, a breath of air that pushed some of the hairs from her shoulders. She could hear someone breathing.

"Princess," a whisper from behind her sent a shiver up her spine, made her shudder in fright. She called out, a scream that pierced the thick darkness and echoed through the halls.

At this her father turned, a slight jump as his head snapped to face her, his eyes wide, his mouth set. Leandra grabbed onto his arm and tried to crawl up him, but he stopped her. His large hand pushed her behind him, into the dim light of the long hallway. She screamed again.

Coarse laughter erupted from the stairwell, a raspy chuckle that subsided as Obelius stepped into the light of the torch. His sallow skin stretched away from his stained teeth into a mocking smile.

"Apologies, sire. I merely was playing a joke."

Leandra knew her father's foremost advisor; knew him more as her private tutor. He turned his hideous smile down upon her, the same smile he gave her when she answered any of his questions wrong. "Apologies to you as well, Leandra."

She gripped her father's shirt, trying to disappear within its folds. She heard her father chuckle, his large hand patting her small one "Perhaps not the time, Obelius."

"Again, apologies, sire." Obelius bent low, his eyes locking with Leandra's before she nuzzled into her father's back. That smile again.

"Lead the way, Obelius," the king said, standing back to allow his advisor to pass. The king bent to Leandra. "Stay close to me, little one." He moved to follow Obelius into the dim light before them.

They walked until Leandra's legs ached. The hallway was lit with torches spaced just at the edge of the previous torch's light. In that dim, flickering light Leandra looked up to the high ceiling, hoping to distract herself from her tired legs. Spiders, bulbous on their webs, stared back at her. She couldn't see their faces, but she imagined they'd have smiles much like Obelius'.

By the time they reached the end of the hallway, her father had given her legs reprieve and carried her in his arms. She liked being in his arms. She liked twisting her fingers through his thick brown beard. She liked the smell of his cologne, even though it burnt her nostrils with its musky scent. Sharp, she'd told him, like his cologne had stabbed at her nose. He laughed then. She liked when he laughed.

"Come," Obelius said as he looked at a fork in the path. "Follow me."

"We are going to the right." The king pointed and set her down. His long stride made her jog to catch up.

"What are we doing in this scary place, Dad?"

A guard peered around the corner and stood stiff as a board upon seeing Leandra's father approach. Her father frowned as they passed. Leandra knew the guard, he was one of the lesser nobles; they were the only people who were made guards. They had to do it even if they didn't want to. The servants couldn't do it even if they wanted. Leandra thought it was all very silly. This particular guard was the father of a boy she knew: a rat-faced boy named Calix who had greasy blonde hair and always walked around with his eyes half shut. Leandra giggled. She'd have to come up with a fun prank to play on Calix later. Her and Edric.

"I've told you, Leandra. We are going to attend a ceremony. It is very important that you see this ceremony; that you understand it."

There were more guards as they moved on. All were dressed in the same outfits, armour under blue cloth, and their funny, pointed metal hats. She didn't know any of these nobles; many of them seemed too young to be a castle guard. She couldn't help but think of Calix as a guard, stumbling around the corridors of the castle, tripping in the too-big uniform. She wanted to laugh, but the thought made her sad.

"Here we are," the king said as they stepped into another dark room. There was a different kind of dark to the hall. This room was meant to be dark; it was better that way. Torches were lit throughout the room, but they did little. It was as though the shadows just absorbed the light; fed on it.

"Where are we, princess?" Obelius' voice slid from his throat, a slithering whisper that hung on the gloomy air around them. Leandra took in her surroundings. Metal bars, bed mats made of straw, old and misused buckets in the corner of each little cube, and a distinct smell that Leandra couldn't pinpoint then, but would later come to recognize as desperation and pain.

"We're in the dungeon?" Leandra said to the nodding Obelius. She turned to her father. "The ceremony is in the dungeon?"

Her father's answer was to point to the other side of the room. Near the end of the cells was a small fire, its flames licking out at the air. There were people sitting around it.

As they moved closer, Leandra could see that there were five men sitting at the fire. Three were dressed in regular guard's uniforms and were huddled around a fourth man who seemed to be stripped to the waist and was looking at the floor, his long red hair covering his face. On the other side of the fire was another man who Leandra thought was another guard, but, as she got closer, she realized that he was wearing black instead of blue and his face was covered in some sort of hood.

All of them, save for the shirtless man, stood rigid as the king and Obelius approached. "Sire," they said in unison, bowing their heads.

Leandra's father nodded to each of them, but his face

was set with grim purpose. His eyes turned cold as they looked upon the man who remained on the floor. Leandra stood close to her father but kept behind him. She wasn't sure of these men; they didn't seem nice.

Obelius had stepped forward and stalked around the shirtless man, his fingers creating a steeple in front of his chest as he did. He took his time, bending towards the man's head, examining his back, and even prodding him with his shoe. With a cursory nod, Obelius moved towards the man in black and they began a whispered conversation that Leandra couldn't understand.

Her father picked her up, and they shared their own whispered conversation.

"Leandra, this man here is a very bad man." Her father kept his eyes on the shirtless man on the floor as he talked. "He has done something that could have put everyone in Appolumi in danger."

"What did he do, Father?" Leandra looked at the man as well. His breathing was coming in short bursts, like her cat when he was sleeping or dreaming. And he shook all over, like he was shivering, but Leandra didn't think that it was very cold, especially next to the fire.

"I know you have been playing with that young boy," he stopped for a moment, his mouth twitching, "what was his name? The sickly-looking boy that is Hesperos' ward?" At the mention of Hesperos the man on the floor flinched. Leandra's father didn't seem to notice.

"That's Edric, Daddy. He's fun."

"Yes, well, Edric and Hesperos are very important to the castle, to our people. Did you know that?" He finally turned his eyes to her. They had softened some and Leandra was glad.

"Is it because they are magic?"

"My, Obelius has been teaching you so many things," her father smiled and tickled under her chin. She giggled. "Yes, it is because they can use magic. And why is that so important, my little genius?"

"Um… because they use their magic to keep Appolumi from falling?" She shrugged, comforted in her father's eyes.

"Yes, that's exactly it." The king tickled her under the chin again. "Well, this man tried to stop the magic that keeps us above ground; that keeps us away from our enemies. That keeps us safe."

"Did he hurt Edric?" She bit her bottom lip, afraid and angry at the same time. Poor, sweet Edric. She couldn't imagine anyone wanting to hurt him.

"No, no dearest. Nothing like that." Her father turned back to the man on the floor. "He tried to take the magic away. Not from Hesperos, not from Edric, but from the whole castle. He wanted to break The Circle."

Leandra was vaguely aware that she gasped. The Circle were very powerful, and everyone knew they kept the castle above the ground. Why anyone would want to destroy them was beyond her. She was lost in the shock of that thought when her father put her back on the floor.

"This is going to be his punishment for trying to hurt the castle." Her father beckoned for Obelius to approach, whispered a word or two in his ear, and said something like, "get it over with." But Leandra couldn't be sure.

"As the voice of his majesty, King Vaselious the wise and powerful, I hereby declare that this man," Obelius' voice boomed against the dungeon walls, drawing everyone to his sneering face. He pointed to the shirtless man with a black-handled knife he'd removed from his shift, "Balthasar Crocus has been found guilty of the crime of treason against His Majesty the King, and the kingdom of Appolumi. For his crimes he will be punished by death." A tight smile crept over Obelius' face and he waved for the black guard to step forward.

Leandra was shocked to see the man in black produce a large axe and brandish it casually as he moved toward Balthasar. The prisoner was no longer looking at the floor. His green eyes were wide over his dirty face. He had dried blood on his chin and his nose didn't seem to be right at all. It was mashed to one side; dried blood rested under it.

The other guards took hold of Balthasar's arms, straightening them out at his sides. The third guard approached from the front and grabbed two fistfuls of red hair and pulled his head until his neck was taut, and Balthasar's eyes were focused on the ground.

"Daddy," Leandra was slapping her father's leg beside her, "what are they going to do, Daddy?"

"He's going to be punished, darling. He's going to be killed." There was ice in his voice, and he held her shoulders firm against him, making her look at what was happening.

"But... but he did something to the magic, right?" She looked up at her father. "Edric and Hesperos are magic. Can't they do something to change him. To fix him?"

Her father stared down upon her then, his eyes changed. They were no longer hard or cold as they had been when he looked at Balthasar. They weren't loving or kind as they were when he looked upon her. They were strange. They held something that Leandra had never seen there before.

"No, dearest. No. I wouldn't wish that fate on anyone," he said, and a slight shudder ran through his shoulders.

The black guard had stopped next to Balthasar and had raised his axe overhead. Balthasar finally broke his silence and he screamed. There were no words in his scream, just pure fear, frustration, and anger — the force of which nearly pushed Leandra back.

Leandra's father held her there, looking until the guard's axe fell and Balthasar had stopped screaming. Then it was her turn to scream.

CHAPTER THREE

Dust rose underfoot as Bijan pushed his way through the crowded marketplace. Gruff-voiced merchants called out their wares to customers who flocked in a rolling wave of sour-scented bodies that pressed around him as he shouldered his slim frame past. He cast a quick look over his shoulder, catching only the surging movement of the crowd, and clasped his hands greedily around his satchel to feel the weight of its contents. He finally had it.

Bijan skirted by a large man dragging an old horse behind him; the creature's ribs, protruding under grey, taut skin, brushed against Bijan's arms as he past. He grabbed up his satchel and held it tight to him to make sure nothing disturbed it. It had been weeks of him searching the outskirts of Hanifakash, and months before that doing research in abandoned and unadorned temples before he had gotten even the slightest hint as to where his prize was hidden — the Tower of Akas Mehul. The Tower was the spiritual centre for Hanifakash, and it housed the worshippers of the Ancient Three and their devout historians. The planning he had to do to get it into his hands was tedious beyond measure.

"Pardon me," Bijan shouted behind him, not caring to look back at the grumbling matron he'd shoved out of his way. He allowed himself a moment to breathe more freely, confident that he had been folded completely into the knot of people that occupied the small square. Of course, his plan hadn't been perfect — his plans rarely were. The few dangling threads he left in them were always pulled loose just when they would do the most harm. He ducked under a rug two men had rolled up and hefted upon their broad shoulders and allowed himself a simple grin. So what if the guards had become aware of his presence, he thought, at least he got away... this time.

"Stop! Thief!" A voice rose above the nattering hum of the crowd, bringing it to an uneasy silence as they turned towards its source. Bijan cursed to himself and turned. Alarmed as he was, he didn't want to be singled out in the gathering: he clung to the satchel.

An enormous man stood above the crowd, his immense weight supported uneasily by a large crate. He wore all black, from the top of his turbaned head to the point of his leather boots, and his right hand rested comfortably on the large hilt of an oversized scimitar that hung by his side. His left hand was extended to the sky to draw all attention to him.

"A thief has broken the sacred laws of Hanifakash and stolen from the home of the Ancient ones." His voice was rough, stripped of any gentleness long ago by constant use of pipe smoke and strong alcohol. "We believe he is hiding as one of your number." He let his left hand fall to his side and Bijan took note of several other black turbans that started to move among those gathered. "We, the Brothers of Samet, ask that you present yourself to us, let us see your faces. This godless coward will be caught," he said, stepping down from the crate with a grunt before moving into the crowd himself.

The crowd stood passively, waiting for the Brothers to make their way to them. Most people seemed resigned to the search, though Bijan heard some grumbling about poor timing amongst the whispered small talk. Ultimately, however, they bowed to the authority of the Ancient Three and the Brothers of Samet. Bijan tried to mimic those around him, tried to seem aloof, unworried, but would make slow steps toward a small alleyway once he was sure no one was looking. Sweat rolled down his forehead and he clutched his prize even closer.

"Horrible timing, eh," a stout man said, leaning in to whisper in Bijan's ear. The man had stopped in mid-trot when the Brothers of Samet had made themselves known. His bright, chestnut eyes danced under his heavy, wrinkled eyelids, but they were alert and there was something wild in them. "I was just about to close a deal with that son of a whore Azimullah." He slung his heavy arm around Bijan's shoulder, a chuckle bubbling up out of his chest. "That crusty old bastard was just about to give me a deal of a lifetime and then this. What if he changes his mind? I'll hang that thief by his balls. Am I right?" His barrel-chested laugh exploded into the silent crowd.

Bijan chuckled alongside of him, his eyes spotting the men in black turbans moving closer and closer, and the alleyway just by his side. The big man next to him continued to jabber on, laughing at his own genius, arm firmly about Bijan's shoulders.

"Yes, yes," Bijan said with a chuckle as he moved out from under the other man's arm, "this is a terrible waste of time, isn't it? Perhaps I will go introduce myself and be on my way."

"That's a strange accent, eh," the large man said with a raised eyebrow, "you're not from around here…"

Bijan darted down the alleyway, satchel cradled to his chest. He could hear the uproar of the crowd behind him, the large man's voice rising about them all. "He's there, he's there," he yelled in a shrill voice.

The alley was dark and unfamiliar. Bijan struggled to find his way, one hand on the pale clay of the building to his right, the other still clutched to the artifact in his bag. He moved as quickly as he could in the dark, stumbling over the refuse strewn amongst the shadows. More shouts came from behind him and he thought he heard the slap of boots echo in the alley he'd just fled. Bijan pushed forward.

He broke through the murky alley and into the harsh light of the sun at the other end. Bijan shielded his eyes too late but moved forward and tried to keep up his pace. As he did, he went headfirst into a monstrous wall of black that grunted as he stumbled backward. Blinking his eyes and rubbing his nose with his free hand, the wall took shape into a giant man with a voluminous moustache and a black turban, a grimace of disgust on his frowning, dark face.

"Pardon me… sir, I was just trying to get to…" Bijan darted again, trying to duck under and around this Brother of Samet's thick arm, but he was caught with a frying pan sized hand that wrapped its strong fingers around his bicep. With another grunt from the wall of a man, Bijan was skidding across the ground on his backside.

Anger flared in Bijan and he lunged at his opponent, cursing and grasping for a throat he saw no evidence of actually existing. More arms emerged from the alleyway and entangled with his own before he could attack the larger man. Bijan flailed and fought against those black figures that now entwined and trapped him, but it wasn't long before they had him subdued and his satchel in their hands.

They forced Bijan to his knees. A man on either side of him held one of his arms behind his back, while a third used a handful of his dusty brown hair to force Bijan's head back and his chin up. Once he was sure Bijan was secured, the oversized wall of a man stepped aside and the leader of the Brothers moved forward, one hand still on the hilt of his sword and the other stroking his wiry beard.

"The Idol." The leader put out a hand and Bijan's satchel was placed in it by another man that bowed as he backed away. The leader opened the bag, studied the contents and handed it off to the wall.

"You are very bold, my friend," the leader said in his booming voice. The other Brothers were silent. "Foolish, certainly, but very bold." He walked around Bijan, scattering those Brothers who were gathered about the alley entrance in his wake. "To scale the Tower of Akas Mehul is a brave, and foolhardy, task in its own right if you are not a follower of the Three," he bowed his head and kissed his fingertips, "but to steal the Idol of Ur Mekhenet," he stopped in front of Bijan and chuckled. "Well, as I said, very bold."

"I can live with bold," Bijan said, failing to crack a smile with his head at such an angle. A thunderous slap to his cheek shook him and dazed his vision; he could feel blood trickle from the corner of his mouth.

"You'll not live at all," the leader said, his voice strained but quiet despite his ragged breathing and bulging eyes. The Brothers holding him tightened their grip on Bijan as their leader unsheathed his massive scimitar and, with the hilt gripped in two hands, allowed the tip to point towards Bijan's throat.

"Chigaru." A new voice rose up outside of Bijan's vision, but he could see black turbans moving and parting in the distance.

The leader allowed his blade to graze Bijan's Adam's apple, sighed, and then turned toward the voice, driving the blade of the sword into the ground and resting his elbow upon the upturned hilt.

"This is not your concern, Iollan." Chigaru yawned and leaned heavily on his sword: his followers, however, were tense; Bijan could feel it in his captors' grip on him.

A small group of men emerged from the black mass of the Brothers of Samet. At the head of their line was a shorter man, his nose and mouth covered in a checkered shemagh, bright blue eyes and messy white-blond hair standing out above the rest. Iollan stood before the Brothers of Samet, his pale, muscular arms crossed in front of him, a broad sword by his side.

"I'm afraid this is my concern, Chigaru." Iollan moved forward to stare up at his counterpart, his blue eyes blazing with a white heat. "You knew what we came here to fetch. Your priests, nor my master, would hardly be impressed if their agreement was broken."

"Yes," said Chigaru, still leaning calmly on the hilt of his blade, "broken from either side." With this he nodded upward at the glint of arrow tips glittering on the rooftops above, where four more men draped in shemaghs stood.

"I'm a careful man, Chigaru." The men exchanged nods. Bijan could feel the grips holding him relax.

"Are you sure you want this, Iollan?" Chigaru stretched, one hand still on his hilt. "I don't know how much good you will get out of it: rather pathetic really."

"We'll find a use, one way or another." Iollan turned

his eyes upon Bijan. "Managed to steal something from your gilded tower, eh?"

Chigaru turned towards Bijan as well, an expression crossing his face as if to say he was surprised to still see him there. "Yes, it couldn't have been easy for him. I'd like to ask him a few more questions about who may have helped him." Chigaru's eyes narrowed and he stroked his beard.

"Impossible. I must leave now, today." Iollan signalled to two of his men, who approached Bijan. Chigaru waved off his own followers. Bijan was lifted to his feet once more and carried to the centre of Iollan's troop. They were all very much like their leader, all wearing shemaghs, their mouths and noses covered, and wearing loose clothing. Each had a broadsword on their belt, and a few had a small bolt-firing crossbow as well. They made little sound when they moved; Bijan didn't even hear them breathe.

"Many thanks to you and your masters." Iollan took a deep bow and his group turned to leave. Chigaru sheathed his scimitar with a great sigh, but spared a scowl for Bijan as he was being carried away. The last Bijan saw of the Brothers of Samet was the Idol being placed back into Chigaru's large, waiting hands, a sickly smile growing under the man's thick beard.

***

It was a slow crawl across the sandy plains away from Hanifakash. Bijan marched amongst the outsiders, silent and miserable. They didn't bind him, though their arrows were trained on his back at all times. They were silent even during breaks in their march, communicating with vague hand gestures Bijan couldn't comprehend. He was fed scraps and was provided water when he asked.

Bijan had not seen the leader, Iollan, since he was taken captive. He assumed he was at the front of the line, but when he asked to speak with him, he would get no response. Those that surrounded him in the march were as faceless and hard to tell apart as the sand grains he tread upon, and he cared little about learning much about them.

It wasn't until the third day of the march that Bijan saw Iollan again. He approached Bijan as he sat away from the outsiders, though under a steady watch by those closest to him: he hardly had freedom from their ever-present eyes. Iollan unwrapped his shemagh, its burgundy tail hanging over one shoulder. He shook out his shock of white-blond hair, rubbing one free hand through it, and crouched before his captive.

"I hear you want to talk," Iollan said, leaning on his knees. His once pale arms now pinkish under the grime of walking sandy trails.

Bijan swallowed the hard piece of bread he had been savouring and pointed a strip of crust at the leader of the march. "Yes, and it's about damn time." Iollan's glacial blue eyes bore into Bijan, his fair eyebrows twitched around scars and dirt. "Perhaps you could start by telling me what the hell is going on, why did you take me from Hanifakash?"

"Rescued," Iollan interrupted and started to re-wrap his shemagh so that it only covered his chin and neck. "We rescued you from Chigaru and his band of slayers. Make no mistake, son, you were as good as dead until we came along." Iollan stared off into the horizon, past the rocky crags and dusty hills that made up the wasteland they wandered through. Bijan made to disagree, but Iollan silenced him by turning his steely gaze upon the treasure hunter. "You still could be," he whispered, "the Brothers of Samet have a long reach." Bijan swallowed his words.

"Bijan the burrower, Bijan the grave robber, Bijan the scavenger. Your name precedes you." Iollan stood and stretched his thick arms out from his sides. "It must be hard for a man of your... talents, being so recognizable and all."

"It does muck things up once in a while," Bijan said and shrugged.

"Yes, I would think it so." Iollan smiled here, a broad and genuine smile but with something hidden behind it; something that didn't seem quite right. "And yet it helped us find you."

"How fortunate for you."

"Fortunate for us both, I think. We need you for a job, and you need us to keep the Brothers of Samet off your back."

"A job," Bijan raised his eyebrows, "what kind of job could I do for a group such as yours?" He ran his fingers through his few days' growth of goatee. "A trained, experienced group, with allies and influence. What could a poor professor do for a group such as yours?"

Iollan laughed, "I'm sure you are many things, but a professor is not among them." He pulled his scarf over his mouth once more. "But you have a knack for finding things, and that's what we need. A man who can find things." Iollan waved to Bijan's guards and walked away.

Bijan jumped up and followed him. Bijan was a taller man, his legs were longer, but it was still an effort for him to keep pace with the leader of the small group of bandits. He looked for any reaction from his guards, but they remained nonchalant and stone-faced under their shem-aghs.

"What have you lost?" Bijan looked down upon the shorter man's pale blonde hair. Iollan did not return his gaze.

"It's not what I have lost, but what *we* have all lost. Everyone." He waved his hand before him as if he was addressing the entire world.

"Sounds tragic." Bijan looked away and took stock of the small camp. Nothing was overly strange, men lazed around waiting for their next orders, relishing the chance to relax. Still, none removed the scarf from their face, adding to their ambiguity. They all blended together as if there was one person who had been copied over and over.

"It is tragic," Iollan said, "but not without its excite-ment." He stopped and looked towards Bijan once more, his strong hands gripping Bijan's biceps, his blue eyes wide. "We are chasing myth and legend. Chasing the cas-tle Appolumi."

Bijan stopped moving, watched Iollan take his leave, and whispered, "the flying castle?"

Chasing myth and legend indeed.

CHAPTER FOUR

"Hurry, Leandra," Edric said in a harsh whisper. "Hurry, before someone sees us." He peered around the corner and looked down another long hallway.

The hallway had been decorated with explosive reds and oranges, and exciting yellows. Banners and streamers strung along the high ceiling, trailing in some places to mid-wall. In regular intervals the flag of the nation was displayed, the coat of arms prominent: an Eagle and a Raven holding a fistful of arrows and a spear respectfully. There was no one else there, no one except them.

"Almost done. It's not easy carving into stone with this little pig sticker, you know." Leandra tossed her frizzy hair out of her face and held up a small kitchen knife, its thin blade now jagged from her efforts with the wall. She blew a stray hair out of her face and went back to work.

"If we are caught, Hesperos is going to kill me." Edric's stomach sank at the thought. He'd only just turned ten, but already he knew Hesperos had a temper. He didn't know the limits of that temper yet though.

"He won't kill you," Leandra scoffed and slapped the stone wall, a dull thud echoed in the hallways. "Besides, I'm all done. What do you think?" She gave him a big smile.

"The arms are a little too short." Edric had pressed his face close to the sigil Leandra had just carved on the wall, just on the outskirts of a long banner. He didn't notice her frown. "He's a wizard, Leandra. He could probably just make me disappear if he really wanted." He leaned back and nodded, finally giving her another look. "Not bad."

"All right. On to the next," Leandra said and pulled Edric along, one small hand gripped around his sleeve.

Edric tried to hide the smile, but it was near impossible when he was around Leandra. Some of his earliest memories were of them playing. In a castle as large as Appolumi, they were the only two children of the same age. The rest were either a year or two older or younger. Not that Leandra or Edric wouldn't have played with those children; they often did, but there was something just the two of them shared. Edric had heard Alethea, Leandra's handmaiden, say there was something special between the two. That felt right to Edric. Special.

"Why are we doing this?" Edric panted as Leandra studied the new corridor they found themselves in. Still empty. The revelries were in other parts of the castle — the great hall, the courtyard, and most prestigious of all, the king's table. That didn't mean that they were out of danger of being found. As the princess, Leandra was closely followed. Edric had no doubts that Alethea and other servants were searching for her.

"You know why," Leandra said, sliding her knife out once more and jabbing at the stone. "These marks —"

"Sigils."

"Yeah, sigils. These *sigils* will help guide us through our adventures. These halls are rarely used; it'll be easy to play without anyone interrupting. Hold this."

Edric lifted the edge of a red banner with a sigh. "I got

these sigils from one of Hesperos' books. What if they, I don't know, hurt someone?"

"Make them disappear you mean?" Leandra said, her tongue sticking out in concentration.

"Maybe!" Edric peered around the corner again. "Either way, hurry up."

They continued on that way for some time, running through seemingly random corridors, Edric keeping a lookout, while Leandra carved the symbols into the wall. Edric complained the whole time, but he didn't want it to stop. Not really. He wouldn't have changed anything that day. Not the nervous giggles as they fled from one banner to the next, nor the feeling that someone might catch them at any moment. He'd have changed nothing aside from when they were actually caught.

"Hey, what are you two doing here?" A shrill voice cut through their laughter. Edric stood straight and tall, as if ice had run along his spine. Leandra's eyes went wide, and she bit her lower lip.

"Shouldn't you be off in the servants' quarters or something?" The boy stumbled out of the shadows. Tall and slim, he towered over both Edric and Leandra, his cold blue eyes focused on them over his thin, pointed nose. He swung a large bottle of wine in his hand.

"Calix," Leandra let out a long sigh, and her breathing returned to normal. "We could ask you the same thing."

"Princess?" Calix asked, screwing up his near invisible, blond eyebrows. "Well that's easy, isn't it? I have this," he swung the bottle of wine in front of their faces. "Father wouldn't be pleased if he saw me drinking one of his finest vintages." Calix chuckled, but his expression was ugly and without humour. "So, what brings you out here with… with… a serving boy?" Calix took a swig from the wine bottle.

Calix was a young noble that would often try to pick on Edric when other noble children were around. He only stopped because Leandra made him. But that wasn't enough for Leandra, she said she had something special planned for Calix. Edric couldn't wait to figure it out.

"Royal business." Leandra said, pushing her shoulders back and putting her hands on her hips.

"Pfft. What's that supposed to mean?" Calix slurred.

"Royal business means that it is none of yours." Leandra stuck out her chin in defiance, practically daring him to deny it.

Calix stood back for a moment; his eyes flicked to either side as if a guard were about to come sweep him up. When nothing happened, he laughed and waved his hand at them. "It's not royal business. What's that there? On the wall? Are you carving up the wall?"

"It's none of your business, Calix." Leandra made her hands into fists but kept them at hip level.

Edric said nothing. Too accustomed was he to avoiding the attention of people like Calix, he slunk further against the wall.

Calix pushed Leandra aside with one thin arm. His finger poked at the gouged stone. "You are carving something in the wall. Not very becoming of a princess. Did your servant put you up to this?" Calix laughed around another swig of wine.

"Leave us be, Calix. Go drink your wine by yourself, just like your father."

Calix's baleful blue eyes narrowed on Leandra. He dropped his bottle to his waist mid-pull, maroon liquid running down his chin. "What did you say?"

"Go away, Calix."

"What did you say?" Calix grabbed Leandra's thin wrist and pulled her towards him. His face was a mask of rage.

Edric stepped forward, his desire to be out of sight, forgotten, but Leandra had pulled her small knife once more and slashed Calix across the back of his hand. The boy pulled back with a shriek, though there was barely a scratch made by the dulled knife.

"You bitch," Calix said and threw the wine bottle at Leandra.

The bottle seemed to move in slow motion as Edric stepped forward, focusing his will into action just as he did every night before he slept. He could see Leandra squint her eyes and cringe away from the bottle, he could see Calix's grimace of satisfaction at the arc of his toss, he could even see the subtle drops of wine that spilled forth from the bottle as it turned end over end.

The smash keyed Edric back into real-time. The glass bottle shattered just inches before Leandra's face, the stream of red wine draining to the floor, seemingly in mid-air. Edric smiled.

"What the —" Calix said, falling back further, his back to the wall. His half-lidded, drunken eyes had grown wide and startled. Leandra, for just a moment, gave Edric an uncertain look before turning to Calix with her large smile full of mischief.

"Edric is a wizard of The Circle. You mess with us, you mess with magic."

Calix began to sputter, but he froze when he heard the far-off call of an adult: Alethea calling out to Leandra. All three children looked at one another for a moment and then began to run in opposite directions. As they began to move, Edric dropped his concentration on the shield and the wine splashed onto the floor. As he ran, Edric looked back at Leandra, but she had already turned a corner and was out of sight, not to be seen again for many years.

PART TWO
CHAPTER FIVE

Edric pulled the heavy oak door from its rocky frame and walked into the open sky. The air was thin, but fresh and cool. It caught and pulled at his long blue cloak, and made his dark brown hair float in front of his grey eyes. The sun was to his left, still high above despite how far the castle climbed each day. There were clouds, white and translucent, floating around the castle; around Edric. A smile tugged at the edges of his young face as he leaned over a stone wall to look out upon the sky, the clouds, the world.

Or what remained of it.

In the distance below, through the haze of cloud and sun he could see the vast blue of the ocean, a mirror of the sky Edric and the castle Appolumi now occupied. Other times he could see the green of forests and the brown of earth that was so far below that even the most nimble-eyed couldn't discern if there were survivors. Even as they passed by the tallest mountains, so close that Edric thought he might be able to just reach out and touch the peak, no one could be seen.

"I thought I'd find you out here." A screeching, uneven voice cut through the blowing wind, an edge of disappointment in it.

Edric cast a lazy look over his shoulder, the corner of his mouth twitching up for a moment. "Master, it's time for lessons?"

"Past time," Hesperos said with a scowl, adjusting his black cloak against the wind. He was an older man, a foot taller than Edric and a shade thinner. He moved to stand beside Edric and placed his skeletal hands on the cool stone wall to brace himself. Edric often thought of his teacher as a talking skeleton; the man's pale and wrinkled skin did nothing to dissuade this impression. What Edric found most fascinating about him, however, was his eye colour. His right was a pale blue while the left was a sickly yellow. Edric avoided the gaze of that eye at all costs.

"I must have lost track of time." Edric turned his head from the clouds, his back resting against the cool wall.

"Indeed," Hesperos cast a sidelong glance at him with his cold, blue eye. "You've lost track of time quite often recently. You feel you do not benefit from lessons lately, perhaps?"

"No, Master. I apologize for my tardiness, please, let's get started for today."

Hesperos turned towards his pupil, a small, humourless smile crossing his corpse-like face, and gestured to the door. "After you."

They entered the castle again, steps echoing on the cobblestone as they moved towards descending stairs. "Tell me, Edric, where did we leave off?" Hesperos walked astride his pupil, hands clasped behind his back.

"Incantations?" Edric flashed a hopeful smile at his teacher.

"No," Hesperos growled with a twitch of his lizard-like eye. One clawed hand shot out as quick as a snake and gripped Edric by the shoulder, turning him on his heel. "Boy, you are heir to The Circle of Magi, a conduit of magic and power, and a saviour to this castle and the people upon it. Show some respect for your position." Hesperos released Edric's shoulder and took the lead.

"I'm sorry, Master." Edric hurried to catch up.

"You certainly are," Hesperos said out of the side of his mouth.

They continued in silence for some time as they steadily moved into the bowels of the castle. They wandered into the cellars, where stone walls stopped and damp earth began, earth that would keep in the cold and fought back the heat. A moss-like smell came over him, a smell of rot and age, of worms piercing the wet, brown dirt, and of trees dying in their search of somewhere to take root. A terrible, evil smell that he had always, and would always, associate with the place they approached. Two large black doors loomed before him, fitted into the earthen wall of the cavernous cellar. They opened onto The Circle. Edric failed to repress a shudder.

"Where are we?" Hesperos' voice was low, muted. He waved one hand toward the doors and eyed Edric.

"The Circle," Edric bowed his head to avoid Hesperos' glance.

Long, thin fingers gripped Edric's chin and brought his head to bear once more. "You're not wrong, Boy. Behind these doors *is* The Circle of Magi, the most powerful wizards known to man. But that's not exactly what I meant. Try again." Hesperos hissed the last part, a whisper in Edric's ear.

"We stand before the reason and the means, Master," Edric quoted, his eyes staring at the dark crease between the two doors he faced.

"Well put. And its significance?"

"It is The Circle. It keeps the castle afloat, keeps us safe from the plagues of the earth and our enemies below." A bluish light seemed to spill from the small gap as he spoke, he was mesmerized by it.

"Too true, Boy. Too true." Hesperos walked around Edric, studying him. "Why don't you have a seat, it's time to start your lesson."

Edric sat and crossed his legs before him, his eyes still fixed on the doors.

"Now," Hesperos said as he continued to walk around his pupil. "Entry into The Circle will be the single most taxing thing you have ever done. It will test your mettle, Boy. It will push you to your very limits. But here's the secret: it has little to do with your magic. Very little."

The blue light throbbed, and Edric stared at it. He was afraid to look away, for fear he may miss it; that it may stop.

"What The Circle requires is utter and complete concentration. Devotion. That's your lesson for the day: Concentration. Sit here and meditate on the —"

"Meditate," Edric brought his eyes up to meet Hesperos. "Master, I hardly feel that is a proper use of my time."

Hesperos grabbed Edric's head and pushed it forward, his eyes facing the double doors once more. "*Your* time, is it? No, Edric, it's *my* time. You will focus, and concentrate, and *attempt* to meditate on The Circle and the powers held within."

Edric sighed, then set about appeasing his teacher. Meditation was something he'd learned when he was a child, fresh in Hesperos' tutelage and still afraid of sleeping alone in the dark. Hesperos taught him to focus on his strength, focus on the magic within, and with that focus would come peace. It didn't hurt that Edric had also learned how to create a small protective bubble around himself as he slept. It never hurt to be prepared.

"I'll come fetch you once I think you've come to fully understand the importance of concentration," Hesperos said, his footsteps moving off into the cellars. "Oh, before I leave. Perhaps you have heard already, but the princess has finally chosen a suitor. You remember the princess, don't you? Leandra. I believe you had some interactions when you were both children. Good news, wouldn't you say?" Hesperos moved on again, a low chuckle following him.

Edric's eyes popped open, his peace disturbed, and curses rising to his lips. Leandra was to be married.

***

It was with an unmitigated sense of dread that she awoke. Throwing off her bed sheets, she rolled to her feet, her breath heaving in her chest. She ran to her window and tossed aside the heavy maroon curtains. Grey clouds, a cool breeze of fresh air. The castle, its courtyard, lived on.

Leandra, Princess of Appolumi and only heir to its throne, sighed her relief.

"Only a dream," she said as she slid to the floor and sat in the grey daylight. A dream she couldn't remember, she thought, and wrapped her slender arms around her legs, hugging herself to try and control her breathing.

"Princess?" A kind, prodding whisper. "Princess, are you all right?" Alethea kneeled beside Leandra, her small hand fell on the princess' own.

"I'm fine, 'Lethe." Leandra forced a smile and a small nod. "Strange dreams."

Alethea's smile brought lines to her face. It reassured Leandra. "You haven't had them night terrors in some-time." The matron helped Leandra to her feet and guided her to a chaise at the far end of her room.

The echoes of their footfalls on the marble floor bounded through the grandiose room. White stone and marble made up its walls and floors, while a strange onyx was inlaid to create a large hearth. Leandra had areas for her clothes, a place for her accessories, and a magnificent mirror that she could sit before and, well, she wasn't sure. Something to do with her hair or makeup, she supposed. A frown etched her face.

She had never wanted the room. The castle had limited space, and her room could have easily housed two families. When she approached her father, the king, about offering up her room he refused. Leandra then offered to house her personal servants with her, but that was also refused. Even kind, old 'Lethe with her grey hair and ruddy complexion had told her it was a bad idea. She had told Leandra that it wasn't befitting a princess to share her chambers with servants. Poor 'Lethe had said this, even though she'd have been amongst those to benefit from the extra space.

"Are you ready for today, princess?" Alethea said after a short pause to fuss over Leandra, brushing her hair, helping her dress, and every other little thing she insisted upon doing, despite Leandra's refusals.

"Yes," Leandra said, not entirely able to keep a shudder from running up her spine.

"He's a fine man, from a good family," Alethea said, nodding behind her. "And not bad looking either." A conspiratorial smile spread across her chubby face.

"Alethea!" Leandra turned on her handmaiden, a

smile touching the corner of her lips. "He's young enough to be your son."

'Lethe waved her off, smile growing. "I'm not dead yet, my darling."

Giggles boiled over to laughter in the easy way that Leandra and her handmaiden had together.

"You may be right," Leandra said through the remnants of chuckles. "He is a handsome man, honourable to his family, and loyal to the throne." She sighed. "And yet, what is the point?"

"I've heard this before," Alethea rolled her eyes, but her smile remained warm.

"Maybe, but it doesn't change the validity. I don't need a husband to rule, it's a silly tradition leftover from when it really mattered. When a marriage would have meant more than two people joining, but entire kingdoms joining together."

"But the two people joining, they're still important, princess," Alethea said, watching Leandra pace in front of her.

"Yes, yes. But in either case, why must I marry Calix? Why must I marry any noble for that matter? Appolumi isn't going to change for the good or the worse for it. It will remain the same. What's the benefit besides tradition?" Leandra balled her fists together.

"I s'pose tradition is a good enough reason, your highness." Alethea had busied herself with tidying the room, a small distraction from the conversation at hand.

"Certainly, for my father." Leandra plonked herself onto her chair, her deep breath exhaled as a heavy sigh.

"Your father is very wise, princess."

"My father is very sick."

"Princess!" Alethea said, her hand clutched to her

chest.

"And old fashioned," Leandra said, trying to smile.

Alethea finished straightening the room and paused for a moment. She looked down at Leandra, a sad smile on her lips. "I'll send in your breakfast. Then it'll be time for your lessons with Obelius."

Leandra sank farther into her chaise. Obelius. The man was as dry as sand. At least that was one reason she could be thankful for in the marriage: a married woman needn't receive private lessons after all. One tradition she could certainly appreciate.

She cast a sidelong glance at the wall next to her and caught a glimpse of something etched into the otherwise flawless white stone. A flower and circle.

Leandra's thoughts immediately turned to the sweet boy who ran the long corridors of the castle with her all those years before. The same boy that aided her in and out of mischief. Her mind turned to the days of her childhood, of days of endless summer. To laughing and playing and... and something else. To freedom. Yes, that was it. Freedom to go where she chose, play as she might, see whom she wanted.

She smiled. She hadn't seen the boy in years. Hadn't been able to. If it wasn't Obelius keeping her occupied with lessons, Alethea practicing her manners, or her father immersing her in the politics of the castle, it was something else she just had to attend to. A gathering of a noble house, the King's Council, or any other number of things required of her station.

Even with nothing on her schedule, with nothing preventing her from her leisure time, she had to contend with Hesperos. She only did so once; baring the full weight of his vicious wolf-like eye one time was more than enough for her. The man made her skin crawl. Her father said it was The Circle, and the magic within, that gave Hesperos his otherworldliness. He told her Edric would be the same in time. Leandra hoped not. The boy had a kind heart, and more than that. He had a light about him. She nodded, yes, that seemed to fit.

Edric. The boy. It had been so long. Perhaps, when she was married and the Queen of Appolumi she would be able to see him again. A Queen could make that happen, Hesperos' evil eye or not.

Leandra walked to the window. Grey clouds gave way to blue sky, sun, and warm breezes. The green of the courtyard garden, the rising chatter from the subjects waking and starting their day. It was all still there.

A horrible thought came to her, unbidden and un-wanted. An uneasy feeling tingled her spine and covered her in gooseflesh. Appolumi was still there, but for how long?

CHAPTER SIX

"And that's what he said, eh?" Gregory's deep voice, hoarse from too many late nights drinking and roaring with his friends in the servant's quarter of the castle, echoed in the stone hallway. A gentle half-smile crept over his plain, overworked face, red from working in fields of the castle, tending the gardens and farming the vegetables of which he and his family would see little.

"Yes, just like that," Edric said with a shrug of his shoulders. His eyes watched the floor. "He actually said 'the princess has finally chosen a suitor'."

Gregory tutted, shook his head, and let the silence guide their path through the halls. Gregory was a young man, stout and gruff, the clay of his body molded through his work, his hands rough and thick. That wasn't how Edric pictured him though. He saw the dirty-faced little boy that jutted his chin out at trouble, right or wrong. The same little boy that scared off a group of noble boys who'd cornered Edric, even though he could have been severely punished.

"Perhaps," Gregory said, drawing the word out. "Perhaps, Hesperos was lying to you." He nodded to himself as they turned a corner and moved into another, more dimly lit corridor, the floor abruptly changing from stone to dirt and gravel.

"Do you think so?" Edric perked up some, his keen eyes reaching out to Gregory for more.

"Well, he has done it before." Gregory shrugged.

It was true, Hesperos had tricked and misled Edric throughout their lessons, but it was often for the sake of motivating Edric to push himself. He'd once said that the castle was not Edric's home, that he'd been brought in from the dead earth. It was an attempt to make Edric angry and force him to lash out at Hesperos. It had worked.

"Yes, but..." Edric stopped moving, thoughts rolled around in his head. "And you haven't heard anything about Leandra choosing a suitor?"

Gregory laughed and gave Edric a small bow. "You'd know more than me, oh heir to The Circle."

"Not anymore. Hesperos has clamped down on my time outside of my studies. The Trials will start soon."

Gregory pursed his lips and stroked his chin.

Edric perked up once more and grabbed Gregory's broad shoulders. "But you're right."

"I am?"

"Perhaps. An heir to The Circle must be somewhat important, right? An heir may even be as worthy of the princess' hand as a noble, don't you think?"

Gregory's dun eyes shied away from Edric's.

"No, perhaps not," Edric said, his arms collapsing to his sides.

"Pity, I was looking forward to being right for once," Gregory said, and elbowed Edric with a sharp jab in the ribs and barked a short laugh. Edric ignored it as best he could and pushed the broader young man away from him before falling into a brief silence.

"Look, I'm not sure about the status that comes from

being an heir to The Circle," Gregory said, wrapping one thick arm around Edric's shoulders. "But you don't know much about your parents. Perhaps you are of noble blood." His kind half-smile had returned as he patted Edric's back.

Edric hadn't cared to think about his parents in years. His life was focused, he had a means to an end; a goal. The Circle. Though he had precious little information about it, The Circle had always been something to look forward too. Now that his final days were approaching, he just didn't know. Maybe it was worth knowing more about his family.

He'd speak to Hesperos about it.

***

Hesperos pushed through the trapdoor with a slam, his old bones still agile despite his years.

"Ah," he said, sizing up Edric, "you've got yourself put together." He climbed into the room, dragging his staff behind him. He walked around the disheveled space, pushing books aside with his foot, leaving them tipped over in his wake. "You've been doing your study, then?"

Edric's room was near the top of one of the turrets of the castle's outer walls. A room once meant for soldiers and guards, for archers who defended the castle, but that was centuries ago, long outside of Appolumi's collective memory, save perhaps the memory of Hesperos.

"Yes, Master." Edric bowed his head, letting his hair fall around his face to keep Hesperos out of sight. He was sitting on his small bed, the wall cooling his back. The room was lonely, separated from the rest of the castle on high, though he couldn't complain about the view. His window overlooked the courtyard, a sprawling green garden that the castle's inhabitants frequented daily. That's the best he could ask for in the days leading up to the Trials — a peek at life on Appolumi.

"Good," Hesperos said in a growl, and kicked aside another pile of books and discarded clothing as he made his way towards Edric.

Edric straightened up as he came, stood from his bed and greeted his teacher.

"You look awfully sullen today, Boy. You're getting your rest, aren't you? The Trials are upon us, after all."

"Yes, rest," Edric said, chewing on his bottom lip. "Master, I actually have a question I've been meaning to ask you." His hands fidgeted at his sides.

"What's that, Boy?" Hesperos sneered, his mismatched eyes exploring the remnants of the bedroom. "Something about the Trials, no doubt."

"Actually, no. It's about my —"

"Not about the Trials? First, I find you daydreaming when you should be attending my lessons, and now your mind is wandering when it should be focused. Boy, you have a chance to become a part of something bigger than yourself, something that is not only important to the people of Appolumi, but to the survival of world itself."

"I meant no offence, Master. I just wanted to ask…"

"If this doesn't have anything to do with the Trials, I don't want to hear it." Hesperos reached into his robes and took out a small tome, its leather binding old and weathered. "This is something to help you prepare for the Trials. Add it to your studies."

Hesperos shoved the book into Edric's chest and turned his lizard eye to him.

"I need to know about my parents," Edric said, his voice echoing against the large stones that made up his walls. Hesperos' sneer deepened.

"Your parents." The old wizard stroked his thin beard, both of his eyes now fully concerned with his young pupil.

"Yes. I've never asked, I've never cared, but I want to know." Edric flopped to his bed, the small book tumbled to the floor. "Please."

Hesperos studied his young pupil, lines of concentration creasing his brow. "You know, Boy, some things just aren't worth knowing."

"So, you know about my parents?" Edric sat on the edge of his bed.

Hesperos gave a dismissive wave of his hand. "I know everything there is to know about you. Everything that matters anyway."

Edric stood and gripped Hesperos' shoulders. "Thank you, Master. I appreciate…"

"I didn't say I would tell you, Boy." Hesperos shook off Edric's hands and moved towards the trapdoor.

So many things crossed Edric's mind in that moment — fear, confusion, disbelief, but mostly there was anger. A red-hot spark was set off in his stomach, his face burned, and he clenched his fists.

"Not to your liking, is it?" Hesperos smiled and twisted his free hand. Edric could feel the air around him warm and the hair on his arms stood on end. He could sense the energy of the room start to change and knew that Hesperos was preparing something. Edric stepped back, but kept his eyes focused on his teacher.

Hesperos nodded and ceased twisting his hand to gather energy. "My, you are motivated by this information, aren't you?" The smile grew on the old man's face.

"I'll make you a deal. The Trials begin in the next day

or so. Delve into your studies once more; prepare your-self. There are three Trials to complete, and for each that you overcome I will give you a piece of information about your parents. That may just suit both of our needs, don't you think?"

Edric wanted to complain, wanted to demand an-swers, but knew it would be useless. He dropped to his bed once more and nodded to his master.

"Very well then. I will return in two days. Be ready, Boy."

After Hesperos left, Edric sank to the ground and picked up the book that his master had left for him. The worn leather creaked as he opened it to the first page, the moldy smell of old parchment tickled his nose.

"Sacrifice," Edric said, reading aloud.

CHAPTER SEVEN

"So, what did you say these books were about?" The barmaid was tall and blond, and her accent tickled Bijan's ears.

"My gentle desert sun cup," Bijan purred, his arm slung over the back of his chair. "These books contain lore. Lore of this particular province, in fact. So much, perhaps it even includes something about you." He touched her hand, a gentle squeeze, and gave her a subdued smile. Iollan sighed from across the table. Bijan shot him a warning stare.

It had been a long trek over rough seas, but Bijan and Iollan's raiders had made it to the Northern Provinces. In the years since the raiders had aided Bijan's escape from Hanifakash, he had been in deep study researching the lost floating city. Iollan had many resources at his disposal and already had many key texts and documents collected for Bijan, who had his own connections and resources. He had always thought of the castle, the kingdom, as nothing more than a dream, a fairy tale told to children around a fire, but now he thought differently. The more he read, the more he discovered the historical links. It took him some time to put it all together: the maps, the accounts, the legends and stories, but he was finally able to uncover something new. It's original place in the world. That's what brought them to the Northern Provinces, to a town called Arnarfell, waiting for a guide that was already late beyond measure.

"Lore, of this place?" The bar maiden looked around her, a derisive snort complimenting her growing smile. She bent over, her ample cleavage in plain view, and whispered in Bijan's ear. "What's lore mean anyway?"

Bijan could feel the roll of Iollan's eyes without having to look, but it didn't stop his own smile from growing. "Merely stories, legends you might say. These books are full of them," Bijan knocked on the top book of the pile. "For instance, have you ever heard of the goat that, once fed thin metal, would tell you your fortune?"

The wench laughed, sorting empty tankards on her tray.

"No? Perhaps you've heard of the man-eating grass, said to be somewhere well north of here?"

The barmaid just shook her head and placed the tray on the bar just to her right.

Bijan gave Iollan a quick glance. The leader of the raiders gave him a practiced look of impatience, his scarred brow furrowed around his ice blue eyes, but he gave a shrug as he tossed back the rest of his ale.

"Hmm, that is very surprising. I would think a young, intelligent woman as yourself would be aware of all of these stories." Bijan sighed and took a sip of his wine. "Perhaps you'd know something about this one," Bijan flipped open the top book and settled on the middle of the book, his index finger tracing the words there. "Ah, yes. The flying kingdom. A very rare tale indeed. I wouldn't expect anyone to know anything about that. Perhaps we could try..."

"The flying kingdom? You mean Appolumi the flying castle?" The girl stood there chewing one nail.

"Well, well, little sun cup, you are full of surprises," Bijan said, his face brightening with a large smile. "Perhaps you could entertain us with the story you know. We have scant few clues about this... Appolumi, as you say, and it does seem so interesting." Bijan held her hand and stroked her fingers with his thumb.

The girl flushed. "Well, I'm not much of a storyteller." She pulled her hand away and moved to another table. Bijan's hand lashed out, a blur of movement, and latched onto the girl's thin, milky wrist.

The bar sunk into a sudden and complete silence. Men covered in grizzled beards and wearing scars upon their faces turned their heads to watch the foreigners, their thick fists twitching on the battered and worn tables in front of them. It hadn't gone unnoticed to Bijan that many still wore hatchets at their belts. He cast a quick glance at his companion. Iollan, the owner of his own share of scars, sat straight, his eyes darting back and forth.

"Please," Bijan said through a strained smile, "we only wish to hear your tale while we wait for a friend." He produced a small bag that clanked with coins as he lay it on the table. "Please," he said and released her hand, motioning to the free chair at the table.

The barmaid gave a hesitant glance at the bag of coin and made a wave towards the rest of the bar before she sat, pulling the bag towards her. The thrum of whispered conversation grew until the silence that had assailed the room had completely disappeared.

"Now, 'tis not a story of the castle proper," the barmaid said as she hid the coin purse somewhere in the folds of her dress. "But it's the best story we have about the castle that isn't centuries old."

Bijan and Iollan shared a glance. They had many pieces of information, even full records of the families associated with the lost kingdom, but not much else. When the castle disappeared, information dried up. There was even some disagreement around its origins. That's where Bijan wanted to start: a logical first step really. A place their guide was supposed to know the whereabouts of. If he showed.

"Might as well tell us, girl." Iollan said and gave her a nod to continue.

The barmaid shrugged. "Well, everyone around these parts knows the tale of the boy who saw the castle and was driven mad. It happened when I was just a wee lass myself, but the tale travelled, as such tales are wont to do. The boy's name was Vali, a poor boy from a small coastal town."

"What town?" Bijan said, leaning closer.

"What?" The barmaid screwed up her nose and then nodded with realization. "Oh, well, that's the thing. No one knows for sure. It was over twenty years ago; besides that's not the point of the story." The girl threw her loose hair back and continued. "Vali, as the story goes, had just lost his mother. Not sure how, but she died all the same. Now, the boy's father, a drunk to begin with, turned his grief into anger with every drop of booze that hit his tongue. The rage from his father sent the boy into the forest."

"It was a garden, his mother's garden," a haggard looking man said as he limped by, wiping saliva or vomit away from his mouth with his sleeve.

"Shut it, Errol, who's telling this story?" the barmaid growled, an annoyed stare following the man as he exited the bar and disappeared into a gust of wind and snow. "Anyway, *some* people say it was the mother's garden, but most say it was the forest. It doesn't matter. The point is, Vali hid someplace that his father wouldn't find him, probably wound up in some ray of sun somewhere, and grief being what it is, he fell asleep from the toll."

"This is a lovely story and all," said Bijan, studying the woman's bodice in search for any unnatural shapes — particularly anything purse shaped, "but what does this have to do with the castle?"

"I'm getting there. I'm getting there. So, Vali was asleep when he was jarred awake by a thunderous rumbling that quivered the earth beneath him. He jumped to his feet, bracing himself against a big oak, his wide eyes scanned the flailing branches and falling leaves. A loud hum tore through the trees over his head and an enormous shadow blotted out the sun. The quaking followed in the shadow's wake and moved further along the forested area. Vali followed the shadow. His eyes still itchy from crying, his breath still caught in his throat from sobbing, but his grief had been temporarily forgotten.

"Vali ran through the forest, as he'd done hundreds of times before, and when he came to a steep bank, he scrambled up it using both his hands and feet, his fingers digging into the soft earth under the emerald green grass. He broke the crest of the bank, sweat streaking his forehead and back, and was able to see through the tree canopy, surprised that he could get a good view of the valley below and the sky above. Still, he couldn't see what was making the noise.

"He ran along the embankment, his bare feet tickled by the long grass until he came to an inclined rock face that he bounded up, his lungs burning. Vali was soon edging along a cliff, the trees he was accustomed to on his left, and a thirty-foot drop on his right. But he could feel the air tremble about him, and he then he saw it.

"The castle breached the trees on the other side of the thirty foot drop he now stood upon. The keep rose first, a great stone construction capped with battlements and adorned with vines that even Vali could see from far off. The four towers followed suit, rounded stone on each corner of the massive curtain wall and portcullis gate that crept past the treeline. Great red and blue flags waved in the wind, the smack of their fluttering indistinguishable under the roar of the rising castle, though Vali imagined he could hear them. Ground came with the castle too, a massive clump of earth that fell in a jagged spike of brown dirt and grey stone. It was as if the castle was simply lifted out of the ground to be transplanted someplace else, someplace more suited. Vali had seen his mother do just that with flowers before."

The barmaid stopped to light a pipe, puffing the tobacco to life. Bijan held his breath, and sensed Iollan's anticipation.

"Anyway," the barmaid continued after another puff on her pipe, "Vali called out to the castle. I suppose he hoped that it would see him or rescue him from his father. But scream or yell as loud as he could, the castle did not hear him. He was forced to sit there and watch Appolumi fly off into the horizon. That wasn't good enough for this boy though. No, he couldn't let it go at that, couldn't live with just a brush of greatness. He decided, right then and there, that he would see that castle again. He decided that he needed to see the castle. Not only see it, but to set foot on it. With that in mind, he turned his gaze to the horizon the castle had disappeared behind and began to walk after it."

"And has anyone seen this Vali since?" Iollan said, leaning into the table, his icy blue eyes on the barmaid's alabaster face.

She shrugged. "It's just a story. May not even be true. You lads want another drink?"

"Yes, please," Bijan said and drained the last of his mug. He watched her walk away with great interest.

"That did little to help," Iollan said with a yawn, his thin arms rippled with muscle as they stretched above his head.

"It's more than we had before," Bijan shrugged. A grimace formed at the corners of his mouth as he peered into his empty mug.

"When the guide gets here —"

"What guide?" Bijan barked a laugh. "Your *guide* is well past due. I think you may have been misled. Besides it's been *my* books that have gotten us this far," Bijan said, eyeing the fresh mug of ale that was slid in front of him.

"Don't forget who provided you with those tomes, Bijan the Borrower," Iollan said, draining his own mug.

Bijan prepared to snarl a retort when the tavern's door slammed open and his eyes were drawn to the largest man he'd ever seen. Whatever he had been about to say was lost somewhere in the distraction.

Snow swirled around the man's feet and onto the tavern's worn wooden floors as he walked into the tavern and closed the door behind him with a flick of his wrist. A long, tattered bearskin cloak shrouded his face with a fur-trimmed hood that he pushed back over his broad shoulders.

"I am looking for Aodhan," the stranger said and raised his hands above his head. "Aodhan of the Southern realms."

The room went quiet, the bar's patrons turning their haggard faces to the newcomer in a series of angry expressions and a general sense of disquiet.

"You are not welcome here, Erland," the barmaid said, her face contorted with hate and fury. Bijan could feel the tension grow in the room, could feel the hostilities grow as men returned their grip to their hatchets, their eyes steady on the man who blocked the doorway.

Though his size was something to behold, Bijan couldn't see much difference in this Erland and his fellow Northerners. Long, dark, straggly hair fell about Erland's shoulders and chest. A beard that was streaked with different colours and may have even been as long as the twisted hair on his head. All things Bijan had noticed in the Northerners that sat around him. And yet, there was still a separation that Bijan couldn't place, as though the man at the door was a different species than those that populated the bar. Perhaps it was as vague and obvious as the difference between a wolf and a dog.

"I will leave, fair Talia, when my query is met. Not before." The newcomer shook his arms and the ragged sleeves of his tunic fell down some. There was an inhalation of breath and the locals took a step back, cursing.

"I am Aodhan," Iollan said slamming his mug on the table before him. Bijan was shaken out of his distraction and gave Iollan a surprised look that he shared with the rest of the tavern's patrons.

"Excellent," the newcomer said in his coarse voice, "I am your guide. Come with me." He turned on his slush-covered boots and left the tavern. In his wake the strained silence grew.

Bijan gathered his books in his arms, each one threatening to tumble to the floor as he hurried to follow Iollan and the newcomer, Erland.

Outside the derelict tavern the two men tromped after one another in the dim torchlight, snow curling about their figures as they drew their cloaks tightly about them. Erland was much taller than Iollan but the raider was almost as broad about the shoulders. The tavern was squat between two snow-laden ironwood trees that towered above it. It had been there for so long that it seemed it were growing into the trees; that they were one and the same. The very edges of the tavern were askew, wrapping themselves around the tree trunks, grasping at them desperately, never to let go.

"Aodhan," Bijan hissed as he came up alongside of Iollan, still juggling books in his arms. "What is this bloody Aodhan business?"

"It is my name," Iollan shrugged, his eyes staring upon Erland's back.

"And what about Iollan?" Bijan said, unloading a book or two into the man's waiting arms.

"That is also my name," Iollan said, arranging the books in his arms without taking his eyes off of Erland.

"A man with two names, how strange."

"Smart," Erland said, his strong voice carrying on the wind.

"And is that your name then, Erland?" Bijan said, sticking out his jaw.

"That's what they call me," he hitched a thumb back the way they came, "but I go by Boon to most. I answer to either."

Bijan and Iollan gave each other a troubled look. They hadn't talked much about their guide; Iollan had arranged for it some time before their landing, through connections of his own. In the months since meeting him, Bijan found that Iollan's contacts, while valuable and useful, were rarely the friendly sort. Bijan's own were often rough around the edges, but more often than not were intellectual by nature. Iollan's connections were brigands and rogues, mercenaries and assassins. They were men who liked to kill and steal. So far as Bijan could tell, Erland wasn't much different.

"Do you know our destination then?" Iollan called ahead.

Erland turned on his heel, studying Bijan and Iollan under his hood. "You're in search of the origin of castle Appolumi," he said, and returned to his trek. "I'm the only one who knows where you're going."

CHAPTER EIGHT

"The Trials are made up of three parts." Hesperos glowered down upon Edric, his staff beating a harsh tattoo that echoed in the stone hallway that they traversed. "Name them."

Edric rubbed a balled-up fist against the corner of his eye, a stifled yawn caught in his throat. True to his word, Hesperos had come to fetch him early in the morning on the second day of his forced study and preparation of the Trials. It had been so early that the sky was still dark and the birds refused to sing. Edric had been dreaming when his teacher clawed his way into his bedroom: a fevered dream that he'd nearly forgotten, save for the faint, hazy image of a boy standing beside a black crystal. The trap door slammed open and Edric sat bolt upright, eyes still bleary from sleep. His skeletal hand gripping the floor gave Hesperos the appearance of a corpse trying to escape a grave. Edric had let out a yelp of surprise, but as Hesperos brought his lantern into the chamber Edric was able to discern the old man's cadaverous features, and his one vulture-like eye.

"Isolation, Transition, and Incorporation," Edric said, holding aloft his master's lantern to help guide their way. He'd studied the book Hesperos had given him, but it had left him with more questions than answers. The first Trial, Isolation, felt as though it were too easy; that he'd already completed it. Certainly, his time spent in his room and separated from the rest of the castle would count towards that. The only person he was allowed to see was Hesperos, and that had waned due to his studies.

"Master, surely I've already completed the first task." Edric cast a hesitant glance at Hesperos as he spoke. "It's easy to see how isolated I've been for the majority of my life, but especially as of late."

"Is it now?" Hesperos cracked a crooked smile and motioned for them to continue.

Edric followed Hesperos' directions deep into the castle. They delved into its oldest sections, where darkness ruled, and sun could not reach. He knew where they were going; Hesperos' chambers lay within the darkest parts of the castle. Hesperos would say that his age, his seniority, and his value to the king won him this place. Edric knew different. No one wanted to live there. They gave it freely to him without question or argument, happy that he would be out of sight more than in.

They crossed into the chambers between two huge and aged oaken doors, so old they were unable to open or close and just hung ajar. Not that Hesperos had to worry about unexpected visitors or thieves so far into Appolumi's depths. Despite its dingy location, Hesperos' personal chambers were quite a spectacle to behold. He had collections of ingredients, glass vials filled with strange liquids, and yellowed bones of long forgotten animals. The walls were filled with books from floor to ceiling, with strange macabre trinkets scattered amongst them. If you looked in one place you'd see a skull smiling at you, another and you'd see a decaying corpse of some reptile the wizard had kept in his younger years. In spite of everything else he knew about his master, Edric envied his book collection. Tomes upon tomes of knowledge gathered in one place was amazing in its own right, let alone the innumerable amount of secrets held within. Edric had once hoped Hesperos would allow him a day alone with the books to study, but it never came to pass. Hesperos was as greedy with knowledge as he was anything else.

"Sit," Hesperos pointed a long, skeletal finger towards a wooden stool. "So, you believe that you have already completed the first stage of the Trials?" Hesperos leaned on his staff and bent towards Edric, his eyes bulging.

"Yes," Edric said with a firm nod. He thought of the days studying, reading, training with no one to talk to but Hesperos. He thought of the quick glances he stole of the courtyard from his room, the people mingling as he was so often prohibited from doing. 'Yes,' he thought, 'I have been isolated.'

"Quite convinced, are you?" Hesperos started to pace around the room. "I suppose I can't blame you. I have really kept you in solitude all these years, haven't I?"

"You were trying to teach me," Edric said, though his heart wasn't in it. Hesperos had subjected him to isolation throughout his life. If he hadn't snuck away from time to time, with Leandra when he was younger and with Gregory as of late, he may not even remember what another human being looked like.

"True, true." Hesperos tried a smile. "You do a kindness for your old master for saying that."

Edric lost sight of Hesperos as he moved around him, the strange triple echoes of his feet and staff still signalling his presence.

"Of course, you know, Boy, that you've always had

me."

The air around Edric went rigid. The hairs on his arms stood, and he felt a transference of energy. He turned around, his face contorted in confusion and anger. His hands flew to his chest, fingers prepared to dance out spells. It was too late. He could feel the push as he was thrown into the wall. An invisible ball of energy held him there, tried to drive him through the books, the stone and the mortar.

Then it was gone.

He fell to the ground. His breath returned to his lungs in long wheezes. "What the hell are you doing?" he managed.

"Isolation." Hesperos smiled. The old wizard's hands began to work again, his jaw clenched, his neck taut.

Edric looked up at his master and winced.

"Stand, Boy. Let's see how prepared you are," Hesperos said, a humourless smile on his thin face.

He couldn't beat Hesperos in a straight magical fight. They both knew that. He'd never be able to outwit the man either; he was too old and too wily. There was a chance that Edric could trick him. It was a slim chance, but it was all he had.

As Edric stood he threw the stool at Hesperos. The elder's mismatched eyes went wide with surprise as he sidestepped the projectile, his smile replaced by a frown. "Come now, Edric, I'm sure that's not what you read in your...."

Edric muttered some words under his breath and pushed his will and strength towards his master. It hit Hesperos in the chest, pushing him back but not taking him off his feet. Edric cursed. Hesperos stood in the centre of the room, leaning on his staff, his breath uneven.

Now! Edric's mind shouted at him. *Now, before he can conjure another spell.* Edric ran towards Hesperos. He cleared the room in a blur, his young legs carrying him with ease. He reached his master and kicked his staff where it met the floor. It went flying into the corner and Hesperos toppled to the side atop of some displaced books.

Edric tried to follow through and jump upon his master. Hold him down, hit him, anything. But as he moved, he struck an invisible barrier and bounced off.

"Enough." Hesperos struggled to his feet and dusted himself off. His face was a mask of disgust. "You're a tricky one, Boy," he said in his screeching and uneven voice, shaking one long, slender finger. "But the use of physical aggression," Hesperos twisted his mouth as he said it, like he had just tasted a bitter lemon. "Well, let's just say that was very... uncouth."

"You attacked me." Edric stood back, his hands ready, eyes on the old wizard.

"I did," Hesperos said and leaned on his cane. "In doing so I finally left you on your own. I isolated you." He stretched out a withered hand to Edric, but the young man only eyed him. Hesperos smiled through a sigh. "I was able to see, for a fleeting moment, how you could handle a situation without support; when you were truly alone."

"So, I won," Edric said, relaxing.

"You what?" Hesperos snatched up his staff. "You survived, Boy, on pure luck. Don't get cocky."

"But I passed the first Trial?"

"Yes, you did do that." Hesperos grumbled and moved to sit in a large wooden chair. "Pick up that stool and sit."

"I wo... I mean to say, I passed. Tell me about my parents," Edric said, arranging himself in front of his master.

"I did promise you that, didn't I?" Hesperos stroked his long grey beard, his eyes drifting to the ceiling.

"Tell me — are they of noble birth? How did they die? Were they skilled in magic as well?"

"I told you that I would tell you something about your parents, Boy, but I didn't say I would let you pick," Hesperos said, waving a hand before Edric's face before returning to his thoughts.

"Oh yes, this should do." Hesperos sat up straight in his chair and locked eyes with Edric. "Your father was a drunk. He'd have sold you for booze the first chance he had, if it wasn't for you mother. She was the one that brought you to me."

The words echoed in Edric's mind but didn't provoke any strong images from him. No answers were provided, none that he had hoped for anyway.

"That's all?" he heard himself say, his voice distant and unsteady.

"For now. Tomorrow you'll be taking part in the second part of the Trials. Succeed and I'll tell you something else." Hesperos dismissed him with a wave of his hand.

The walk back to his room was plagued by a pain in his back and ribs, but Edric hardly noticed. Instead he focused on the information that Hesperos had given him, as small as it was. His mother hadn't let him be sold, but had been the one who'd given him up. Did that mean he was given up when his magical abilities had been noticed? He'd read in one of Hesperos' books that the common age for the onset of magical properties was four or five.

Questions riddled his brain, more questions than answers and more theories than evidence. He cursed under his breath.

His room was as he left it, untouched and uncared

for. The sun was still in the blue sky, and the fresh scent of grass floated through his window and welcomed him home. Laughter and chatter filled the courtyard beyond his window and begged for Edric to look out. He allowed himself a quick glance, taking in as much as he could — the dull shine on the guards' aging armour, carefree nobles walking arm in arm without a care, and a young girl running through the grass, a small army of children chasing after her, their laughs a constant utterance just above their good-natured cursing. A smile rose to his lips as he remembered doing something very similar as a child, chasing the young Princess Leandra through the castle on one of her scams. Or, as she would have called them, adventures.

He paused when he saw the old book Hesperos had given him lying page down on his bed. Edric was drawn into it, forgetting the rest of the world, focusing on the Trials. He needed to learn more about his parents; about his past.

CHAPTER NINE

The morning wore weary on Leandra's head; her list of responsibilities was heavy and cumbersome. Still, it was made all the more light being done with Obelius and his lessons full of sanctimonious, broad-scoped messages that always returned to something inherently about him as he flailed about with his favoured black-handled knife to make his point. This most recent lesson devolved into an unwarranted and unwanted discussion on his success with women in his youth. Leandra shuddered at the thought.

"I wouldn't mind," Alethea said through wheezing giggles, "but he's been stuck on this castle just as long as any of us. And, let me tell you, none of the women I know would be beating down his door to play the pyrdewy."

"Alethea!" Leandra brought a hand to her mouth to conceal her urge to laugh.

"Well, it's true." Alethea smiled, her chin in the air, defiant.

Leandra took her old maid's arm into her own and pulled her along the bright hallway. Sun poured through the open windows, a warm breeze carrying fresh air scented with the flowers and trees that bloomed in the courtyard. 'This,' she thought, 'if only it were just this all of the time.' The thought was gone almost before she had finished it. A Princess of Appolumi didn't have idle time to waste, even on a beautiful day with good friends.

"So, my dear Alethea, where am I required next?"

Alethea tried to dampen her smile some; getting back to business. Leandra squeezed her arm all the tighter because of it.

"Well, my princess, we have options on this fine day, neither of which I am sure you will overly enjoy. Would you rather me present you with the exciting option first, or the... droll option?" Her emerald eyes peeked sidelong at Leandra, her smile still a faint curl on her lips.

"My, my. Presented like that, Alethea, I suppose I will have to hear the..." Leandra placed one delicate finger over her pursed red lips. "Droll option first."

Both women laughed, a joyous sound that rolled around the corridors they passed through, their sandals making no sound on the carpet runner that ran beneath them.

"Dress fitting," the old maid said, stifling more laughter.

Leandra shot a horrified look that brought another bubble of laugh from her maid.

"Well, on to the exciting option then."

***

The tournament had started long before Leandra was dragged into the Bailey, the air pungent with the smell of sweat and blood, aggression and desperation, victory and defeat. Alethea led Leandra to the king's booth, a small wooden tower that stood looking down upon the festivities. Her father was already there, propped up in his throne, one of the many that were scattered around

Appolumi. King Vaselious' deep blue eyes flitted at their approach and rested on Leandra, wet to the point of over-flowing.

"Hello Father." Leandra forced a smile and bent to kiss his sagging cheek. The salty taste of tears greeted her lips. "Now, now, don't be like that," she whispered. "I'm here. Would you like some wine, some bread?"

The king grunted and turned his head away from her.

"All taken care of, princess," Obelius' chilled, silken voice crept out of the shadows, the man himself emerging with a plate of soft foods and a chalice of something dark.

"Thank you, Obelius," Leandra said, falling into a chair beside her father, carefully hiding a deep roll of her eyes.

"My heavens, Obelius, you certainly made your way here awfully quick," Alethea said pouring something up for her mistress.

"I didn't know that the king's chancellor had to report to a handmaiden." Obelius turned a poisonous smile on Alethea. "Besides, it is my duty and pleasure to be at the side of my king."

Vaselious grunted and Obelius bent to give him a sip from his chalice.

"I'm surprised you weren't here faster. I recall you having some *shortcuts* when you were a child, princess."

Leandra opened her mouth to respond to the smug look that crossed Obelius' face, but was interrupted by an-other grunt from her father.

"Ahh, you are right, my liege. The last duel of the day. Look, princess, your beau, Calix, is on the field."

A tall, lean man approached the centre of the field

from the right. His black leather jerkin was immaculate and untouched, as always, and was in stark contrast to his pale skin and blonde hair. A sword was strapped to his belt, the hilt long and slender. It was his preference, the handle, and Leandra knew that; she hated that she knew that.

From the opposite side of the field a broad-shouldered man approached the centre, his brown leather jerkin slightly more worn and aged than Calix's, but it seemed stout enough. Leandra recognized the man but couldn't quite place his name. It didn't matter, he was the same as Calix; he was of the same stock. He may have worn more wrinkles on his face, his hair parted more sparsely, but they were the same. Nobles playing at war in a kingdom where no war had been waged in centuries.

"We need to keep our guard up," her father had once said to her, before succumbing to his affliction. "We never know when we may encounter agents of the enemy." And then he tutted her off to bed.

He never once answered her questions about it. How could we meet the enemy, if we can fly? How can they find us so high above the earth? Not even the simplest question — why is it only noble boys who join the militia?

The king didn't answer her questions, but she figured the final one out herself. It was to keep the noble families busy. Keep them entertained.

The crowd cheered as Calix and his opponent met in the centre field. They bowed to each other and then turned to face the king.

"We hope these bouts do you honour, great King Vaselious," they said in unison before taking a deep bow. Standing tall again, Calix took his helm from under his arm and placed it over his face and head, his pale, angular features hidden now, save for his steady, piercing blue eyes.

"He is a handsome lad though," Alethea whispered in Leandra's ear as she handed over the glass of wine. "He certainly grew into his features from boyhood."

"And he's quite a warrior," said Obelius, giving the king another sip from his chalice. "He's won all of his bouts today and did exceptionally well in the archery competition earlier."

As much as it pained Leandra to admit it, Obelius was right. Calix was a fierce warrior. While most nobles took to their militia duties as a pastime, as head of the militia, Calix took it deadly serious. He would often be the first to his morning duties and last to leave at night. It earned him some favour and brought him some attention in the tournaments.

After that, Calix and Leandra saw much more of each other, much to her chagrin. Of course, when Leandra thought of Calix, it wasn't the handsome and fierce warrior who stood ready to duel on the field of tournament that she pictured. Instead it was the rat-faced, greasy haired boy that often tried to torment her and Edric when they were children. The same rat-faced boy whom Edric and herself played pranks upon as often as they could; dullwit that he was.

"Why him?" Leandra said, casting a wave in the general direction of the grounds. A roar went up from the crowd as Calix's opponent rushed toward him with a slice of his thin-bladed sabre.

"Not this again," Obelius said. It was his turn to roll his eyes as Alethea tutted somewhere behind her. Her father never moved. Calix fended off the attack, blocking with his own sword and pushing his opponent off-kilter.

"Why do I have to marry at all?" Leandra said over the angry grunt of Calix as he was thrust backwards with a stiff shoulder from his opponent.

"Princess, as my pupil, I *know* you are aware of the traditions of the Appolumi throne. When a first-born son is not produced, the first-born daughter will be married to a man of appropriate lineage and worth, to ensure the crown is bestowed upon a strong and noble king," Obelius said, wiping the saliva from Vaselious' chin.

The crowd roared as Calix recovered and slashed his opponent's jerkin open across the chest. The elder fighter stood back, his breath coming in heavy gulps, and nodded to Calix. A point well earned.

"I can rule on my own." Leandra stood, her fists by her side, anger rising in her cheeks.

Another cheer went up. His opponent had anticipated Calix's barrage of attacks, sidestepped them, and tripped Calix to the ground with the sweep of his foot. None in the royal box witnessed this as they all stared at Leandra.

"You...you what?" Obelius said, almost dropping the plate of food he held under the king's nose.

"I can rule without a husband," Leandra said. "I'm the only child of the century-long King of Appolumi; I have learned more about ruling watching him than anyone else on this castle. I can rule on my own."

"It's just not done," Alethea said, coming up on her side. "A kingdom needs a king."

Leandra shot her handmaiden a fierce look.

"Too right," Obelius said, laying the tray of food down behind him. "And the people of this kingdom could not stand that sort of change."

"Of course, it's been done. Obelius, it's in your history books. Father, you told me stories of your great, great grandmother ruling with an iron fist. I am sure the people of this kingdom will rally behind the true heir to …"

"No," the king's voice rolled from his thick chest, his weary eyes bearing down on his daughter.

Applause went up amongst the spectators. Calix stood over his opponent, sword placed next to the man's neck. A position of power; he'd won.

Leandra glanced out on the field, her cheeks flushed and her temples throbbing. "I *can* do it."

"But you *will* not," said Obelius, his slender hand on the king's thick shoulder. "The king himself has spoken." A salacious grin took over his face. "You *will* be married to Calix. Preparations have already been made for the coming celebrations. I urge you to put this rebellious streak behind you, princess. For your poor father's sake, if nothing else."

King Vaselious continued to peer at her, but whether he comprehended anything around him at that moment, she could not say.

"Come, Alethea," Leandra said as she made her way to the exit. The resounding cheers for Calix followed her into the grand corridors beyond.

CHAPTER TEN

The Northern Provinces were misty and cold. Despite being outfitted for the travel, Bijan shivered under his cloak constantly. Boon and Iollan seemed not to be bothered by the weather, and never commented on it. The rest of the raiders were equally as frustrating.

It had been two days since they left Arnarfell, heading north on another silent march. Bijan hadn't gotten to know many of the raiders, even though they'd been together for several years. They were as stubborn and reticent as their master. One raider, a young man named Adun, would speak to him sometimes. He was the man tasked with keeping Bijan fed and happy. Sometimes Adun would ask about Bijan's origins, about his people. Bijan loved to converse, could go on about any topic. Whether it was truth or not depended on the mood he was in. Bijan's mood during this ungodly trek did not lead to his speaking many truths.

"I didn't think these cursed islands were big enough for all this walking," he said, catching up to Iollan at the head of the raiders. Iollan, spry and quick, was always at the lead. He set the pace for his raiders and was untiring. Today Boon was ahead of them all, his long legs making up distance over the uneven, grassy terrain.

"There are no straight lines in this accursed country." Iollan stared into Boon's back. "We are constantly walking around marsh or thick brush, or some sort of obstacle of this hellish landscape." He sighed and let out a long breath. "Erland does tell me that our destination should be within our grasp. No more than another day's trek."

Boon was far ahead, his cloak barely visible in the fog that clouded their trip. Bijan lowered his voice to a whisper, "how did you come in contact with him?"

"He was a contact made through my master. It is not my place to question him, or his choices."

"Very well, but can we trust him?" Bijan felt foolish asking; there was only one of this man and dozens of Iollan's raiders, and yet it was a question that had come to his mind unheeded.

Iollan gave Bijan a strange look, his mouth a fine thin line, pale even for his white skin, and then marched ahead leaving Bijan to ruminate on the question himself.

***

"Welcome," Boon turned to Bijan and the raiders and spread his long arms at his sides. "Welcome to the Valley of Appolumi." It had been another cold night huddled around a dwindling campfire for Bijan, another night of little sleep and poor demeanour. Still, tired or not, he surged forward with the rest of the raiders to take in the sight of the legendary valley.

It was a huge canyon that was before them, a canyon that angled itself further and further down into the blackness of earth and rock. It was as if the gods themselves had cut a piece of land out of the ground, an enormous piece of cake to devour. It was certainly a spectacle to behold, but the gods made the earth any way they saw fit.

This did not prove the existence of the castle that took to the skies.

"How do we know this is the right place?" Iollan asked from Bijan's side, as if he was reading his mind.

"I'm afraid that is not my problem," said Boon, lowering his arms and turning towards them. "But I can assure you that this is the valley that you seek. If the castle Appolumi took flight, it was from here."

Iollan's features hardened. His thick hands folded in on themselves and his mighty back began to heave. He stepped toward Boon, a quick step that closed the distance between the two men faster than Bijan would've believed possible. Boon stood his ground and merely shook his forearms as Iollan approached.

Bijan just stared on, watching both men as they stared at one another. Boon's face was relaxed, almost bored, but his eyes did not move from Iollan's. The raiders sensed the tension as well and they began to shuffle and pace, the sound of some unsheathing their weapons reached Bijan's ears. "Is there anything in the books that can verify this place," Iollan's voice was quiet, his tone restrained. It took Bijan a moment to realize that he was talking to him and not to Boon. He dropped his bag and began to sort through his books.

"I... I can't say for sure, but there may be a passage or inscription somewhere that will clear things up."

"Let's find some place to set up and keep warm. Bijan, start reading through your books." Iollan turned and signalled to his men to follow; a sigh fell through the air as the tension lifted. Boon smiled at Iollan's back as he left, his arms relaxed now, his sleeves still.

"This is the place," he said to Bijan, turning toward the valley before him. "This is where the legend starts."

***

"This place is amazing." Bijan emerged from a dusty hole in the ground, the sun, cutting through the mist, cast sunbeams around him. Bijan held up a broken urn, his eyes wild with excitement. He turned it over in his hands, images of men huddled in a circle surrounded it. "Fascinating."

"I'm not sure this is what we hired you for," Adun was staring down at him from a close-by mound of dirt. The young raider had his scarf down over his nose, his eyes smiling.

"Oh, my young friend, this is the very reason you hired me." Bijan crawled out of the hole, being careful with his new prize. "Everything I find leads me closer and closer to discovering the nature of the people of Appolumi."

"How could that possibly help us track a flying castle?" Adun tossed a dagger in the air and caught it with little flourish.

"First of all, Boy, the castle surely isn't flying." Bijan blew some dust from the urn.

"Well, I think that this gaping hole in the ground tells me otherwise," Adun said and spread his arms wide to emphasize the valley.

"Boy, the only things that fly are the birds in the sky. There's nothing magical about this mystery. The castle was likely ransacked by a rival nation, savages perhaps. Or, they simply died away. Lucky for you, and your employers, I'll discover it before too long. All of this will tell me." It was Bijan's turn to spread his arms towards the valley. He pointed to the urn, "for instance, this tells me that they revered a group of sages, or wisemen. Magi perhaps."

Adun slid down the mound of dirt and took a closer

look. "This doesn't look like a group of men. It looks like a squiggly line."

"A squiggly line!" Bijan raised his voice and hid the urn under his arm. "Don't you have food or water to fetch me, perhaps a cup of wine?" He turned away from the laughing Adun and walked towards his tent.

Weeks had passed since Boon had led them to the Valley of Appolumi. Despite the cold weather and the ever-present mist, Bijan soon began to discover little relics of the kingdom that once rested its laurels in that very spot. Little things at first: jewelry, disintegrating baskets, cups that did little to prove the castle had once resided here, but it succeeded in holding Bijan's interest. It was when he started to uncover pottery, urns (some in better shape than the one he just discovered), coins, and even weapons that proof started to reveal itself. Proof that the castle of Appolumi was here, proof that it had an advanced culture centred around a king and, now, this group of Magi.

Iollan hadn't been impressed. He studied everything Bijan put in front of him, listened to Bijan's explanations, theories, then nodded and walked away. Bijan hadn't seen him since. Boon had also been missing since their arrival. At first, Bijan had seen him on the outskirts of the valley, roaming the edge, looking down at them. It had been quite some time since even that had occurred. Not that Bijan was overly upset, he was left to his own devices and able to do what he needed to do, and he had a small band of raiders at his beck and call. "Piss on them," Bijan said to himself, placing the urn next to another very similar to it. He sat on his makeshift bed, studying the artifacts he had already found. As joyous as it was for him to discover all these rarities, Adun was correct. As hesitant as Bijan was to admit it: none of them gave him many clues in how to find the wayward kingdom, at least to Iollan's desires. He leaned forward studying the urns. A circle of wise men, a king in power, a war on the horizon. The tales were all there, but what did any of that have to do with flight?

"You have quite a collection there." The voice, dry and cracked, startled Bijan and he jumped to his feet, facing the opening, one hand on his sword. Boon stared at him, his ice blue eyes calm over his abundant beard. "Are your trinkets telling you anything?"

Bijan hadn't taken in the sheer size of Boon before the strange guide blocked the exit of his tent. He stood before Bijan with his wide shoulders slumped over a broad chest in the tradition of those Bijan had seen in the North. Burly and hairy, the lot of them. He was brutish compared to the lithe and agile Iollan and his raiders, but middling when compared to the sack stomached Brothers of Samet. And yet it wasn't his size that made the world-weary scavenger pause. It was something else, something Bijan could not name. One thing he could say, Boon gave off an eerie energy. It crackled in his presence.

"You sneak about like that, Boon, and you'll get yourself stabbed through the gut," Bijan huffed as he made a show of sliding his scimitar into its scabbard.

"Why should I fear anyone here. We're all friends." Boon walked further into the tent and sat in a squat chair Bijan had set up next to a small table. "How is the hunt, Master Bijan?" Boon's head rolled on his shoulders taking in the tent and its contents, a lazy smile on his face.

"I've found some interesting pieces," Bijan said, picking up a particularly nice bracelet he'd found the day before last.

"Oh, so you'll have conquered your goal soon? You'll have reason to leave?"

"Er... I'm afraid not so soon." Bijan placed the bracelet back on its perch. "There is much yet to discover."

Boon nodded his head, one hand twisting his beard. "Did you people ever hear the actual tale of the castle?"

Bijan scoffed. "Of course. Even my far-flung people have heard tell of the flying kingdom; its majesty and treasure."

"Is that so? We have a slightly different story in this part of the world." Boon began to pick his teeth with his finger. "Would you like to hear it?"

"This should be good," Bijan rolled his eyes and sat on his bed, "go on then, if you must."

Boon unravelled the tale, his cadence relaxed, the voice of a man who had told this story dozens of times. The castle Appolumi was under attack. The neighbouring lands took exception to their practices, to their dominance over the land, over the people. They despised the king and his Circle of Magi. That was who they hated the most, the Magi. They sought to kidnap every child who was born with some magical inkling. Sought and accomplished. Under the king's orders, sons and daughters were taken, screaming, from their parents' arms and forced into The Circle of Magi.

The people banded together and set out to take the castle, overrun it and bring about its demise. The king and his Magi held council and decided that with all their might, with all their power, they couldn't hold off their enraged neighbours for long. A new plan was made: The Circle of Magi would lift the castle out of the ground so that their enemies could not reach them. They would be steadfast in their ways, constant in their practices. The castle would endure, its people remain.

"Of course," Boon said, tapping the bowl of a pipe

onto the table before him, "that is only one story. No one knows the truth for certain. Not unless they live on the castle, of course."

"You Northerners have a very negative view of history," Bijan said, troubled. True, he had never heard Boon's version of the tale of the castle Appolumi, but the information, new or old, didn't seem to help clarify a way to find the ever-moving castle.

"In this case, we are probably the closest to truth," Boon said with a grunt. His eyes were cast downward, studying the urns. "You Southerners, your story is so diluted by the magical and the amazing that it forgets the basic truth of it. The lesson hidden within."

"Bah! Magic," Bijan spat. "I've heard my fair share of tales about magic. I've delved deep into ancient caves, cursed temples, sorcerer's tombs. I've held all sorts of magical items in these hands. Do you know what I've discovered?"

Boon turned his shaggy head to the side, a funny sort of smile on his face, as if he were aware of a joke and he wouldn't share the punchline.

"There's no magic, Boon. Just relics and dust." He waved his hand toward his prizes.

A silence fell between the two men then. An awkward thing that kept them both on guard.

"And what lesson is hidden within your story?" Bijan said, breaking the stalemate that had followed his diatribe.

Boon looked up at him, surprised. His calm, half-lidded eyes replaced by a fiery stare. "To fight. To kill. To punish those that would cause you or your kin harm."

"As I said," Bijan ignored the gaze of his uninvited guest, "you Northerners are very negative."

"Perhaps," Boon said, calming, "but it is a good lesson all the same." He stretched his arms in an elaborate yawn, and for the first time Bijan noticed the markings. Lines of scarlet and obsidian trailed his arms in elaborate pictures and symbols that even Bijan had not seen before. It was such a strange sight that Bijan caught himself staring, just as Boon did the same and rolled down his sleeves. "I'd better be leaving you," he said, making way for the entrance. "I hope you find what you're looking for."

After he left, the tension in the air dissipated and Bijan felt as though he could breathe freely once again. 'What a strange man,' he thought, running his hand through his dark hair. As he looked around his tent one more time, he caught sight of a small leather-bound book sitting on his table that had not been there before. He opened it, the leather spine creaking, and began to read.

He read through the night and into the early morning hours. He couldn't put it down until he had finished.

***

Iollan looked at Bijan with furrowed brows. He was hesitant, Bijan could understand that, but they may not have the time of hesitancy. It was all laid out for them, they just needed to find it. Cast their line and reel it in.

"So," Iollan said, repeating it for the third time, "you believe there are some sort of markers that guide the path of the Castle." He took his time with his words, rolling them over in his mind as he spoke.

"Yes, yes —" Bijan started, but was halted by Iollan with an outstretched hand.

"And you've come to this conclusion, not because of the digging around that you've been doing, but because of a book of scrawlings given to you by Erland." Iollan dropped his hand, his cold eyes rested on Bijan, as did those of the three raiders that were sitting behind him, and Adun's dull eyes from behind.

"Well, partially," Bijan said, scratching the back of his head, eyes on the ground.

Iollan cursed; his men shuttered back a step. "Well why didn't we hire that infernal tree pirate and leave you to the Brothers of Samet?" His face burned and he slammed his fist into his own leg with a thud of flesh on flesh.

"Wait, wait," Bijan held his hands out before him, seeing a look he didn't like grow on the raiders' faces. He picked up the small book and held it in front of him. "This is just a book of stories. Legends, fairy tales. One such story says that the castle itself is alive! But, these stories often have an element of truth in them." Bijan began to flip through the pages. "Each of these has a different view of how the castle took to the sky, each has a different reason for the people of Appolumi to exile themselves to the clouds. Some say it was coming war, some say it was to flee an evil beast, but in either case The Circle was involved. A group of people gifted with magic who needed to replenish their ranks. Most stories say they stole children, others say they were given up freely. Whatever the case, The Circle needs to keep itself whole. They still take children." He closed the book, satisfied with himself.

"So?"

"So? So? Isn't it obvious? We have to find one of the towns that sacrifice to the castle. We will know because of an ancient marker that is housed there to draw the castle to it, keep it on its path."

"Very well," Iollan nodded, "I see your point. Though, how do you expect to find a town that may not have been contacted in over a century?"

"Easy," Bijan's face broke into a shameless smirk. "I've already found it."

PART THREE
CHAPTER ELEVEN

"Those were some lovely dresses, princess," Alethea said, her ruddy cheeks twitching into a broad smile.

Leandra sank into a pile of cushions, a scowl on her face. "I suppose," she said, tipping her head back and closing her eyes. The events of the day flashed before her darkened eyelids, the clash of swords on armour still ringing in her ears. And above that the whispered growl of her father, the king. 'No,' he had said. As simple a word as there was, but with it came a finality. The king hath spoken, his word was law.

The problem was that the king hadn't spoken in weeks, months. His condition, whether it was age or sickness or something else entirely, was getting worse. His once strong hands now sat folded across his growing stomach. His once keen blue eyes were now glazed over and lifeless. His mouth, once quick to smile, now drooped under a layer of dried saliva. The thought brought tears to the brink of Leandra's eyes.

"No need to sulk, princess," Alethea said as she did some mindless tidying. She'd been taking care of Leandra for longer than she could remember, and she was the closest thing Leandra had to a mother. Still, dealing with her was sometimes a chore.

"Leave me," Leandra flicked her hand toward her chamber's door.

"As you wish, princess," Alethea said and hurried out of the room, a pained echo under her breath.

'It's getting too easy to do that,' Leandra thought, looking toward the closed door, hoping that her old handmaiden had ignored her orders. Perhaps she wasn't cut out to be a ruler, after all. Her father always said that a king needed to be able to give orders and accept their consequences. But a skinny, noble boy was going to do a better job leading than her?

Leandra kicked her pillows and stomped to her window. The courtyard was quiet; empty. The sun was setting, the sky turned into a surreal, violaceous painting. Before his sickness, her father was against her marrying. At least, he hadn't been impressed with the crop of eligible nobles that had begun to present themselves to him. How many times did she and her father laugh at the nobles' sons? How many times would he point out their faults and weaknesses, laughing all the while? A smile creased her lips.

Admittedly, Calix had impressed King Vaselious with his combat prowess. As a consequence of that, Calix had been brought into the inner circle, as the king was fond of saying. Aside from his ability to play with a sword, what did he have? High cheekbones perhaps, and charming blue eyes, but not a personality, that was certain. The boy was as about as exciting as a wet mop. And where were his leadership skills? Sure, he led the castle militia, but what use is a militia on a castle that flies? Aside from keeping the drunks from harming themselves, Leandra couldn't say.

The princess laughed aloud and kicked her way out

of her dress. She left it crumpled in a pile on the floor and pulled on a comfortable pair of trousers and a loose tunic. Darkness had almost truly fallen, the dim lights from the braziers and the pale light of the moon would be all that illuminated the courtyard. Her hands itched to open her window, but the time wasn't right.

'No,' her father had said. The same man that had broken into tears at seeing her just a few minutes before he said it. Just as he had said when she wanted to learn the use of a sword herself. She sighed. Hadn't he taught her to be strong, to be independent, to be a leader? And for what? To be married off to the noble that can best handle a sword. Leandra scoffed.

She peered out the window, into the dark, orange flames that began to appear across the castle as the braziers were lit. The moonlight was dampened by the clouds; a smile flashed over her features anew. She doused the light in her room, flicked the latch on the window, and crept out onto the window ledge. The familiar feel of the handholds in the worn brick welcomed her.

What would her father say about that, she wondered, scaling the wall as comfortably as she could walk? It had never been a habit that her father indulged. He'd often scolded her for it, that and her interactions with Edric — the boy with all the magic. The king kept Edric and Edric's master, Hesperos, at arm's reach. At choking distance — a comment that Obelius had once casually offered.

Leandra jumped to a new ledge. Spanning the gap in an instant, her calloused fingertips gripped it with a practised panache. She grunted through a smile. Magic was important on Appolumi. Her father knew this more than most, the King of Appolumi would need to understand it as such. She understood it too. Her father made sure of it.

***

She looked down, the courtyard far below her barely visible. The wind took her hair and tossed it around her neck and back. It was a cold wind and she shivered. Just above her a dim light peeked out from the small turret window.

It had been a long time since she'd visited Edric. Their life had grown apart, more from the influence of her father, Obelius, and Hesperos than anything else, she suspected. He'd always remained in her mind, thoughts of the fun they had with their childhood games and their pranks remained through everything else she'd had to learn since then. Through all Obelius' lessons on history, Alethea's lessons on ladylike behaviour, and her father's approach to leading, Edric had always been there. The young boy she remembered peeking out around a corner, his mischievous smile only matched by the cunning in his bright eyes.

Leandra pushed herself upward. She'd soon see him again.

CHAPTER TWELVE

"You are on your way to reaching your full potential, Boy." Hesperos cast his lizard-like eye upon Edric. "You defended yourself ably, if without finesse." He'd moved behind Edric, the clinking of glass and the pouring of liquid giving away his location.

"You're strong, physically, and have the will to engage as needed." Hesperos reappeared in front of him, a small glass vial pinched between the long fingernails of thumb and forefinger. A dark purple substance was contained within.

Edric had spent the previous night preparing for today. According to Hesperos, the second stage of the Trials was especially hard and focused on the mental preparation of the postulant. He'd prepared through the night by alternating between reading his master's ancient tomes on the matter and inducing a deep meditation to buttress his mental fortitude. It would have worked, Edric thought, if he hadn't been so incredibly focused on his parents. His father was a drunk, but what of his mother? She'd delivered Edric to Hesperos, perhaps, but she had to be hoping to see her son once again. Isn't that what all mothers want?

"But physical endurance is not all that's needed in The

Circle. How is your mind, Boy?" Hesperos passed the vial to Edric and stood back. "Drink."

Edric tilted the vial back and forth, watching the tar-like residue film over the glass. It reminded him of something he'd seen before but could not place. He looked to his master, a cold expression staring back at him, and he drank the contents of the vial in one pull. It was tasteless. Thick and warm, it coated his mouth and throat and made him gag as it did. He managed to stifle his urge to vomit and the potion made a slow crawl into his gullet and stomach. Edric's eyes watered, a sweat had broken out anew on his forehead and lower back, but he could feel no further effects of the sickly liquid. Hesperos stared at him impassively, leaning an elbow on his staff.

When the potion took effect, it was indisputable. Edric curled over, clutching his stomach and clawing at his chest. A scream tried to gurgle forth, but he couldn't utter a sound. It was as if the ooze from the vial simply grabbed it and held it tight. He closed his eyes against the flood of tears and whispered for relief inside his own head, even as rainbows caught in the periphery of his vision. And then everything stopped.

***

There was an ache in his stomach. It felt empty and growled with hunger, but Edric feared even the thought of eating. He stumbled forward and tried to open his eyes, but the complete blackness continued unabated.

"Hesperos," he said, panic beating against his temples. "I can't see." His voice echoed in emptiness, and he groped about with flailing hands.

"Hesperos," he tried again. He cursed and moved forward. It was when his hand touched on the rough bark and fragile leaves of a tree that he realized he was not in Hesperos' chambers anymore. Once he found the tree, it guided him to more of its brethren, their branches bending and slapping, their bark sticky with sap. Edric pushed through them until, in the distance, he could see a small light.

"Not blind after all," he muttered.

It was a cold night, and snow floated to the ground at its own leisurely pace. Edric wrapped his cloak around his arms and crossed them in front of him. It did little help. The snow began to seep through his boots and pants, and each little breeze would chill him to the bone. The snow did not crunch under his feet, nor did it give any resistance. It was light and airy, but there was plenty on the ground, gathering in heaps and hills. As he got closer to the light source Edric could tell the snow wasn't white, but a slate grey; it looked dirty. He held out his hand and caught a large flake in his palm. He crushed it in his fist. When he opened his hand again, streaks of black and grey were all that were left. It wasn't snow.

The source of the light slowly came into view: a tall black spire, expelling light as a fire gives off heat. He took up place in some trees not too far from the hill the spire stood upon. In the haze of the dim light he saw the boy. The boy, chained to the iron ring that protruded from the flawless ebony surface, looked back at him.

On the air, Edric could hear the boy's wails for help. His young, fragile voice carried above the breeze. He wanted to run to him but couldn't. He slumped into the trees, his feet unable to move as he listened to the boy's sobs.

There was a slight quake in the air, a tingle at the edge of his senses. Edric turned, but saw nothing. A sudden

feeling of unease gripped him, and he knew that something else was amongst the trees. A low growl started in
the brush before him, a cavernous moaning that shook the
trees. Four creatures emerged then, at the same time and
from different directions.

The first he saw was a brown fox that flitted and
danced from the direction of the spire to sit at his side. Its
curious, luminescent green eyes kept looking at the obelisk, its tongue lolling from its jaws. The next beast was a
sleek, white wolf. The wolf emerged to his left, its teeth
exposed and its back up, as it moved in on him. Its pink
tongue shot between its bared fangs tasting the air and
the fear within it. Edric heard a noise in the trees to his
right; a giant black owl sat there, feathered horns bobbing
up and down as it took him in with its enormous eyes.
They looked hollow and empty, but they were ever present, and always watchful. When it turned its head at the
sound of the boy, its eyes seemed to change in colour for
the briefest moment. The final creature to emerge from
the trees was a mountainous grizzly bear, its dark, matted fur showing some grey, its muzzle scarred and ugly.
It roared as it emerged, its massive teeth taking up all of
Edric's vision. As it came forward, Edric stood back, his
hands out in front of him, until he came up hard against
the tree, the branches and bark scratching at his back.

It took a mere moment but Edric noticed two things
about the creatures. First, they were not interested in each
other nor were they particularly drawn to Edric. Their aggression was directed somewhere else. Secondly, their intent was the obelisk and the boy chained to it. Even the fox
that sat by his side looked over its shoulder at the obelisk,
small pink tongue dashing out to lick its lips.

Edric's breath came in large gulps. His wide eyes darted between the eager animals. Edric fought the urge to look at the obelisk; he didn't want to betray his intentions. He didn't know if he could release the child, but he was compelled to keep the boy alive. He couldn't let the beasts reach the obelisk. If he did, that would mean the end. Of what, he didn't know.

The wolf made the first move, ducking its head and moving forward one slow paw at a time. It growled as it came, a low guttural sound that pushed Edric further into the open arms of the tree's branches. The brown fox danced away from Edric's side and met the wolf, an eerie howl emerging from its snout. The wolf fell back, a confused sneeze gave it pause before it snapped at the fox, foamy saliva spraying as it did. The fox jumped out of its way and bit one of the wolf's hind legs. It wasn't more than a nibble, but it worked. The chase began. The fox fled into the woods and the wolf followed, snarling. They both cast a quick glance at the obelisk as they ran, one after the other, into the black trees.

The owl made a quick dive as Edric was distracted by the others and, screeching, it sliced at him with razor-like talons. Edric was able to bring his arm up in time to save his eyes, but the weird-eyed bird dug into his arm, ripping cloth and flesh with ease. Edric screamed and tried to shake the bird loose, but that only caused more pain, more damage. He batted at it with his free hand and swung it into a nearby tree, feeling its hollow bones crunch. It squealed and let go, its misshapen wings taking it back into the trees.

Hunched over, Edric grasped his wounded arm. He exhaled through clenched teeth in a short hiss, the blood dripping from beneath his fingers. It was then, with a grunt, the bear pushed through the trees into the field of the obelisk, bending and crushing the finger-like branches that lashed out at its thick hide. Edric made to grab at the beast, not sure what he would do to stop it, but was swept away as if a leaf gliding from the sky. With a scramble, he got back to his feet and rushed after the bear, through the carnage it left in its wake.

The bear pushed its way into the clearing and started to trot towards the obelisk and the boy. Its enormous paws thumped on the snow-sodden grass and revealed a rich brown mud underneath. Edric couldn't keep up with the beast. He ran with his wounded arm tight to his chest, his feet slipping where the bear had not. He gathered his energy into his fist and sent it outward toward the bear. He could see the ripple of air, feel the movement in the atmosphere, and he knew he'd cast the spell correctly. When it hit the bear there was a slight rustle of its matted fur but nothing else. It closed on the boy.

"No," Edric rushed forward, gathering more energy, scraping for his reserve store. Instead of forcing it outward he pushed it down within him. He felt the energy filling his legs, moving him faster and faster. Edric slipped in front of the bear just before it reached the boy. "No," he said once more, facing the bear down.

The bear reared back, red eyes wide with surprise and rage, it roared an earth-quaking growl and bared jagged and sharp teeth.

"You can't have him," Edric said between gasping breaths.

The bear stared down on him, its red eyes glinting with a savage intelligence. A low grumbling laugh poured forth from its immense chest. Its shoulders twitched from on high.

"I don't care about the child," its voice struck Edric's

mind, jostling him. "I don't care about you or your mystic powers." The bear's voice assaulted Edric, pain crawling through his brain like a spider. "My rage is an old one, beyond your comprehension. Should you, or anyone, stand in my way," the bear slammed Edric with the back of its shield-sized paw, sending him through the air. "Should that happen, I will raze you to your very marrow." The bear stepped forward again. "To your very soul."

Edric watched as the bear approached the obelisk, his nose bleeding and a taste of iron in his mouth. The child cringed away from the beast, pulling at his chains, trying to keep as far as possible. The bear paid little attention to him, letting out a snort as he passed. Instead it moved closer to the obelisk, rising on its hind legs once again. It placed its paws on the purple crystal and started to push. Its whole body rippled as it moved, its claws digging into the surface of the obelisk. A grinding noise echoed in the field; the sound of glass cracking. It overwhelmed Edric, his heart raced, and panic rose in his stomach. The obelisk was falling.

It fell in one smooth motion. It fell like water cascading down atop of everything, the bear laughing even as it was being covered in shards of crystal. The boy was there too, wailing above the rain of glass. Edric felt the shards fall on him, felt their jagged edges slice his flesh and blood flow from his wounds. The end was near. He closed his eyes. The end of everything.

***

"Wake up, Boy," Hesperos said with a slap to the side of Edric's exposed face. A sting, like dozens of small cuts, exploded along Edric's cheek and he drew his head up from his chest, breath catching as he looked around him.

"Ah, there you are." The old man gripped Edric's chin in his hand and forced him to look in his eyes. "I was afraid I'd mixed the potion too strong." He turned his pupil's head from side to side, never breaking the gaze of his mismatched eyes. "So, tell me Boy, how was your dream?"

Edric shuddered at the brief remembrance he had at its mere mention. He twisted his head out of his master's grip. "It was a dream. Nothing more."

"Oh, but it was most certainly something more," Hesperos said with a crude smile. "It is a sign of your transference to The Circle. It is a sign of how prepared you are to join it. The mere fact that you survived with your mind intact certainly says something of your grit. I will admit, I had doubted your ability to make it through." He continued to smile, pacing before Edric. "But I'm glad you were able to prove me wrong. Finally, a new member of The Circle." Hesperos clapped his hands together. "Well, if you manage to survive the last Trial."

Edric squirmed. Something about Hesperos' glee put him off. The old man was never excited, even happy. For Hesperos to be so absolutely joyful made Edric think of only the worst of things. "Are my Trials at an end for today, Master?"

"Who, or what, was in your dream, young Edric? Do tell before you scurry off."

"I... I can't remember." Sweat draped Edric's torso, and he tried to conceal the shiver that ran down his spine.

"Can't remember," Hesperos said, mimicking Edric's voice. "I find that very hard to believe. The elixir makes the vision oh so vibrant. Please, do tell me what you saw."

"I can't remember, Master. It's just a blur."

Hesperos spat. "Bah! Stupid Boy. Return to your quarters and reflect upon your dream. Perhaps you'll be more willing to talk tomorrow."

Edric stood next to the open door, waiting.

"Well?" Hesperos said, cracking open a large, leather-bound book and letting his fingernail guide his reading.

"I passed the Trial. You owe me more information about my parents." Edric could hear the waver in his voice. He could feel the shaking in his limbs, but he forced it out of his thoughts. He stood facing his master. Waiting.

"I owe you," Hesperos said in a slow purr. "Imagine, this whelp believes that *I* owe him anything." He closed his book with a slam and pointed a long finger at Edric. "Boy, I owe you nothing."

"We made a deal." It felt like a whisper, as if he were a child begging for a toy.

"A deal? The deal is that I tell you what to do and you do it." Hesperos stroked his thin beard. "Now, if you were to tell me something of your dream, perhaps I would be a little more open to —"

"We made a deal." Edric took a step forward, his fists clenched. "I upheld my end of it, now you owe me."

"Boy, I would suggest that you mind your to —"

"Tell me about my parents." Edric could feel the energy whip off him, could sense the crackle in the air, and the hair standing on his arms. A rage built within him, sloughing off in invisible tentacles of power.

Hesperos' eyes went wide for just a moment but settled quickly as his scowl reverted to a small smile. "Since I see that this is very important to you, let me tell you a little something about your parents." Hesperos walked around his desk and stood before Edric, his hands crossed behind his back. "Your parents were nothing more than squalid peasants, barely making a living. The only thing that saved them was *you*. See, *you* had magical gifts. *You* were worth something, where your beggarly family was worth scarce more than the fleas on their backs. And so, they sold you. They sold you to me, to the kingdom of Appolumi, for a paltry few shillings and a goat."

"But, where —"

Hesperos stood straight and shook his finger at Edric. "Ah-ah-ah. I've lived up to our deal, Boy. One more Trial to go. Maybe once you're a part of The Circle I will tell you more."

Edric turned to leave, his mind muddled with Hesperos' words and the images that he'd seen in his dream. As much as he attempted to think about his father who sold him, to feel hatred, sadness, or any sort of emotion towards him, he couldn't. He could only picture the boy and the crystal rain of the falling spire.

"Oh, and Boy," Hesperos called as Edric walked into the waiting hallway. "The next time you want to threaten with your powers, be prepared to learn a harsh lesson."

"Yes, Master," Edric said as he left Hesperos' chambers, trying not to think of the obelisk.

***

Edric stumbled through the halls of Appolumi in a daze. His thoughts were jumbled, his body weak. Hunger gnawed at his guts, but he couldn't fathom eating; even water seemed a repulsive thought.

One moment his mind would rage against the betrayal of his family, for selling him. The next moment he shook in fear for the boy in his dream and the bear that threatened to end everything. Somehow, he knew that the bear meant to raze the castle, to destroy it. Was he an image of the ancient enemy? Could the bear be someone who survived the plague? Edric didn't like to think about the possibilities.

He pushed open the trap door that led to his bedroom and fell to the floor, moving his legs out of the portal just before they could be struck by the falling door.

It was dark. The sun had gone down during his time with Hesperos, which seemed ludicrous, but was something he'd become accustomed to. Working with magic often played with the senses, the world, even time itself. Still, there was an initial stab of incoherence.

Edric sighed; the thought of moving pained him. "Things to be done," he said as he pushed himself to his knees.

A quiver of something crossed the nape of his neck, a stir of energy. Edric pulled at his depleted will, hoping it would be enough, and squinted into the darkness of his room.

There was a scratch and a spark, and a lamp lit next to his bed.

"Hello Edric," Leandra said.

CHAPTER THIRTEEN

In truth, Bijan hadn't expected Iollan to offer much support in the new direction the dig had taken. He imagined the man, growing as curt and temperamental as he had been, ordering Bijan's immediate and painful execution. Instead he was offered ten strong men, including Adun, and two weeks' worth of supplies. Perhaps pushing his luck a little too far, Bijan also requested Boon's guiding services to help them navigate the land and find that which he had promised Iollan — a path to the castle Appolumi. Boon and his ever-decreasing interest in what was happening around him, just shrugged his shoulders at the offer and readied a small bag.

In a half-truth, Bijan didn't exactly know where to start looking, despite what he told Iollan. This was, in fact, the main reason he had pilfered Boon's services. He needed a bloodhound to track his clues. He didn't see any reason to explain this to Iollan and his foul mood. After all, the results would be the same. A new hiccup was the last thing that he needed to present to Iollan.

"All right, you gave me that book for a reason," Bijan had said to Boon their first night away from Iollan and his raiders. "Now, I need to find one of these bloody markers. You know where they are don't you?"

Boon sucked his teeth and gave Bijan a half-lidded glare. "I may know of where such things exist."

"And you'll guide me to them, correct? You are a guide after all." Bijan sipped his tea, feeling much less anxious.

"Perhaps," Boon said, staring at his fingernails. Stalling.

"Perhaps? What is that supposed to mean?" Bijan could feel his temper rising. It was a simple thing, the man already knew where they had to go, he could just show them. Hell, he could even just write it down for them if he felt so inclined.

"It means I can show you if I have some assurances."

Bijan cursed under his breath. "What sort of assurances?"

"One, really. A fairly simple thing I'd imagine."

"Spit it out." Bijan laid his cup down on the floor next to him, feeling the need to pace in his squat tent.

"I want to be taken to the castle. I want to be one of the first to set foot on it." The ease at which he said that astonished Bijan. He stood there, gawking at the Northern guide in his fur-lined cloak, and wild, bushy beard. He was trying to find any sense in those disinterested blue eyes, but only found calm.

"Are you mad?" Bijan paced his tent with reckless abandon.

"Just a man who knows his people's history but has an urge to live it." Boon leaned forward. "I deserve to be on that castle. More than you, more than Iollan, and more than his master. I deserve to be there. I deserve to see it, to feel it, to sense it with every aspect of my being."

"I… I can't guarantee that sort of thing. I'm just helping them break the puzzle, find the prize. They run the show," Bijan said sitting back down, his knees bouncing unwarranted.

"I'm sure you can find a way. Besides, is this really about your obligations to Iollan or is it about the discovery? You're a man who can make legends reality. A man who can experience the impossible. I've heard tales of you, Bijan the Borrower, I know what you really want out of all this. I hold a key that can bring you closer. Will you guarantee me entry onto the castle or no?" Boon's blue eyes were whirlpools, fierce and intent. Bijan stroked his beard, eyeing the man across from him. It would be no easy task to make Boon a part of the finding crew. Iollan had no love for him, and his usefulness had run out in Iollan's eyes some time ago. But, if he held a secret to the castle, he would only smooth their way and make their task easier. Besides, Bijan was a singular man. He'd scaled the Tower of Akas Mehul, had stolen the Idol of Ur Mekhenet, he could certainly sneak a quiet fellow like Boon into a raiding party.

"Okay. I will do it, somehow. But just as I will follow your directions now, when the time comes, you will need to follow mine. Are we agreed?" Bijan extended his hand and Boon grabbed it.

"Agreed." Boon stood and moved to exit the tent. "The town we will need to reach is Haugr. It is but a two-day trek. Have your men ready by sunup."

Bijan watched Boon exit into the mist, tendrils of which crept in under the closing flap of the tent. He sat back and drained the rest of his tea. Boon was completely right. He'd done and seen so many things, but this was his chance to bring legend into reality. All the other baubles and treasures he had found were surrounded by some superstition: a curse, a god's appendage ripped asunder, a ghost of its previous owner. None of them were real.

However, none could touch the pure significance of the castle of Appolumi. All the corners of the world, all of its people, knew of the castle, dreamed of it. It was a bedtime story for children, a fantasy for adults. Bijan even heard that there were those in the west who were searching for a way to prove flight could be accomplished. Many had seen it over the years or claimed to see it. Many believed that it was a sign from the gods, or that it was the home of their deities. Boon's book proved that there were more than a few theories that ran through even these Northern Provinces. If Bijan could find the castle, could discover the true nature of its flight, of its people, then he could become a legend himself. He leaned back in his chair and stared up at the cloth ceiling.

"Bijan the Borrower, indeed."

***

Boon was true to his word and led Bijan and the small band of raiders at sunup. He had returned to his insular ways, only speaking when relaying directions or warning of pitfalls. To Bijan's chagrin, the mist and cold persisted. It swirled about his feet at all hours of the day and made his already substantial cloak heavier in the cold, damp air. As always, the raiders showed no discomfort, and Boon seemed as born to the weather as a fish to water. Bijan shuddered, walking behind the large Northerner, Adun at his side.

"Do you people have no blood?" Bijan said through chattering teeth, his eyes giving Adun a sidelong glance.

The young raider turned his smiling eyes to Bijan; he seemed as chipper as ever. "It's not our way to show weakness. It is better to keep our enemies guessing."

"You're not very good at keeping your secrets are you,

Adun? I have but to ask and you tell me everything," Bijan scowled at his young compatriot.

"Are you an enemy?" Adun said. Bijan grunted and pushed forward, trying to keep up with Boon.

Haugr was a small village on the outskirts of the area once considered Appolumi. They marched into the town square at midday, the little sun allowed in that misty Northern realm was on their backs. That was as warm a reception as they would receive.

At first, the town appeared to be deserted. The small wooden houses seemingly boarded up or empty, and there was an almost complete silence, only gently broken by the muttering of livestock from somewhere further within the small town. And yet there were signs of life if one observed close enough. A catch of whispered conversation, a sound of a glass banging on wood, and even the low growl of a dog. Bijan pointed to his ear and said to Adun in his own whispered tone, "not completely deserted then."

Boon took up a position in the middle of the town, surveying it in full, and waited for the others to crowd close to him, waving those who wandered back to him. "They are a shy people," Boon said, "they don't trust strangers. What we seek is on the outer reaches of the town, in the forested area." He pointed a finger to the far side of town. "We shouldn't disturb them if we keep moving." Boon nodded once, his eyes scanning the company with him, and without further discussion he moved on toward their goal.

"Why have you brought these outsiders here, Erland?" A large man with a heavy grey moustache stood beside the closing door of a house directly in front of them. He had an axe held between his two hands.

"Merely passing through, Halvar. I doubt you'd have noticed our arrival if you hadn't left your dwelling." The man reminded Bijan of one of the brigands they'd met in Arnarfell, big and burly and easily offended.

"You're not welcome around here, Erland. Nor are your friends." More men seemed to appear from behind the small homes, equally armed with axes, clubs, and a few swords. At first it was just a half dozen men, but it soon grew to almost two dozen. Older men were in the majority of those gathered, but both young and old were represented in their number.

"Let us pass then," Boon said, any drop of pleasantry gone from his voice.

Halvar looked around at his brethren, the rough-looking, haggard bunch, grumbling under black eyes. "Nay. Go back the way ye come. We know what you're after, Erland, but you shan't have access twice."

Boon shook out his sleeves and stepped forward, a growl rising in his chest. The men of Haugr responded in kind, brandishing their weapons and hurling curses and threats across the small space of town.

"Excuse me," Bijan's voice rose above the ruckus, his hands raised upwards as he stepped around and in front of Boon. "Excuse me, fine people of Haugr. I know not what issue you may have with our guide here, nor do I care. If he has harmed you or wronged you in some way, I will not stand in the way of your well-deserved justice." Bijan cast a sneer at Boon, who's utter confusion was laid bare on his face.

"However," Bijan continued, lowering his hands and modulating his voice, "we are trying to reach Arnarfell and are not accustomed to your province. If our guide is to be punished, perhaps one of you fine people may show us the way?"

There was a low whispering amongst the townspeople, surprise present on more than one of their expressions.

"Is… is that the only place you seek?" Halvar said after a moment's consultation with those around him.

"Yes, yes. To be honest with you, we are making our way back to the sea. Our ship waits for us just past there, but the crew wait in Arnarfell. We've already paid this man as our guide, and though we have no such money on us right now, we'll surely be able to pay one of you guiding fees once we get to our crew."

"Is this true, Erland? You do not seek to enter the plain?" Halvar turned his eyes to Boon once more.

"Obviously," Boon said, his voice lowered to a growl.

Halvar and his men conferred once more. Bijan made a show of barely withheld impatience, rolling his eyes and tapping his foot. Oh, the men of Haugr must have thought him a dandy indeed.

"Very well, you may pass through. Calder will accompany you to the edge of our town to ensure your good intentions," Halvar pointed to a large young man holding a sledgehammer in two hands, his blond beard just growing on his cheeks.

"Many thanks, people of Haugr," Bijan said with a low bow. He then turned to Boon and in a whisper said, "you're welcome."

As the other men went about their business, Calder stood waiting for the outsiders to approach. Boon led the way, grumbling to himself as he went.

***

The stern eyes of the men of Haugr followed them as they moved through the town. Some stood outside their homes, brandishing their weapons, while others stared from the shadows of their windows. Bijan was confident that he'd convinced the simple townsfolk they were just moving on to another town. If he didn't, they'd be walking into one hell of a trap.

"What were you thinking?" Boon said in a hiss when Bijan caught up to him. Calder, the town's assigned delivery boy, was just up ahead, his massive head turning from side to side.

"I was avoiding bloodshed and death. It's called diplomacy, you may want to try it in the future," Bijan said in equally hushed tones.

"Diplomacy is not one of my strengths. And we still have a problem to deal with," Boon nodded his head towards Calder, "even if it is a slightly smaller problem."

Bijan just smiled and walked ahead of the Northern guide, a plan formulating in his mind.

***

"Calder, is it?" Bijan said from behind the large man. Getting only a grunt in response, he pushed on.

"Where does this path lead?" Bijan was standing next to an open trail, a break in the trees that had sprung up around them as they left the town. It was a well-used path, widened with care and beaten down by frequent foot traffic.

Calder turned. He had passed the trail without a second thought, and now looked back at Bijan, who smiled at him as he played with his moustache. The rest of the raiders stood somewhat back from where Bijan stood, waiting.

"That's none of your concern," Calder said, his voice a rough monotone. "The path to Arnarfell is this way."

"I see, I see." Bijan crossed his hands behind his back. "The only thing is, my guide here, if I can even dare to call him that, doesn't seem to know anything about this path. Not a name or idea has come into his head since we left your town. Now, normally it wouldn't bother me much, I am of your mind as well in trying to reach Arnarfell as soon as possible, but I am also an inquisitive soul. Perhaps you could tell me something of where this path leads?"

Calder gave Boon a wary glance and heaved a mighty sigh. He swung his hammer over one shoulder and walked the short distance back to Bijan. The large youth stood before Bijan, looking down upon the smaller man, a glib smirk crossing his features. "This path is none of your concern, little man. Now shut your mouth and let's get a move on."

Bijan felt his jaw tighten and his fists clench, but he forced himself to maintain a semblance of calm. "As you wish," he said with a small smile, and motioned for Calder to lead the way.

Adun was waiting for the young man to turn, and as he did he placed his sword at Calder's belly, the sharp point almost piercing the skin. The unwilling guide froze in his tracks, his eyes wide with surprise. As he froze, another raider struck him in the back of the neck with the hilt of his scimitar, sending him to the ground like a sack of rocks.

"Subtle," Boon said, pushing past Bijan and starting down the other path.

"You're sure this is the right way?" Bijan called after him, moving slower to let the raiders catch up.

"This way will lead us to the marker of Haugr. Now, hurry along. We don't have much time."

Bijan pressed forward, eager to see the marker, and to be a step closer to the castle.

CHAPTER FOURTEEN

She could hear him fumble his way into the room, and her first thought was that he was drunk. It had been a mistake, she thought, coming to see Edric early in the evening darkness, unannounced. Of course, it wasn't like when they were children and Edric, the boy, was awake and deep in his studies. No, the Edric she saw now — barely avoiding the trap door that he'd undoubtedly traversed hundreds of times — that Edric was not the same as she'd remembered. In his cups... She just couldn't picture Edric drunk.

He rolled about on the floor, a groan creaking out of his chest. The best thing Leandra could do now was to leave as she came, in the darkness, through his window; he'd be none the wiser. She just had to wait for the right moment —

Edric went still. Leandra couldn't rightly see him, he was nothing more than a dull outline, a shadowy figure, but she could feel the change in the room. It was like a chilled breeze tickled her neck, a cool breath blowing softly; Edric knew she was there.

"Hello Edric," she said, lighting the lamp to her right.

The boy she knew faced her, barely hidden by the layers of years. He'd filled out, his chest and shoulders broader than she'd expected. He was taller too, though he looked barely a hair over her own height.

"Leandra," he said with a grim nod, his eyes a hard grey. "It's been a long time."

"Too long." Leandra could feel a weak smile growing on her face. This was not how it was supposed to be. In days long passed, Edric would welcome her with open arms. He would smile (a genuine, toothy smile), and grip her in a tight embrace before he'd reveal some of the parchment paper and ink he'd squirreled away unbeknownst to Hesperos. Some nights they'd sit, draw maps, and write stories until the sun made a fire-like haze of the far clouds.

Edric stood, his legs unsteady beneath him. He gave her another curt nod, his stone-grey eyes, rimmed in purple, squinted away from the lamplight as he pulled a small wooden stool toward him to sit upon. He stared at her, a shrug rippled the blue cloak around his shoulders, urging her to get on with it.

Leandra frowned and readjusted herself on his bed, moving a loose book from beneath her. At least that hadn't changed. Edric had always had a thirst for learning, a desire to read and to gain knowledge. She always thought that it was a part of what made him an ideal candidate for Hesperos' apprentice. After all, who had more knowledge and wisdom than a wizard?

"How have you been?" she said in a low voice, her eyes darting from his cheeks that were thick with stubble to his unkempt hair that needed a wash.

"I hear you're getting married," Edric said, his voice low and bone dry. He turned his bleary eyes on her face, their focus making her uncomfortable.

"It seems so." Leandra couldn't restrain the drop of

her shoulders, the roll of her eyes. "Not that anyone consulted me about it," she said with a snort and immediately regretted it. She hadn't crept out of her room to confess her problems; she had just wanted to see an old friend.

"'The princess has chosen a suitor'," Edric said in the same high-pitched voice he'd used to mock Hesperos when they were children. "My master is many things, but fanciful is not one of them."

"Is that what he said?" Leandra said and felt her cheeks flush. "And since when have you believed your master's words at face value?" She clenched her fists around the thin blanket gathered beneath her.

Edric dismissed her question with a wave of his hand. "I'm in the middle of the Trials, you know."

Leandra's shoulders slumped, her back leaned against the cold, stone wall next to the window of which she had entered. "The Trials? Already?"

Edric nodded, the forefinger and thumb of one hand rubbing the bridge of his nose. "Only one more Trial to go, and then —"

"The Circle?" Leandra rose from her seat and wrapped her arms around Edric's shoulders. She knew what The Circle meant to him. It was the pinnacle of his craft, a signifier of power and prestige, and it was something that he'd been working toward since she could remember. It was also the end of his life as he knew it. The Circle, and the magical work they did, was important to the entire kingdom of Appolumi and its future, but no one knew what happened once a member went beyond those doors. Whatever it was, they were never seen again.

"Yes," Edric said and patted her hand.

"You must be studying extra hard these days," Leandra said lamely, sitting on the floor, her back against the bed.

A smile, faint though it was, finally appeared on Edric's worn face. A glimmer of the boy he once was appeared with it. "I rarely do anything else. Haven't had much chance since —"

Since they'd played together all those years ago. Leandra frowned. She'd been angry when her father had banished her from seeing Edric. She'd put up a fight, vowed to see him, and often snuck out to see Edric in much the same manner as she did now. Skulking, her father had called it when Alethea had found her sneaking back into her bedroom early in the morning.

"That poor boy," the king had said, his wet blue eyes bent to the ground and her chin small between his finger and thumb, "he'll have a hard enough life without you giving him false hope."

"And it's not becoming of a princess," Obelius had added with a sneer. Alethea nodded her agreement from behind both men.

Leandra didn't understand it then and was still confused at how the men of Appolumi, with such moral and intellectual regard, clung so fiercely to such ancient ideals. She'd grown to understand the logic, the tradition, but she hated that they'd made it that way. That her father, and his nobles bound her and the kingdom to such archaic thoughts of propriety.

"...We all have our role —"

"Sorry?" Leandra turned toward Edric, their faces close. It was the boy's eyes that looked upon her, soft and full of wonder; her face flushed again.

"We all have a role to play on this castle," said Edric, his hand squeezing hers. "It has always been that way. The peasants toil away in the Quarter, serving the nobles for food and shelter. At the same time the nobles, the king, sets rules and laws and ensures they're enforced. Why one differs from the other," Edric shrugged, "is beyond me. Us gifted folk have it much simpler. We live and die for The Circle. The Circle keeps the kingdom in one piece. It's not ideal, but it's what we pay for living on a castle that travels amongst the clouds."

Leandra laughed. It was unbidden, but pleasant. She squeezed Edric's hand. "What if," she said as the seed of an idea grew in her mind. "What if we weren't on the castle?"

"You can't be serious." Edric shook his head and disentangled his hand from hers.

"Why not? You said it yourself, we pay a price for living here. For you, it's The Circle. For me, it's this... this marriage. If we leave, we wouldn't have to follow the rules. We could make something for ourselves. Live by our own rules." Leandra rose, gripped Edric's shoulders and stared into his eyes, willing him to believe her; to agree with her.

Edric stood, knocking over his stool. "Leandra, we can't."

"I know it won't be easy, but —"

"Easy? Leandra, what about the plague? What about the enemy? The castle keeps us safe. It's all that's left. If we leave, we'll be dead."

Silence overcame the small room, Leandra and Edric staring at one another with incredulity.

"Edric, that's not true," she said after some time. "It's a story told to the peasants to keep them happy. It's like the scary stories we're told as children, meant to keep us in line."

"That can't be true... why would the castle stay away

after all this time if —"

"Well, there was an enemy. Perhaps there still is, but they are only looking for the castle, the kingdom. They wouldn't pay attention to two people. It's a big world down there, Edric."

A flicker of excitement flared in Edric's stomach. Could he find his family on the surface?

He ran a hand over his face, propped up his stool again and sat with his elbows on his knees. "Even if what you are saying is true, how would we escape? We're in the sky; I haven't seen the surface in… well I don't know when."

"Let me figure that out," Leandra said, a bow-shaped smile growing on her face.

CHAPTER FIFTEEN

Edric woke to Hesperos' bilious face. The old man's scowl had penetrated Edric's sleep and made him rise from his bed with a start.

"I hope that the reason you're late for lessons today involved a lot of study and preparation," Hesperos said, jabbing at Edric with one end of his staff.

The plans he and Leandra had made the night before were still fresh in his mind; thoughts of leaving the castle, fantasies about freedom lurked too near the surface. If he wasn't careful, if he gave any indication, Hesperos would pluck those thoughts from his mind as easily as he would an apple from a tree.

"Yes, Master. Apologies," Edric wiped the sleep from his eyes and made to stand, but Hesperos' staff held fast to his chest and kept him in place.

"Well, Boy, how are your ruminations?" the old wizard said, pushing the staff into his pupil's sternum.

"I still need to do some research, Master." Edric winced and gestured towards the books on his bed.

"Indeed," Hesperos' thin face cracked a smile, "good. Very good. And your vision? Have you remembered anything from your vision?" Hesperos stroked his long beard, his good eye on Edric.

"Nothing has revealed itself, Master," Edric shrugged.

Hesperos grunted and stamped the floor with his staff.

"Fortunately, for you, our preparations have been put on hold for the day. We've been invited to the king's table for a special dinner."

"The king's table?" Edric ran a hand through his dirty hair and stroked the scruff of growth that ran along his chin. Hesperos watched him and his expression soured.

"Yes. The princess has decided to gather the entire kingdom for an official announcement of her upcoming nuptials. Sadly, despite all your preparation late into the night, the celebration is tonight." Hesperos looked out the window, his focus on the courtyard below. "It seems that the king, in his infinite wisdom, has decided that his only daughter's engagement party is more important for this castle than a new inductee to The Circle. But what am I to do? He is my king after all." Hesperos' thin and gnarled fingers gathered together in a fist and thudded down on the stone outline of the window. It was a quiet smack that resulted, but it still surprised Edric to see Hesperos resort to a physical outlet for his frustration.

"Really?" Edric thought of what Leandra had said to him the night before. Her father seemed to truly be pushing her hand into marriage. It wasn't something unheard of in the history of Appolumi, but it was certainly odd. Women and men were historically equal in marriage in Appolumi. Many of the greatest nobles and leaders were known to be female. If the king were to continue along this route, it would upset an ages old balance between the genders. Then again, it was an even rarer historical event if a wizard initiate of The Circle refused his place.

"Stop your smiling, Boy. Pull yourself together and try to look at least halfway presentable tonight." The old wizard sighed and jabbed his staff into Edric's stomach. "At the very least, bathe and shave."

***

Edric strolled through corridors of the castle that he hadn't traversed in over ten years. A wave of nostalgia came over him as he remembered the tiny landmarks that only a child could find important in a castle the size of Appolumi: a loose stone in the floor that made a strange noise when it was stepped upon, a crack in the brick of the outer wall that looked like a spider, the off-pattern stitching in the tapestry of the castle's coat of arms, and of course, the jagged carvings meant to be sigils that he and Leandra left just under cover of the hanging banners. All these things he remembered and were still here. A smile grew on his face.

Hesperos had waited for Edric to clean himself up and put on more respectable clothes, but he was all the more cantankerous because of it.

"Wipe that smile off your face, Boy," Hesperos said from just ahead of him, his staff offering its offbeat to the staccato rhythm of his gait. "You are my ward. Present yourself as such." Hesperos turned and fixed his beast-like eye on him, enunciating his point.

Edric had seen the castle decorated for many celebrations. Some were pristine yet sombre decorations, running the colours of the nation: blue, white, and orange. Others were more festive with explosive reds and oranges and exciting yellows.

Whatever the celebration, the king always ensured that food was readily available to all people, servant or not, and would often open the wine cellars for the occasions. The particular occasion they were now taking part in, however, was another story entirely.

The halls he now ambled through were covered in banners emblazoned with the Chalice of the king, its green and yellow hues drawing the eye. Servants walked throughout the maze of corridors, offering food and drink to those they came upon — Edric had to stave off two such men already on his short walk. The king had even seen fit to fly new flags from the parapets and towers so that even the birds would be aware of the celebration at hand.

"When will the real celebrations begin?" Edric ventured as his eyes darted about, trying to reignite some more of his old memories.

"They will begin with supper. Most will be attended to here in the halls, or in their homes or places of work. We, on the other hand, have a king and princess who have asked us to join them for the formal meal." Hesperos didn't break stride to speak with Edric, and continued to talk with him, expecting his pupil to catch up. "After the meal the festivities will begin. Games, wine, mead. All very droll." He gave Edric a quick look over his shoulder, "Not that you will be able to enjoy any of that. The Trials will resume tomorrow."

Edric nodded to his mentor's back. The final Trial was delayed, but not for long. He needed to speak to Leandra. He needed to know what she had planned.

CHAPTER SIXTEEN

The forest was thick with tall but slender trees, their white bark peeling under thin, finger-like branches that jabbed Bijan when he wasn't looking. He pushed on, ever following the solitary figure of Boon, who seemed immune to the trees affections and passed through them undisturbed.

The raiders were suffering in the same way as Bijan, the branches catching in their shemaghs, their equipment, their blades. Not that anyone could tell by their appearance; they remained as quiet and calm as they ever were.

"Just up ahead," Boon said from his place in front. Through the spaces in the trees Bijan could see tall grass and flat land not encumbered by birch wood. He said a silent 'thank you' to whatever god might be listening.

Boon was waiting for them as they broke through the wall of trees and into a wide, expansive field. Bijan noticed a slight scratch and trickle of blood on Boon's cheek. Not so immune to nature it seemed.

"We're almost there now," Boon said as the last of the raiders fell from the tree line. "It's lodged in the centre of this field, nearly embedded in the ground now, but still of use." Boon began to move again, his long stride putting space between him and the raiders quickly. Bijan made to stop the forlorn guide but knew it would be of no use. Boon was set in his mission, the goal of which was just within his grasp. Instead, Bijan turned to the raiders and motioned them on. None of them showed emotion one way or the other.

Boon took a diagonal path in the broad circle that was the field. He cut through the tall grass as easily as he did the forest, moving through it as if he were a spirit, both intangible and untouchable. As before, Bijan and the raiders found the trek to be considerably harder. The grass bogged down their legs, seemed to creep up and wrap itself around their ankles.

All around Bijan, the raiders took out their swords, as if in unison, to cut a path in the tangling grass. Adun slithered up next to Bijan and prepared to clear the way for them both.

"Don't," Boon said, his voice stern. Bijan's eyes were drawn to him, as were those of the raiders. The big Northern man was facing them from his place at the front of the line. Bijan was amazed at how far ahead he actually was. Was it ten feet? Twenty?

"Don't disturb the grass." Boon's eyes were cold with warning. Bijan could feel his stare and knew that the others could as well. Was there a shade of green dancing in those glacial blue pools?

To Bijan's left he heard a grunt and a blade slicing through the air. The reaction was immediate. A scream rose from behind him and the sound of people scrambling, muttering, cursing. He tried to turn and see what was happening, but he was stuck where he stood. The curling and twisting grass now were latched to his ankles and legs. It was twisting tighter and tighter and pulling him down.

Adun's arm was caught in midair, the grass lashing out like a whip, gripping it, biting into flesh. Bijan heard the man's scream of agony as he dropped his sword and tried to free himself with his other hand. He too was being dragged to the ground.

Bijan tried to pull himself free, tearing at the wrapping grass, but it was growing and thick and its grip was steel. His hands and arms became entangled as he moved, and he could feel the strange grass wrap itself around his neck. It was cold. As cold as the dead.

"Enough," Boon raged, his voice now closer to them. Bijan's face was being pulled closer and closer to the ground, his neck and back strained against it, but it was no use.

Over his own groaning, Bijan began to hear some whispered mutterings. They weren't a language he could understand, but he was certain it was Boon speaking. Chanting.

The grass stopped, its grip relaxing on Bijan's neck, arms, legs. He was slowly being allowed to move, to sit, to stand. Bijan stood, as they all did, disheveled and sweating, their limbs shaking from spent effort. They all faced Boon. The large, bearded man stood before them, his own face lined with strain, his thick corded neck muscles stuck out in effort. His sleeves were pulled up around his elbows, his tattoos now on full display for the first time since Bijan met him. They were beautiful, scrolling pieces of art in strange symbols and images that were too close together for Bijan to understand with just a quick glimpse.

"There," Boon said between breaths, his eyes flashing. "We should be fine now. Just don't attack it again." Boon covered his tattoos and started to move once more. Bijan and the raiders were left to ponder what had happened and how Boon played a part in it.

***

They walked the rest of the way in silence. The swish of the tall grass as it rubbed at their legs was like a promise of more violence to come. Bijan could hardly contain a cry of fear each time the grass happened upon his bare skin. He looked to Adun; his demeanour was impenetrable, but he held his sword arm close to his chest, droplets of blood leaving thin lines on his skin.

"There," Boon said after another half hour of walking. He pointed one large hand towards a small and gradual hill just within their sight. "The marker is there."

"Are you sure?" Bijan said, squinting and straining his eyes. "I only see the hill."

"It's there," Boon said without looking at him, and moved off.

In a few minutes they had scaled the hill. The flailing, tall grass had receded around the hill, leaving the group to traipse through grass the colour of wheat matted with dried mud. Boon stood at the base of the hill studying his fingernails.

If Boon hadn't said there was a marker on the hill, Bijan would have dismissed it for a lost cause. Even with that knowledge he had a hard time picking it out. He found it in the centre of the hill, a black rock that was just barely sticking out of the ground. There were other rocks surrounding it, dull and dusty, covered in mud. The black rock shined through despite the mud or grass or dust. It looked perfect once you were able to see it.

Bijan knelt before it and brushed some of the dirt from around it. The marker was hard and sharp. It was most certainly a crystal and not a rock, and it was definitely bigger than it appeared.

"My things," he said and stretched his hand out behind him. His bag was given to him. He did not see by who, nor did he care, but he began to dig through it, looking for his tools.

A moment later a brush was in his hand and a flat metal spade. Bijan dug furiously around the object, bits of grass and dirt clumps began to pile up around him. The raiders stood watching him, save for Adun who crouched by his side.

"No use," Bijan said clambering to his feet, and threw his tools into the pile of cast-off dirt. "We'll need the shovels." Two particularly broad raiders came forward, shovels in hand. Bijan motioned to the marker. "Dig around it," he said. "Here and here," he motioned to areas around the crystal, giving it plenty of space from the shovels' blades. The air was filled with the grunts of the two men and the slicing of earth and grass. They all watched, and Bijan held his breath.

***

"Enough," Bijan said, raising his voice above the noise of shovels at work. The sun had set, and the night taken over, the pale moon hanging overhead behind wisps of fog and mist.

Several of the raiders has taken their turn at digging around the crystal, each more careful than the last; afraid of damaging the exterior of the marker. A dull glow from lanterns lit the excavation as it bled into the night.

"Enough," Bijan said again as the shovels were slowing to a stop and those in that company stared. "That's as much as we need now. Take a break," Bijan shooed them away and took stock of the scene.

The dig hadn't been right to begin with. The ground was hard and thick. The crystal marker was bigger than expected and unexpectedly fragile. Finally, the raiders believed the field to be a cursed area and deemed unclean by the gods. Many of them had stopped engaging in the excavation at all and stood on the edges of the small hill, watching the process unfold.

Bijan squatted on the balls of his feet to take stock of the dig. A crater had now formed around the perimeter of the black crystal, almost as tall as a man and twice as wide. The raiders had done well in keeping their shovels away from the structure and only once did the sound of metal on crystal echo in the air. Bijan studied that area now, and it seemed little more than a scratch on the surface.

That, in and of itself, was the problem. There was nothing on the surface of the marker, nothing besides the scratch inflicted by a weary raider. Without markings, it would not give away any secrets, and no clues; it created more questions than answers. Bijan sighed. "Boon, come."

The burly guide lumbered over the small embankment and stood at Bijan's side. He stared into the hole, appraising the marker in its uncovered glory.

"What else do you know about this marker?" Bijan stood and faced him. He stared into the half-lidded eyes of Boon's mask of disinterest.

"Everything I know about this place, its purpose, was in the book." Boon's eyes were drawn to the crystal. Bijan had to concede that there was something mesmerizing in the crystal's surface. The black so dark it almost seemed purple at the edges where the light hit it. The more Bijan stared upon it the more the purple seemed to move and swirl. Though he knew it couldn't be true, he began to see shapes, letters, float through and within the crystal. Messages in the dark.

"What in the hell is this thing?" Bijan said under his breath, trying to draw his eyes from it.

"It's very ancient. Very powerful. Only those of Appolumi remember its true purpose now." Boon turned away from the crystal and looked out in the field that surrounded them.

"It isn't just a marker?" Bijan attempted to follow Boon's lead, to turn away from the crystal. It fought for his attention. He could feel the pull of it as he looked away, and relief when he finally did.

"No. It acts as one now, but it was so much more. The power it expels is dark and tantalizing. It makes you feel warm, at ease. In reality, it is very cold. It was a terrible power that was not used for pleasantries." Bijan nodded along to this and shivered at the pull it had on his own attention just a moment before.

"So, how do we make this thing work?"

"I don't know, but we'll need to figure that out sooner than later. Calder has most certainly returned to Haugr. The villagers will be coming, and they won't be happy."

Bijan looked around at the raiders, tired and wary. None would look at the crystal, and most wouldn't look at Boon or Bijan. Their stoic facade had faded just a little. They had to find the solution to this puzzle quickly. Their time ran short.

CHAPTER SEVENTEEN

"A dinner party?" Leandra fumed. Alethea stood before her, the handmaiden's ruddy, wrinkled face blank before her mistress.

"Yes, princess. Your father was very adamant —"

"My father is little more than a vegetable!" Leandra's words rebounded off the high ceiling of her room, the stone acting to reflect them back to her own ears. Her cheeks flushed.

"T-that's to say," Leandra collapsed on her bed, "Obelius was adamant, Alethea. Obelius, and not my father."

Alethea sat beside Leandra and ran a small, cool hand through the princess' long hair. "I'm sure you're right, princess, but what are we to do? He has been the voice of the king for as long as I can remember. His word is the king's command and the king's command is law." Alethea's voice was soft and kind. There was no blame or anger or guilt or fear in her words. Even so, it did little to placate Leandra.

"Why would he want me to marry Calix anyway? It would just ensure my place on the throne. He must know that he'd be out of a job." Leandra rolled her eyes.

"Well, princess, perhaps it isn't Obelius."

"Alethea, my father is —"

"Yes, yes. I know. But he has been lucid at times. Even just yesterday, at the games…"

Leandra waved off her handmaiden and rolled to her side to face away from her. "It's nothing more than a latent reaction to something," she said, but she knew that wasn't true. Her father had always been a strong man; a fighter; a champion. If anyone would be able to fight through the disease that was trying to sink its claws in, it was King Vaselious. Leandra didn't know if that was more comforting or disconcerting.

***

"Honestly, princess, you'd think you'd be accustomed to this by now." Alethea helped Leandra gather her dress skirts to descend another set of stairs.

"I'm afraid I'm not so comfortable in anything so… puffy." Leandra grabbed her skirts in one hand and pushed down on the lace collar that surrounded her neck. "I can't see the bloody stairs," she grumbled as she carefully placed her slick-soled shoes on one stair after another.

"I've had you in dresses since you were a mite," Alethea said with a sigh. Leandra was well aware of this, but her old handmaiden had forgotten what she often did with them once they were worn. Alethea and Obelius often called her stubborn or, if they were feeling kind, strong-willed. Her father would often laugh it off and tell them it was a sign of a born leader.

Leandra's strong-willed ways didn't end at getting dresses filthy, of course, and though her father would often overlook many of her indiscretions, her handmaiden and her tutor would not. They wanted her as princess-like as she could be, even if her nature pulled her in other ways. She had wanted to play in the dirt, climb, wrestle, and play jokes. She wanted to do what the other children did and come home filthy with a smile on her dirt-scrubbed cheeks. And so, she did. She played the toughest, and the roughest. Her pranks were unrepentant and merciless. Her dresses were torn and dirty. Each time, Obelius and Alethea would scowl down upon her and tell her she wasn't acting like a princess. When she was young this wouldn't bother her, she'd just continue to do as she pleased. No matter how many dresses they made her wear, no matter how many baths she had to take, she was having fun and that's all that had mattered. Until her father fell ill.

She hadn't realized it was happening until it was too late. She gave in to the paltry demands of Alethea and Obelius, she was paying attention in tutoring sessions, and she wasn't dirtying up any more dresses. Her father seemed pleased, but he was too far gone in his illness to say it out loud. Instead he smiled and gripped her hand whenever they saw one another. Leandra grew to accept her place. Her father continued to smile as she continued to meet expectations. Even as his once vibrant blue eyes, full of cunning and mirth, turned flat and vacant, he still smiled when she told him what she had accomplished. But that would end soon, too.

Leandra had grown into the role, but it was never something that she had wanted.

With a grunt, Leandra kicked off her uncomfortable shoes; the silky dress fabric alighting on the tops of her feet was refreshing and new. The stone floor underneath her feet was cool. Miniscule pieces of dirt clung to her skin, and it felt like sand — or what she thought sand might feel like. Warm, soft, but there; always there.

"Princess!" Alethea scurried forward and tried to pick up the shoes.

"Leave them, Alethea." Leandra walked on and let her bare feet slap an echo down the hallway. "I'm already dressed in this ridiculous thing; I'm not going to bear the discomfort on my feet. Besides, no one will see it anyway."

Leandra could hear Alethea huffing and puffing behind her as she struggled to keep up. A smirk grew on Leandra's face. A little freedom, she thought, keeping her lead. She'd been awake all night thinking of how to flee the castle. Going over escape plans in her mind, routes and detours, but it was missing just a little freedom. Just a little to gain so much. Unfortunately, a princess wasn't allowed much freedom. Still, she had been able to sneak out of her room to see Edric. Couldn't she do that again? Perhaps, but how long did she have?

"Princess, your feet will be filthy," Alethea said, but she already sounded defeated.

"And I'm sure they'll be all the better for it." She tossed a playful glance over her shoulder at her handmaiden, a smile hidden beneath her scowl. Alethea had been a light sleeper in her youth, but now she slept like the dead. Leandra could use that.

"Finally," Obelius' sleek and caustic voice greeted them as they turned the corner. "Really, princess, you know how to make a crowd wait." He nodded his head in a mock bow and turned a sour look to Alethea. "You were supposed to have her here ten minutes ago, woman."

"Yes, well, you try to wrangle this sort. See how much luck you have."

"Let's just go in." Leandra made to push her way past Obelius, but he grabbed her arm tight with his long, skeletal fingers.

"Not just yet, princess. First, you must wait for your prince." Obelius stretched his lips over his teeth in a mockery of a smile and pointed further down the hall. Calix and his family were making their way up the corridor, their happy chatter carrying ahead of them.

"Seriously, Obelius…"

"Seriously. This is your big night, let's make it special, shall we?" Obelius moved into the dining room, the roar of polite conversation falling into the open hallway. Leandra took a glimpse within and her eyes fell on Edric. She hadn't expected that he would be here, hadn't even considered it. She wanted to run to him, talk to him; discuss her ideas, see if he had any plans of his own. Wouldn't that just teach Obelius a lesson. To have the crown princess abandon her so-called betrothed to speak with an apprentice of The Circle. Perhaps even Calix's sallow face would redden at that one. Leandra had a sudden jolt of glee at the thought and she could feel a giggle bubble up her throat.

Leandra swallowed the laugh. She *could* rush to Edric's side and teach Obelius, Calix, and even Alethea a lesson. She could do that, but at what cost? Propriety be damned, but what would she accomplish aside from a cheap thrill? Less freedom, she guessed, a sigh escaping her parted lips. Less freedom when all she needed, all she wanted, was just a little bit more. Just enough to escape.

No, it was too much of a risk. As much as it would hurt, Edric would have to understand. They were playing a game now. A game of inches, and with every step forward they would be plagued by dangers. If they were going to win it, they had to play their parts. She would have to be the very model of a proper princess.

The door closed and with it so did Leandra's view of Edric. The boy she once knew was lost in that young man's face, lost in his thoughts. They'd be free. With some planning, and a little work, they'd be free.

CHAPTER EIGHTEEN

Vaselious was old. That was Edric's first thought when he saw the king, a man that had been so prominent and awe inspiring in his youth. The king had been a large, jovial man. His piercing blue eyes had danced with a playful fire over a toothy grin and curly, brown beard. Edric had never actually spoken with the man, but had seen him from a distance and, like the rest of his subjects, admired him.

Edric now bowed before a sagging husk of the man he remembered, with a face that was cracked and lined above a scraggly grey beard. All the life seemed to have drained from the joyous hulk. Now he just sat, uninterested, as Hesperos and Edric bowed and kissed his ring.

"Welcome honoured Hesperos and Edric," Obelius, the king's magistrate, said, guiding them to their seats around the large table. "The king is pleased you were able to join; he knows you are very busy in the Trials." Obelius gave a weary nod towards Edric. The magistrate had gotten older as well. The tall and lanky man was stooped over, and his hands were covered in age spots; his skeletal fingers danced over his arms.

"Many thanks to his highness, Obelius." Hesperos bent his head to the magistrate and took his seat, motioning for Edric to follow suit. "We are very honoured to have been asked to be here on this special occasion." Hesperos stroked his beard and turned his eyes to the king.

Vaselious, for his part, seemed to be staring at his own stomach. That or he was dozing with his chin on his chest. Edric tried to get Hesperos' read on the king, but the old wizard was tight-lipped around his usual sneer. Perhaps it was only Edric who was alarmed by the king's appearance, having been without His Grace for so long.

Edric sat beside Hesperos, his eyes roaming around the ornately decorated room. Abstract paintings lined the walls, their subjects looked vaguely familiar to Edric, though he couldn't be sure if the painting across from him was a bowl of fruit or of people circling a fire. The room was smaller than he had anticipated, and it was mostly taken up by the large, dark wood table that he now found himself taking up space at. There were enough chairs and place settings for twenty people, most of whom had already arrived. Edric himself sat next to a small, sour-faced man who was altogether too pale and stank of putrid perfume. A noble of a smaller house, Edric thought. The head of the table, on the opposite side of the room, was set for three: The king, his daughter, and her betrothed. Leandra was not here yet, though. Edric found himself cheered at the thought. Part of him wanted her to refuse to come, wanted her to go into open rebellion of the expectations placed upon her. After all, it was that exactly which they had been planning just the night before in his room. In that brief moment of remembrance, he knew that she wouldn't come to the dinner. He knew that she would rebel against their expectations of her and would begin to forge her own path. He knew that the plans they had spoken of just the night before would have officially begun.

"Ah, finally," Obelius croaked after a few moments. He cleared his throat, a mighty smile defiant on his old face. "Presenting Princess Leandra, and his lordship Calix, son of Alastair." Obelius bowed low as Leandra and her fiancé stepped into the room, arm in arm.

Edric's heart sank.

Leandra was more beautiful than Edric could have imagined. Her raven black hair fell around her strong, bronze shoulders and framed her oval face. Over peach-coloured lips, her glacial blue eyes engaged the entire room. He could tell that she was studying everything around her, making quick notes and thoughts as she turned her head from side to side, a small smile hiding any nervousness or calculation. Despite himself, Edric could feel himself falling into the same old trap that her eyes had set for him all those years before when they were just youngsters playing jokes. Still, he yearned for her gaze to fall on him again and hoped that when their eyes met that she would give him some notion, some idea that their plans were not just an act at reliving a lost childhood. He wanted her to give him a signal that it wasn't all some sort of hollow game like something they did when they were children.

Edric frowned as Leandra's handsome fiancé, Calix, started to lead her through the room. If Edric recalled correctly, Calix was a relatively minor noble from a small house. Memories of Calix's blond hair and sallow face as a child came to Edric without heed or desire. Studying the man he had become, strong, and lean, and confident, Edric couldn't help but recall the many pranks he and Leandra played on Calix in their heyday. Then again, they had played pranks on many.

Obelius walked them to their seats at the head of the

table, on either side of King Vaselious. Leandra laid one long-fingered hand on her father's arm as she sat, a warm smile beaming down upon him. The king raised his shaking head, his eyes bright as they fell on his daughter's face. A smile creased the corners of his mouth, and for a moment Edric could see the man he had once been.

Leandra's eyes never fell upon Edric. Or, if they did, she never showed any signs of recognition. Despite his efforts otherwise, he couldn't contain his disappointment. He balled up the serviette in his lap over and over.

"What are you doing?" Hesperos leaned into him and whispered out of the side of his mouth. "Have you no manners?"

Perhaps not. Edric had never been to a formal dinner before, had never sat in the presence of the king as an adult. He knew little of what he should be doing but was very aware of what he'd like to do. "I'm sorry, Master," Edric said, smoothing out his serviette and laying it flat in his lap once more.

More people came in. Obelius introduced them and showed them to their seats. Most were nobles from Calix's family, including a handsome elderly couple who smiled broadly at their introduction and took some extra time speaking to the king, his daughter, and her fiancé. Calix's mother and father perhaps, Edric hadn't bothered to listen.

The dinner went on flawlessly. Silence reigned supreme between the guests, the fervent clicking of utensils on the tableware displacing the illusion of an empty room. Despite his upset, Edric found himself eating ravenously. He savoured each course and cleared each plate that was put in front of him. Hesperos jabbed his elbow into Edric's ribs at times, trying to get him to slow down or to remind him of his manners. Edric took little heed of this. By the end of the dinner, Edric was bloated and uncomfortable and hoping for a nap.

Obelius led the servants in and out. He coordinated the cleanup of dishes and provided tea and coffee where desired. Conversation finally started around the loud clicking of plates during the cleanup. Even so, it was measured and quiet like whispers in the dark. Edric tried to listen in on Leandra's conversations, but could hear little over the rumble of Alastair's droning voice as he spoke to his son.

"Well, didn't you make an oaf of yourself," Hesperos leaned in close to Edric's ear, "and your antics will most certainly reflect poorly on me and my station."

"I didn't think you cared much for politics or stations," Edric said, his eyes still on Leandra.

"Yes, well," Hesperos peered around at the gathered group of nobles, "be that as it may, we have a reputation to uphold. Magi are wise and skilled, they are not savages who believe it is right to club a woman over the head and drag her back to his cave." A sharp sting erupted in Edric's left hand. He pulled it back with a low inhale of breath and a sucking of teeth. His eyes fell from Leandra and saw Hesperos brandishing a spoon in his hand, a cold smirk on his ancient face.

"Mind your manners, Boy. You have not entered The Circle yet."

If only it were an option, Edric thought as he slid his stinging hand under the table. After a few moments of avoiding it, he turned his attention back to Leandra. Her eyes met with his for a brief moment. Was there something in the way her blue eyes flashed when they held his own? A message that he missed? Edric could feel the heat of his face as it flushed. He needed to talk to her. She'd know a way, she had to have a plan. The Trials began again tomorrow and plans for the marriage couldn't be too far off. They needed to speak.

With a plan, they'd save each other.

***

"The Princess Leandra and Lord Calix have prepared some words for this occasion," Obelius said above the hushed conversation around the large table.

Leandra and Calix stood and, hand in hand, moved to a small stage that stood just behind the head of the table. They looked radiant. Even Edric had to admit they were a handsome couple, well-suited to one another. Their embrace, however, told another story. It was formal, their hands linked but their bodies apart. Thin, fake smiles adorned their unblemished faces as they addressed the crowd.

"Thank you, dear friends, for helping us celebrate this blissful occasion." Calix had a sturdy voice, smooth and elegant, with a practiced tone for these types of get-togethers. "I would personally like to extend my limitless gratitude to His Highness, the king, for arranging this celebration. That is doubly so for his consent of his daughter's hand in marriage." The young noble bowed low to the elderly king, who did little more than nod in his direction. There was a quiet applause that followed.

"Born politicians," Hesperos said, "no wonder Calix and Alastair were able to weasel themselves into the good favour of the king." Hesperos scoffed around his limp-handed clapping.

"I would like to echo the sentiment of my betrothed." Leandra stepped forward, releasing her grip from Calix, a more genuine smile growing across her chestnut face. "Thank you all for coming, we appreciate your kindness and hope to pay it back tenfold." She reached her father, bending slightly to look him in the eyes and caress his cheek and chin. "Thank you, Father, for everything you have provided to your people; to me." She straightened, her smile large and beautiful. "Please, enjoy the rest of the festivities for tonight, there is plenty to take part in. And, don't worry, we will have even more planned for the wedding." She let out a dry laugh and extended her hands to those around the table. Louder applause came this time, with some chuckles mixed in. Edric clapped more enthusiastically than needed, if only to gain Leandra's eye, which prompted another jab to the ribs by Hesperos, but he couldn't help himself. Leandra had learned well from her father, the jovial, rotund man that he had been. Edric could recall him saying something very similar when he was a child. Leandra would make a remarkable leader.

The thought sobered him a little. Leandra would never become Queen, would never get to be a leader. Or would she? Her speech seemed heartfelt enough. She seemed to be going through with the plans to marry. Edric's mind raced, his heart thudded against his ribcage.

The nobles had begun to stand and mingle with one another. They seemed a little freer now and were boisterous with one another, though Edric could make out little of what they said. Craning his neck, Edric could see Obelius escorting the king, Leandra, and Calix out of the room with the aid of some servants. Edric thought he recognized one of those helpers, but he couldn't be sure. He started to move towards the door, when a cold hand gripped his wrist.

"Come, Boy, it is time we take our leave of this revelry." Hesperos had regained his footing and seemed bent on dragging Edric out of the room.

"We aren't going to see anything else, Master?" Edric watched as Leandra and Calix exited the room behind the king. "Perhaps we could go see the fireworks, or enjoy some games of dice, try our luck."

"Have you forgotten that you have the Trials to complete, Boy? We don't have the time for games or cheap spectacles. You need to return to your studies and rest." Hesperos made a pull on Edric's arm and started towards the door.

"Please, Master. Let me go enjoy some games. I won't be late. It'll be my last chance to enjoy anything before the end of the Trials. I'll be prepared tomorrow. You have my word."

Hesperos turned his yellow eye on him, a sneer crossed his creased face and he released Edric's arm with a push. "Don't test my patience, Boy. Enjoy your fun as you will, but come prepared tomorrow for a long, painful, day." Hesperos stormed off.

Once he was sure Hesperos had gone, Edric made for the door himself, hoping to catch up with Leandra and steal a moment to speak with her, and to plan their escape.

CHAPTER NINETEEN

The raiders had made camp on the far side of the hill, a small fire burning in the middle of their huddled circle. None talked, and there was a conscious effort to avoid looking in the direction of the black marker.

Bijan crouched low and looked at the crystal marker in the dim moonlight. Purple veins seemed to run through the crystal when the moon hit it at the right angle. At times Bijan was sure he saw something moving within, eels or snakes, perhaps tentacles. The thought made him shiver.

Boon sat close by, on the edge of the fire's orange light. His face was only half illuminated, but Bijan could see that he stared at the marker, intent on it. Adun had joined them for a short time, providing food and water, and even sat studying the crystal with them. This didn't last, however, and he soon returned to the raiders' fold, warming around the fire.

"Think this has any answers?" Bijan said, removing the small journal that Boon had given him from inside his tunic. He cracked the spine and began to read through it in the gloom.

Boon shook his head. "No. There are only folktales in there — stories. Responses to the castle, not reasons." He chewed on his thumb nail, eyes still on the marker.

Bijan groaned and leaned forward to caress the marker. It was smooth, near flawless. It rose in a sharp tipped point, the lines easy to follow with his hands. In the moonlight it looked like the purple veins were following his movements, mimicking him. He knocked on the surface, a sharp thud rang out and there were purple marks left where he'd struck it with his knuckles. He turned his head. "Well, we haven't tried hitting it with anything yet." A smile stretched over his lips.

"I think that would be a bad idea," said Boon, though he had leaned forward some at Bijan's knock. He was probably right, of course. Bijan had never been successful with brute force. Often that would leave his treasures unusable.

"You said it was some sort of evil power, right?" Bijan stood and moved in a slow circle around the crystal. "Maybe it needs something to wake it up. Blood, or some such thing." Bijan's mind whirled back to some of the stories he'd heard about other artifacts he'd dealt with. The stories of the Idol of Ur Mekhenet surfaced. In those accounts the Idol needed some sort of sacrifice, physical or spiritual. It was supposed to be able to sense the pain and absorb it. In doing so it would awaken and allow the holder to use its powers as their own. The Idol of Ur Mekhenet was a crock of shit, but it was a great story.

Bijan let his hand slide along the smooth surface of the crystal marker. As Boon watched, he slid a knife out of his belt and turned the blade to the moon. In a quick movement he slashed a shallow wound across the palm of his hand, a trickle of blood that began to pool in its centre. He returned his hand to the surface, feeling something in the air between his hand and the crystal that made him pause. It was a warm feeling, electric. It pulled at his hand, as if the crystal wanted it back on its surface. Bijan raised his eyes to the crystal and could see purple outlines squirming in the area that his hand was approaching. He looked to Boon and saw that he was standing now, standing and moving closer to him. Bijan slapped his hand back on the marker, felt his blood slick on the surface as he ran it around the sides of the crystal. The warmth under his hand continued, though he could not see any blood when he moved his hand from place to place. It was as though it were absorbed somehow: as if the tentacles from within drained it from the smooth, crystal surface. The purple anomalies continued to follow his hand around the crystal, Bijan could see them now even without the moonlight. They were getting brighter.

"We have company," Adun said from the fire, his words followed by the sound of swords being unsheathed.

Bijan's eyes were pulled away from the crystal, though begrudgingly, and he moved back to the crest of the hill to see what had happened. Boon remained fixated on the marker.

The raiders had readied themselves; Adun pushed himself through their ranks when he saw Bijan's approach. His eyes were fiery, his voice rough.

"Looks like the villagers," he said, gesturing over his shoulder with his thumb. "They mustn't have appreciated their man being misused so."

Bijan grunted and wrapped a spare piece of cloth around his palm. "How close?"

"Just in the trees. They seem to be hesitating at the edge of the tall grass."

"Smart, but I'm sure they know the secrets of the land this close to their home. They'll have some tactic, I'm sure." Bijan ran his fingers through his beard. "How many can you make out?"

"At least twice our number. They must've cleared out the whole damn village."

"Or brought friends." Bijan tried to get a look at those gathering at the edge of the grass but couldn't quite see anything but shadows. "Let's hope their tactic to avoid the grass keeps them a while." Adun nodded and returned to his place amongst his fellow raiders. Bijan moved back towards the ebony crystal.

Boon had moved up to the marker. He walked in the small space around it, his face so close to its surface that his nose almost touched it. And yet he didn't actually touch it anywhere. His face, his hands, they just hovered before it. The shapes that had been following Bijan's movements had doubled their efforts with Boon. Though no noise emanated from the crystal, the shadows within seemed to slap and claw the inner space, trying to get out. Or drag something within.

"Making friends?" Bijan stifled his immediate revulsion to the tentacle-like appendages that moved within the crystal and moved next to it himself.

"Hm?" Boon's eyes were fixed on the crystal, but he angled his head more towards Bijan as he approached.

"Well, we certainly aren't making friends out here." Bijan leaned into Boon's vision in an effort to draw him out.

Boon made a tentative poke at the surface with one thick finger and drew it back quickly. His eyes scanned the crystal. A shadowy purple tentacle slapped the crystal where his finger had just been. Boon made a quick movement and stood straight and away from the marker. Bijan jumped in place, startled.

"What the hell is this thing?" Bijan said, still standing

away from it.

"Nothing good," Boon said in a growl. "What's been happening?"

Bijan detailed what had happened and drew a grunt and a small smile out of Boon. "Halvar must have gone out of his mind," Boon shook his head, "Haugr can't afford to lose its people to an unneeded fight. I wonder what has gotten into them?"

"Perhaps they're just thoroughly pissed at you. Halvar seemed to have a special hate for you," Bijan said, his keen almond eyes staring sidelong at Boon.

Another grunt. "That was a misunderstanding," Boon said with a sigh. "I had led some people through this plain before. It was unintentional. I just thought it would be a quicker route. It's how I found the crystal marker in the first place." His face became clouded with an unseen exertion, and he gave a quick glance behind him before moving on, his face calmed. "I've come back many times since, but so have those I brought here before. Halvar didn't like that."

Bijan nodded. It seemed reasonable enough for an unhinged half-wit like Halvar, but he couldn't help but think Boon was holding something back.

Adun was waiting for them as they approached. "They've started to move through the grass." He pointed out into the field. Boon immediately caught sight of something and tensed. Bijan could barely make out anything and he cursed himself for it. When he strained, he could just make out movement in the grass.

"They don't fear the grass," Boon said, moving towards the small group of raiders. "They come here often, and they know its secrets." He pulled a small axe from his belt and let the blunt end of the blade bounce in his hand. "Let them come," he said, but a frown clung to his bearded face.

Bijan mirrored his frown and went to join him and the rest of the raiders.

***

They moved in on the hill quickly, and they talked the whole way. Bijan picked up small conversations here and there about farming harvests and hunting trips in the coming days. He heard the reckless, confident bragging of the intoxicated, bold, and foolish alike. And he heard their gentle footsteps through the grass, it swished against their legs. As they got closer, Bijan could see the glint of their blades in the moonlight.

"Erland," Halvar said in a booming voice, suited to a leader, "you gave us your word that you would not return here and yet you have." Halvar stepped ahead of the others, a long-handled axe held down by his side. "Leave the hill and marker now and that will be the end of it. If you choose to stay, we will have no choice but to remove you." He slung the axe over his shoulder and gave a subtle nod to the crowd of raiders that watched him with passionless eyes.

"Take your people and go home, Halvar," Boon's voice rang across the plain, loud and fierce. "You have no hope of winning here." The raiders shuffled within their ranks in anticipation.

"We outnumber you."

"Not where it matters, Halvar. These men are trained killers, hardened in battle. You have nothing but farmers playing at warriors. Go home," Boon said, "save the lives of your people."

A murmur passed through the men of Haugr. In the

dim light Bijan could see fear and anxiety grow on their faces, could see it build behind their eyes. And yet, they still stood facing those that had trespassed on their land and their secrets. Bijan respected the men of Haugr, even if they were engaged in folly.

There was no further conversation. Nor was there a curse or a yell, or a grunt. All that came next was the whomp of an axe having been tossed at the raiders that had huddled together. The wayward axe hit nothing of consequence, but it played its part. The two opposing sides moved against one another in a clash of swords and axes and bodies.

The raiders had the higher ground, as slight as it was, but it added to their advantage. The raiders whirled like spin tops, their scimitars slashing at legs and stomachs and throats. In the back of the group was a sole archer using a quick loading crossbow to dispatch those men of Haugr who were still on the outskirts of the battle. Bijan stood next to him, his own scimitar drawn and bouncing between his hands. He kept watch for anyone who might break through the crowd, or anyone who may resemble a rival archer.

Adun was with his brethren; his blade flashed as he dodged and slashed, dodged and slashed. Bijan didn't know if it was because Adun was a horrible swordsman or a brilliant one, but while each one of his foes ended up on the ground unconscious, hurt, or unable to move, none died. Boon on the other hand was meeting the farmers head-on: axe for an axe. Bijan could see Boon carve a path through the men of Haugr, using his axe like a scythe. He may have been just a farmer tending his fields, if anyone from afar was watching the melee.

It soon became obvious to Bijan that there was nothing

for him to spot. There were no archers in the line of broken farmers that stood before them all, nor was anyone able to make it past the first line of defence.

The men of Haugr seemed to realize this as well and began to change tactics. They fell back, Halvar waving his axe above his bald head to draw them to him. The raiders, for their part, let them go, happy to keep the higher ground. Boon remained apart from them both, standing in the field of grass, his thick shoulders and back heaving under his fur cloak.

"They'd be better off going back to town," the archer said from next to Bijan. It was true. Though Adun seemed to miss the killing stroke, the other raiders were not so lenient or lucky, and Boon certainly wasn't. His bear-skin cloak was splashed with blood, his axe dripped with it.

It didn't take long for the men of Haugr to regroup and charge into the field again. Boon let slip a bestial yell and charged to meet them. It was a mistake. Bijan tried to tell him, tried to scream above the charging villagers. Boon didn't hear or didn't care and he was soon swarmed by Halvar and the men of Haugr.

***

Bijan couldn't see Boon anymore. All he could see was a thick circle of Haugr men piled on top of where Boon had fallen. Their weapons jabbed in and out of the pile.

He called to Adun, pleading with him to send the raiders to Boon, but more of Halvar's men had reached the hill and the raiders were dealing with them. Bijan cursed and ran from his position with the archer and into the field.

Most of the Haugr men were preoccupied with the raiders left on the hill or with Boon in the field, but some stragglers made for the lean Southerner, perhaps thinking he was an easy target; an extra kill to notch on their axe and tell wildly exaggerated stories of to their grandchildren.

Bijan cut through them. His speed matched that of his sword and completely confounded those that opposed him. He made it past two men with ease, slicing across their calves or stomachs and putting them to the ground in pain, if not death. He was about to make another run for Boon when a large hand grabbed him around the wrist and swung him around. Calder looked down on him, his blond hair greased with sweat, and an ugly looking bruise growing on his face. He smiled at Bijan through bloody gums and split lips.

"No more tricks," he said in a grumble and brought a foot into Bijan's unguarded stomach, pushing him back and making him suck for air.

Buckled over and grasping at his aching stomach, Bijan rolled himself forward and out of the way of Calder's swinging axe. A curse erupted from the young man as he stalked Bijan yet again.

Readying his sword, and forcing himself to stand straight, Bijan made to meet Calder head on. As the two men brought their weapons into the air for a violent meeting, a terrible growling sound carried on the wind, careened over the battlefield, and turned the participants towards it source.

Even as he turned, Bijan became aware of the battle around him. The scuffling, grunting, and slashing accentuated by the ringing of sword on sword, axe on axe. It was deafening, and then it all stopped. The growl erupted once more, and men began to flee before it. Raiders and farmers joined in the effort to escape the source of the guttural threat. Someone ran into him, pushed him, shoulder on shoulder and spun him to the ground with a grunt.

Bijan crawled toward the sound, a continuous growl

that rose and fell with exertion. A large form took shape through the running legs of those retreating from the grey presence. "Boon," Bijan whispered, his hands digging into the rich soil, the long grass wrapping gently around his forearms and wrists. An unknown set of legs tripped over him, their owner tumbled as they sent Bijan into a sprawl. The bodies around him cleared, though Bijan sensed that they were still nearby, just out of reach, and huddled to gether watching, waiting.

He pushed himself to sitting, the grass caressing him as he did. He put one hand to his head, his fingers came away slick with blood. Bijan focused on what was before him, trying to clear his head and vision as he wiped the blood away with his forearm.

It was a bear.

The biggest bear he had ever seen, standing on its hind legs, its snout open in an endless roar that bared too large teeth. Its grey fur was spattered with blood around its huge paws with razor-like claws. Bijan pushed himself backwards and away from the beast, cursing the loss of his scimitar in the previous confusion. He knew that the sword would do little more than piss off the gargantuan creature, but at least it would give him some sense of security.

Not all of the farmers had fled; instead they stood before the bear with makeshift spears and pitchforks. They shouted and cursed the bear, sticking it with the pointy ends when they could. Some men tried to provide distraction and jumped in front of the bear, waving their hands. It worked but for a moment; the creature swung its strong paws towards them as they danced away. When the spears found a home during the distraction, however, the bear made them pay. It was over before it had really begun, the men of Haugr lying on the ground in piles, the bear roaring in triumph. Then it turned toward Bijan.

The bloody snout bent forward, the deep hazel eyes meeting Bijan's own. The bear moved forward, walking as a human might, its long, thick arms nearly dragging on the ground. Its fur was matted, but not with blood. Bijan squinted his eyes and could see the bare patches where the thick fur hide should have been but wasn't. Instead there were intricate drawings and swirls, pulsating between their natural black and incandescent red.

"Boon?"

As if in answer, the bear grunted and fell to its forepaws. It turned to the ebony marker and moved towards it. Bijan looked behind him: the men of Haugr had moved back towards the tree line, Calder leading the way. Adun was bent with his hands on his knees, what was left of the other raiders surrounding him and eyeing the hill suspiciously.

Getting to his feet, Bijan returned to the marker himself. Boon, still as a bear, was standing next to it. His forepaws gripped the crystal with gouging claws, and his tattoos burned an ugly red. The marker itself began to glow purple, radiating out from its centre in rays that seemed to focus on the beast before it. Boon's hulking grey form started to shrink in the purple light, changing from bear to human in a transformation that Bijan struggled to understand. It was like reality switched his human self with his bear self as easily as a con man moved the ball during a game of cups. Too quick for the eye, but just slow enough for the performance. The man Bijan knew stood before the crystal. His face was a mask of pain, his body tensed, and his muscles strained.

Adun came to a stop next to Bijan, his arms crossed before his chest.

"I didn't know," Bijan said, his eyes still on the purple

light and Boon.

"He's cursed. It's a bad sign." Adun's eyes were hard and unmoving as they took in what was happening before them.

"It's helped us. We need not worry," Bijan said, and knew the words would provide little comfort.

"I've sent someone back to the Valley of Appolumi. Iollan should be told."

Bijan nodded. Iollan would certainly enjoy the turn in events. His disdain for the rugged guide needed little to push it into hatred, but the information that Boon could harness this kind of power would certainly complicate their relationship further. "Good idea. It seems like we've figured out how to power the crystal." He walked closer to the crystal and Boon, "if the legends are right, the castle will come."

As his words escaped his mouth a steady thrumming noise began within the crystal and a purple beam of light sprang into the sky, colouring the area immediately around it in unnatural hues. Boon stared up to the sky, following the beam with his shaggy head.

"He is a cursed man," said Adun, "the raiders will not help him any further."

"I didn't think your men scared that easy." Bijan turned back to the young man who had become something of his ward.

"He is an abomination. The raiders will keep their distance, or we will kill him. When his usefulness comes to an end, we still may." Adun returned to his brothers in the tall grass. They would spend the night there amongst the creeping weeds. Bijan turned to Boon and the crystal yet again. The large man was laughing, a low chuckling that barely rose above the thrumming of the crystal. He was laughing.

CHAPTER TWENTY

"Princess Leandra and her husband-to-be, Lord Calix," Obelius announced as the two entered into the great
hall to a roar of applause. While the private dinner may
have been subdued, the festivities in the great hall were,
by contrast, uproarious. Leandra greeted the people gathered to see her and Calix, a broad smile masking her fear
and complete lack of preparation. She looked back at the
small entourage they had gathered after leaving the dining room and had a moment to note that Alethea wasn't
amongst them before they were engulfed by the people
who pushed in close to get a better look at the new couple.

This part of the festivities was for everyone in the
castle; peasants, servants, and nobles alike. For many this
was their first time seeing Leandra, and they moved close
to get a good look. The room was an open dining area that
the kingdom used for special occasions and honoured celebrations. It was a large stone room, much like the rest of
the castle, but the standards of each noble house hung at
each corner, forever looking down upon the people who
gathered there.

Lesser nobles and peasants gathered around them, Leandra's unbidden and unwanted entourage. She greeted

them all with a smile and a word. Calix's smile faltered from time to time, but she thought he maintained a pleasant enough facade — for him.

Dinner had been torturous. She hated being forced to sit at the head of the table just so she could be ogled by the lecherous noble elite. Leandra knew what it was really for, the dinner, to placate the ruling classes. Her father had kept her safe as long as he could, kept her away from their conniving eyes, behind his protective, intimidating shadow. Deep down inside she knew that he had kept her under glass, his special prize that was for display only. The problem was, when she came of age (and even before that) the nobility had noticed her. She was no longer a little, mischievous girl. Whether it was solely due to her beauty or the power she represented, Leandra couldn't say, but the nobles wanted her. They yearned for her. It made Leandra feel dirty. Like their unwanted looks marked her with filth and soot. Their sideways glances were like handprints that she couldn't wash off. Calix took her hand and she withdrew it with fright. He gave her a strange look and she shuddered.

On top of all of that, she'd forced herself to ignore Edric. She had felt his quizzical gaze, his piercing stare throughout the meal. That was harder than she'd imagined it would be. Each time she felt his glance she wanted to give him a knowing stare, a wink, a nod. She wanted to wave and tell him she'd speak with him later. She didn't though. If they were to escape, the first thing she'd need was some wiggle room. To get that, she needed to play Obelius' game, Alethea's game, her father's game. Edric would understand. She hoped.

Leandra turned and took Calix's hand into her own, a placating gesture under a demure smile. Calix's stern exterior cracked some, and a smile formed at the edges of his mouth. She gave him a nod that she hoped was reassuring and gave the crowd a brief look. There were few that she recognized in the throng. Some nobles that she'd become acquainted with through the smaller social gatherings Obelius had thrown for his students; some of the common folk who had served in the royal quarters; militia members in their full regalia standing guard throughout the hall, hands on their swords and an eager nod for Calix, their leader; but the grand majority were unknown to her. Their eager smiles beamed up to her, their hands reached out to touch her. She couldn't see Edric anywhere. Was her act a little too convincing at dinner? She bit her lower lip.

The great hall was lined with tables to allow for the multitude of people and their mingling throughout the room. Each table had its own assortment of food: roast pig, beef roast, stuffed turkey, apples, carrots, potatoes, all cooked in several different ways. Wine and mead were laid out next to the food, and servants waded their way through the crowd with their own supply of already poured wine. Leandra stood at the entryway, unable to move further with the surging of the crowd. Obelius was suddenly behind her, thin fingers on her shoulder. He wasn't pushing her, not really, but that's what he intended. That's what his presence meant. She could practically hear his whispered hiss, "move ahead, princess. Meet your public." Calix gave a short nod to his right and members of the militia flowed around her, intermingling in a fluctuating shield that kept the peasants and servants away from the noble couple. They started to move forward.

It was a slow walk through the crowd. The militiamen helped push their way through, their armour harsh on the reaching hands of those surrounding them. Leandra could feel the tension rise in Calix beside her. At some other time, some other place, Leandra would have had to stifle a giggle at Calix's impatience. Even his ruffled noble sensibilities could not raise her spirits. Instead she continued to fake a smile and tried to ignore him.

She eyed a young woman, red hair bouncing behind her playful gait, a serving tray balanced on one hand and shoulder. Of everyone in the room, that servant seemed to be giving them the least attention. An easy smile was on her lips, her green eyes flicked with something akin to flirtatious as she delivered drinks throughout the crowd. Leandra was amazed at how deftly the woman joined the throng of revellers and how she faded into the crowd. Amazed and jealous.

Leandra and Calix continued to move through. Her practised smile still resided bright on her face. In contrast, Calix's face was sombre. He twisted his moustache with a white-gloved hand, his face stern and unimpressed as Leandra offered a hand and a word to those she could, a smile and a wave to those she couldn't. He put his mouth next to Leandra's ear and whispered, "Amazing we have to put up with these peasants, isn't it?"

Leandra gave him a quick glance, her false smile cracking some. Calix's smile, on the other hand, seemed to only grow. It was still cold and hard, but the smile grew. She turned back to the crowd.

It was a common enough belief by the nobles of Appolumi; the common folk were nothing but a means to an end. Just parts to the machine that made Appolumi the kingdom it was. Nobles had the belief that the common folk were disposable, that if one died another would be ready to step up in their place. Of course, this all hinged on the legend, the myth, that there was nothing left to the surface world, and that the only thing that kept the common folk from a sure and horrible death was the protection of the nobles, and the floating castle that they somehow controlled. That last part was a tenuous truth at best.

The Circle ensured the castle remained afloat, and as much as the nobles wanted to believe that they controlled The Circle, they didn't. Hesperos made that perfectly clear whenever he met with Leandra's father and Obelius. Not in so many words, but in his actions. There was more than a healthy fear that leached out when Hesperos made his presence known. Power exuded from him. Leandra had only shared his presence a handful of times and she hated every minute of it. Her skin crawled around him. Almost as if it was trying to find a way to stay as far away form Hesperos as possible. Leandra didn't know how Edric could live with and train with him for as long as he did.

"Leandra," came a voice from the crowd. It wasn't particularly strong or powerful, but it cut through the other voices all the same. The voice addressed her by her actual name and not by princess or my lady. She turned her head in time to see Edric as he pushed through the crowd. He wasn't as efficient as the young server had been, but he made it through all the same. He was stalled for just a brief moment as the militia who were pushing the opposite way stood before him, but it was only a moment. Edric slid past them somehow and stood before Leandra and Calix.

Calix's face dropped a sour glance upon Edric as he blocked his way and tried to wave him off with a roll of his eyes. Edric stood speechless for a moment and stared into Leandra's sea mist eyes. Her peach-coloured lips twisted into a slight smile; she couldn't help herself.

"Princess and Lord," Edric said, bowing a little too low. "What an honour it is to greet you on this joyous day." He gripped Calix's hand in his own, shaking it up and down as Calix attempted to pull it away. Leaving the noble lord's hand be, Edric turned to Leandra, who had taken to covering her mouth with one hand in an effort to stifle a laugh. He grasped her free hand in his own, and he dropped his head once more, bringing it level with her outstretched hand. Edric stayed like that a moment too long but it was only when Calix cleared his throat that Edric straightened right away.

"And who might you be?" Calix said with a sneer.

Edric was focused on Leandra, his eyes locked on hers. "I... I am Edric." He still held Leandra's hand in his own.

"Yes, and *who* might that be?" Calix took Leandra's hand from Edric's grip and held it in his own gloved hand.

Edric gave Calix an impatient look from the corner of his eye, "Edric, apprentice to Hesperos, and initiate to The Circle." Once Edric had uttered these words there was a palpable change in the room. A slight tension appeared, or was revealed, as if the room had taken a collective breath and was awaiting its release.

"Edric," Leandra finally said, breaking the uneasy silence that had gathered. "Young Edric who I had played with all those years ago?"

He nodded and stared about him. Leandra could tell that he wasn't expecting such a response to his own introduction. Nor was she, for that matter. The revellers were watching, their conversations had halted, and their paths were paused in mid-step. Calix had even stopped, one glove posed next to his chin as if defending a punch or caught mid-gasp.

"Yes," Edric turned his eyes back to Leandra; she allowed a genuine smile to break the surface. It felt good to finally let it go, to finally get the emotions out

"How long has it been, ten years?" Leandra leaned into him, her raven hair falling around her shoulders. Leandra hoped that Edric would understand what she was doing. That he would get that their plans had to remain a secret.

"It feels like an eternity." Edric smiled and nodded.

"Wait," Calix butted in, "weren't you with the old wizard at dinner?"

"Dinner!" Leandra wailed and slapped Edric on the shoulder, "You were at dinner and didn't say anything before now?" Her eyes were wide with mock fury, her bow-shaped smile still etched her face. Calix frowned and pulled her closer, but the room relaxed.

"Well... you were so busy. It's an important day for you, I didn't want to interrupt."

Leandra straightened. "Yes, you are right." Still smiling, she turned to Calix, "Lord Calix, I have known Edric since we were little more than babies. Perhaps you remember him?"

Calix grimaced and forced a small smile, "I can't say that I do."

Edric nodded to Calix. Leandra had no doubt the two remembered each other.

"You said that you were still the apprentice to Hesperos?" Leandra said, turning back to Edric.

"Yes, not for much longer I'm afraid."

"The Trials! You are completing them now?" Leandra grabbed his arm with her free hand.

"Yes. We took a hiatus in order to attend your party and wish you the best."

"Well, thank you, Edric." Leandra blushed and dropped her eyes.

"Indeed, thank you for your sacrifice," Calix said, attempting to draw his future wife further into the room. Edric shot him a hard look.

"We must take our leave," Leandra said, following Calix's lead. "I hope I am able to speak to you before the Trials end."

"Wait, Leandra. May I speak to you in private?" He grabbed her hand as she left, drawing a sharp inhalation from those around them; Calix's eyes were blue fire.

"Edric…" Leandra said, her own eyes sad, her face pensive. "I must go. Return to the Trials. You are so very important to these people, to this kingdom. Without your sacrifice our way of life is at an end." She looked around the room. "Please, everyone, let's give young Edric, Apprentice of the Magi, a sign of our gratitude for his important work and sacrifice." Leandra started to clap, and the rest of the room started to join in slowly, even Calix, his clapping muted by his white gloves. She sighed a brief relief. 'Edric, you idiot,' she thought.

"But… I need to speak to —" Edric said, but was cut off with a sudden hug from Leandra, her arms tight around his neck and shoulders.

"We will always be grateful to you. Go to your master, finish your Trials. When I am queen, perhaps I will visit you in The Circle." She let go and returned to Calix, her false smile returned as she moved through the rest of the room.

She could feel Edric's gaze on her back, and all the hurt that was contained within it. Maybe he hadn't understood after all. She'd have to visit him again. It was risky. If she was caught, her current plan on earning freedom around the castle would be all but lost. At the same time, she hated the thought of leaving Edric on his own and without confirmation from her. He'd been alone for far too long.

Leandra sighed, resigned.

The alarm bells went off with a sudden shockwave that stilled everyone in the room. Glasses and mugs dropped to the floor, smashing and spreading their contents all around them. By the second peal of bells, madness had taken over the room.

Leandra turned back to Edric and their eyes met.

CHAPTER TWENTY-ONE

The alarm bells rang in his head as Edric made his way through the narrow corridors of lower Appolumi; a trilling, metallic, sound that shook him with each reverberation. He'd contemplated running to find Hesperos, but he knew that his master may not be the most forthcoming. After all, now that the wedding announcement was done, the Trials were the focus of Hesperos' mind. Still, Edric had his own resources within the castle that his master would not deign to consult. Edric wasn't sure if Gregory had been called away to perform duties for the festivities, but he would take his chance.

The servants lived in relative comfort in the lower levels of the castle. It was certainly a far cry from the lavish accommodations the nobles had carved out for themselves around the courtroom, but it was something. Unlike Edric, whose own quarters had been an afterthought, the servants' quarters were proper rooms. Granted, they didn't have the view Edric had, but they were proper accommodations all the same.

Edric pushed on, passing few people on his way. Gregory enjoyed his life as a servant, living in the Quarter, as far as Edric could tell. It was no surprise to Edric that Gregory was a housekeeper and handyman, his broad shoulders and strong hands were ideal for that position, and he seemed to enjoy the work as much as he did anything else.

He reached Gregory's chambers and pounded on the thick oak door.

"Gregory," he said, head leaning into the door, straining to hear any response. The door opened suddenly, and he fell forward into the muscular chest of his sought-out friend.

"Edric," Gregory picked him up by the shoulders and helped set him straight again. "What's brought you to these dregs again?" Gregory was quick to smile, a genuine, toothy grin that lined his cheeks and eyes.

Edric grabbed the larger man's shoulders, returned his embrace. "Did you hear the alarm?"

"Aye, but that's none of our concern down here," he cast his arm in a wide, including, motion meant to convey the entirety of the servants' quarters. "Not unless it is made our business, of course."

"What does it mean?" Edric said, squeezing the other man's shoulders, "Is the castle in danger?"

Gregory took Edric's hands into his own and patted them. "If the castle were crumbling or falling groundward, we'd all know by now." His smile was gentler, a flash of concern in his grey eyes. "What's got you so upset?"

"I just need to know what the bells mean." Edric turned from the bulky servant, leaning on the wall to the side of the doorway. The bear from his vision, its matted fur and red eyes, flashed through his mind as he leaned his forehead into the stone wall, letting the cool brick overcome him.

Gregory patted him on the back. "I don't rightly know what happened, Edric, but let me ask some friends." He guided Edric to a chair and helped him sit. "You just stay here and relax. I won't be gone long." Gregory shut the door behind him as he left, leaving Edric in the silence once more.

Gregory's chambers were quaint. Edric was now sitting upon one of the supper table chairs, which itself wasn't far from the bed that Gregory must have just arisen from. It stood unmade and ugly, much like Edric's own bed. The room was unlike Edric's in just about every other way, however, as Gregory seemed to be as proud of his work at home as he was in his service to the nobles.

Though the walls were constructed of rock, the noises of neighbours trickled in from outside. The joyous roars of children playing, the friendly banter between those that passed; it was truly wonderful to Edric. Having spent most of his time in his studies and the rest of it secluded to his tower away from the rest of the castle, even from Hesperos, Edric began to envy the servants more and more. True, they were bound to the nobles, but he was bound to The Circle. His life would soon only be that of the Magi. Nothing else, if he and Leandra didn't plan their escape soon.

Edric had begun to fear this final Trial. Everything up to this point had mentioned a sacrifice. Even the people in the great hall had thanked him for it. What did that mean though? Was he meant to die to become part of The Circle? Would they tear his magic out of his body just to power the castle? If any of that was true, did that mean that Leandra had already known what was supposed to happen to him? If so, why hadn't she already told him? There were too many questions, fuelled by so many fears.

Despite that, Edric began to feel that his only escape was with Leandra. She had seemed so aloof earlier. He figured there was reason enough to be quiet about their plans, but they had little in the way of plans just yet. And now there were alarm bells to deal with.

Throughout his entire life on the castle he had never heard those bells. Never. Just days ago, Edric would have feared that it meant that Appolumi was falling into the plague-filled lands, now it could be a route to escape for both him and Leandra; a route to discover his past. And yet, his senses played against it. His senses and his vision. There was something strange at play. Whether it was part of the castle, part of him, or something else completely, he couldn't be sure.

Edric's head was in his hands when Gregory returned, opening the door slowly. He peered in, "Edric, are you still here?"

A new day had emerged but Edric hadn't noticed; he sat in near complete darkness. Once Gregory had left, he had drawn all the curtains to block any light that found its ways to the depths of the Quarter. He also hadn't bothered to light any of the candles or lanterns.

Gregory lit a candle that stood by the door and walked around the room to light the others from the first's flame.

"Well," Gregory said after he was seated on the edge of his bed, "the alarm bell we heard was indeed due to a special cause." Gregory's smile was infuriating now. It was a teasing, cocksure grin that only meant to mock and never to encourage.

"And what was that cause?"

"Seems we had an intruder. An interloper, if you will." Gregory's smile grew.

"That's impossible." Edric's jaw hung so slack he was amazed he had been able to put together such a coherent sentence.

"Of course it is, and yet it's the truth."

Edric jumped from his perch on the small kitchen chair. "Where is he? How'd he get aboard?"

"Well, I imagine he's in the dungeons. How he managed to get aboard, I have no idea."

Edric nodded, yes. This was certainly something worth the alarm bells. Perhaps it would be something that he could use to his advantage as well, if he worked fast enough and swift enough. "Thank you, Gregory. You are a good man." Edric gripped hands with the stalwart gentleman before him.

"Remember that the next time you are able to sneak some of your master's wine away from him," Gregory said with a soft chuckle before shooing Edric through the door.

Edric doubted very much that he'd have an opportunity to repay Gregory's kindness. With any luck he'd soon be rid of his master, his master's wine, and the castle itself. He pushed his way through the narrow corridors once more, heading towards the dungeons and his key to escape.

***

Edric hadn't been to the dungeons. Ever. The only time he had come close was with Leandra when they were only children. It was a day set for a grand adventure. Leandra had planned it for weeks. She had created a treasure map, clues in the form of riddles, and even commandeered some old clothing to better fit the task at hand. Leandra dressed as the cunning pirate captain; a bright red shirt bundled around her head to create a bandana. Edric was dressed as the lowly navigator and first mate, his pants already had holes in the knees, so he didn't need any extra accoutrements. It was a secret game, more for Leandra's sake than for anything else. Obelius didn't like to let her out of his sight for too long and had been fond of dissuading her from playing games that involved roughhousing or vulgar language. This was far too much of a chore for Obelius alone, so he took Leandra's personal maid, Alethea, into his employ. Always one who wanted Leandra to dress properly and appropriately, Alethea was quite adept at stalling games in her own right. For an immense woman, she was quite fleet of foot and sneaky to boot. If either one of them had learned of the secret plot to explore the dungeons, it would have meant trouble for Edric and Leandra alike. Thinking back on it, however, Edric thought he may have been the one to suffer the most.

The pirate adventure saw them battle imaginary foes through the courtyard, find treasure in the market, sneak by guards in the great room, and, finally, hunt and kill the monster that resided in the dark, empty dungeons. The creature Leandra had dreamed up was long, tentacled, but amphibian in appearance, with a face marred by one eye and hideous sharp teeth that would forever click together. The monster was ridiculous in proportions, and silly sounding to Edric now as an adult, but as they'd both crossed the darkened threshold of the stair that led to the lower levels of the castle, there'd been a cold feeling of fear that had prickled at his spine. With each echoing step, young Edric felt the hot, foul-smelling breath of the creature warm on his back. His child's imagination told him that the monster was stalking him from the shadows, ready to lash out and eat him whole the instant his guard was dropped. Edric hadn't been able to tell what Leandra was feeling, and he never had the opportunity to ask her after the fact, but she moved down the darkened stairs at a cautious pace, a wooden sword held aloft to ward off attackers, and her breathing was rapid.

They stopped at the bottom of the stairs, under the only lit torch that they had encountered on their descent. With shaking hands, Edric had checked the homemade map Leandra had gifted him earlier that morning. He remembered thinking that the map was a fairly good representation of the castle. It had contained all the major landmarks that Edric had come to know, even though he had been there a much shorter time than anyone else. As he had looked upon it with his child's eyes, he saw that the dungeon ended with the stairs on which they had taken their break. As a dutiful navigator he told his captain, Leandra, that if they were to continue into the shadows, they would be going off map. As children, they hesitated in the flickering orange light. It gave them time to look about themselves in nervous anticipation of some real monster breaching the darkness before them, their young faces burdened with frowns of worry.

The dungeons were on the westernmost side of the castle, in the depths of the earth that still clung to the foundations of Appolumi. Aside from The Circle, it was the area of the castle that ran the deepest downward. Edric ran through the same halls he'd tread with Leandra all those years before and tried to remember the order of the sigils that would guide him to the entrance once more. It was difficult; Leandra had been the map maker, the guide.

Much like the militia, there was a rare need for those cages that were housed in the earth. From what Edric was able to glean from the servants, peasants, and Hesperos, it was mostly used to house drunkards or young nobles that were too obnoxious for even their families to address. Essentially, the dungeon had become a place to teach a lesson. It was representative of a slap to the back of the hand and a scolding, rather than any true punishment. If there were any crimes of a serious nature, it was often dealt with outside of the cells. Often this involved theft in one form or another. In each case a peasant was blamed, and a sentence was handed down. The punishment often went from dismemberment to death, and no actual time in the dungeons. Servants were needed to run Appolumi and the nobles couldn't handle being without them for that long.

Edric stopped at a sigil and bent over with his hands on his knees. He struggled to take a deep breath and get his wind back. Of all the things that Hesperos had tasked him to do, there was little in the way of physical activity. He'd been able to get by on youthful exuberance most days, but he would certainly need to make a change soon. Especially if he and Leandra were to make it on the surface world. He wondered if there'd be a difference. He'd read about land legs and sea legs, was there a such thing as air legs?

Edric ran his hand over the sigil, a slight curve like a crescent moon with a line etched through it. It came to his waist, which surprised him. Had he really grown that much since he and Leandra owned these hallways? A smile crept to his lips.

"So, you've come, Boy," Hesperos' cold voice seeped out of the shadows behind him. "And early at that." Edric could feel the old man stand at his shoulder, arms folded in his baggy robes. Now he recognized the sigil. A sigil of warning that Leandra had created all on her own. A warning to Edric of his own fears, it signified something much more frightening than the dungeons; it warned of The Circle.

"I... I didn't..."

"The Trials call, Boy. They call to you. I suppose it was the alarm bells that sent you here. A call was made that may have threatened your place within The Circle after all. Never fear, Edric, it was false. Those that perpetrated it will be punished. Your destiny still awaits within The Circle."

Edric felt weak. The meal he'd devoured in the king's dining hall was stirring in his stomach, and he wanted to sit. His knees began to waver, but Hesperos gripped him under the arm, helped him stand.

"I don't want to do this," Edric said. It was too soon.

"What?" Hesperos said in a whisper, his grip tightening around Edric's bicep.

"I'm not going to finish the Trials. I know that this isn't..."

Hesperos pulled up Edric's wrist in one quick motion, using more physical prowess than Edric had ever seen from him before. "Listen here, you petulant child," Hesperos said, saliva dripping from his lips and chin. "You are going to complete these Trials." He wrenched Edric forward. "You are going to pass them, and you are going to become one with The Circle." Hesperos twisted Edric's arm again, his long nails digging into the younger man's soft flesh.

Edric's look of surprise must have amused Hesperos, because a harsh bark of laughter exploded from the older man for a moment, frightening Edric as he stood there in disbelief. *Smack* — the sound of Hesperos' hand slapping Edric across the cheek echoed in the corridor and Edric's mind. He put his hand to his face.

Hesperos released him with a push that landed Edric on the floor. "Now," the old wizard said, "follow me to

The Circle. We will finish the Trials." He sauntered away from the shadows and moved ahead to breach the corridor, and Edric followed.

The old wizard, stooped at the shoulders, led them on through the narrow stone hallways. It wasn't a path Edric was accustomed to, though it had been one of his and Leandra's shortcuts in their youth. The path led on to Hesperos' chambers, the walls becoming more and more dreary as they proceeded. In places it seemed as though the stone walls were crumbling down to dirt and rock. Thin, choking vines crawled out of shadows and cracks, lining the fear-inducing part of the floating castle.

When they finally stopped, Hesperos flashed an evil smile over his bowed shoulder. Edric wasn't surprised that they had stopped before the large wooden doors that closed on The Circle.

Edric and Hesperos had been down in this section quite a few times. Hesperos always gave different reasons for it. At times it was due to the quiet that was abundant in this area. Later it became a good, secluded place to practice physical manifestations and manipulations. Edric had no doubt about the real reason he and Hesperos stood before this place time and time again: the power. The air was charged with magic that made it lighter and more pleasant to be within. Edric felt it, but he feared mentioning it as a child, afraid that Hesperos would discover that he enjoyed the atmosphere and take it away, or use it against him. That fear still remained.

"Here we are, Boy. This room, and what lies within, is everything to Appolumi." The old man turned and pointed one crooked finger at Edric. "Oh, some would say the king and his nobles have held us together. Some would say it was the determination of our people to see this exercise in power through to the end. Know this, Boy, they are blissfully, stupidly wrong." Hesperos pointed his gnarled finger towards the door. "This room is our past, present, future. You are included in that, of course, like it or not. This is the room where your final Trial will take place. It is the beginning of your end, but a continuation of the castle."

Edric shuddered as the old wizard gripped the door handles to push the door open. The room had been a part of his life since he could remember, a symbol for the magic he studied, an altar for the religion he worshipped, and a focus for the fears and anxieties he felt. The door creaked open the smallest crack; Edric's eyes were transfixed on the opening. Waiting, afraid. He had only glimpsed the inside of the room once before, as a child. Hesperos had ended their lessons in the presence of The Circle and told Edric to wait as he entered the room to check on things. The door creaked open, just as it had a few minutes before. Edric's nerve, however, was not the same as a young boy, and fear got the best of him. A stream of light had exited the door before he looked away, closing his eyes tight so he couldn't see anything more until Hesperos exited, smiling his sickly smile.

Edric dared not repeat that mistake again.

A bluish white light fanned across the stone floor as Hesperos pulled open one of the dark oak doors. The room looked as though it were made entirely of crystal, glowing by some pale, absent light. Jagged fingers crept up from the floor's uneven surface, stabbing at the air in crystalline points. From where he stood, Edric could just make out the swaying shoulder of some white-clad figure just past the entryway. Hesperos stood back and motioned for Edric to enter. Fear tugged at Edric's stomach, a gnawing pain of unease that followed him as he entered the cold, sterile light.

Ten men stood around the small room. They were all clad in the same flowing, white robes, their heads exposed and turned toward the crystal spires that grew from the ceiling. Edric walked among them, keeping as much distance as he could to avoid their touch. They were motionless, their eyes, open and blank, were faded to white. It was their mouths that bothered Edric the most. They fell open, gaping, their teeth and tongue exposed, but their blue lips continued to move, continued to speak wordlessly, spells and incantations lost to the ether.

At the end of the room, he walked around the last member of The Circle. He was a tall man, gaunt like his compatriots, blue veins lining his eyes and mouth. One long, gnarled hand was wrapped around a crystal offshoot, and the crystal seemed to have grown around the hand, or the hand had somehow become part of the room. This man was older than the others, his face lined with strain and age in equal measure. He swayed from his tether to the crystal, pain disturbing his decrepit features, and a wheeze escaped his thin throat and sunken chest. He was dying.

The door closed with a clunk; Hesperos stood in the shadow at the other end of the room, his yellow eye glinting in the crystal light. "Welcome to your future home," he spread his arms before him. "Have you been curious about what it would be like?"

Edric nodded; he couldn't find words.

"I see that you've found your predecessor. Magus Vitalis." Hesperos pointed to the man Edric stood beside. "He was the leader of our sect for quite some time." He turned and stroked his beard, "Quite powerful, too. Oh yes. It was he who thought of sending Appolumi into the skies, you know. He thought he could do it alone, that his knowledge and unyielding power could sustain the needs of the castle and its people." While Hesperos walked toward Edric, his hands clasped behind his curved back, he looked in on each member of The Circle in turn. "The legends say that he very nearly did it: lifted the castle into the sky. But that wasn't all that was needed, was it?" He looked at Edric and his mouth twitched up at the corners. "No, of course it wasn't. People who intended to stay upon the castle would need food, resources, luxuries."

"And it takes ten Magi to do all of that if one could lift the castle?"

"He could lift the castle, but it wouldn't move. It would float, but not fly. Also, mighty Vitalis was only so strong. His power would eventually disappear, and the castle would fall. Five men could do it, but they'd be... used up rather quickly." Hesperos flashed a quick glance at Edric, his yellow eye alight. "No, Boy, ten was the right number. Power in reserve and in extended use."

Edric looked around at the ten Magi of The Circle. Each had a hand encased in crystal, a fluctuating light pulsing through the room stemmed from those crystalline shackles that held them in place. They swayed in unison, moving to some unknown, unheard song. They stood in awe of the crystal room, worshippers before the altar.

"It was quite a sacrifice for our brotherhood."

"This wasn't a sacrifice," Edric turned on Hesperos, "this was torture."

"They are so similar, aren't they?" Hesperos began to walk back to the door. "Come, Boy, follow me."

At the back of the room, in the shadows, a singular concrete pole stood to Edric's waist. It was etched with lettering from different languages, a spell that Edric couldn't quite comprehend. He ran his hand over the rough surface, could feel it thrumming with power underneath.

"This is your last Trial, Boy: the Proteus Stone." Hesperos patted the smooth top.

"What do I do?" Edric sighed.

"You make it fit with the rest of the room." Hesperos waved a hand at each Magi with their arms fused with a crystal stand. "You make it a part of yourself."

CHAPTER TWENTY-TWO

The purple beam that extended from the black crystal darkened the sky; it spread through the clouds like milk in tea. Bijan stepped back, covering his face with his arms, and fighting to keep his breath in the growing whirlwind. Dust, grass, and rock assaulted him, his hair, blown free of its bindings whipped at his face, his cloak doing the same to his legs. His feet were unsteady, but he forced his eyes skyward. Clouds were swirling around the beam, drawn to it but unable to touch it; they circled it like sharks to blood.

"We cannot stay here," the forced voice of Adun said at his shoulder, a firm hand on his tunic trying to drag him away. The raiders had already retreated to the tall grass, some had even started out towards the trees, for cover and safety. Bijan didn't begrudge them that. He would have been with them if he wasn't so preoccupied trying to see through the insanity before him.

Bijan shook Adun's hand off. "Where's Boon?" He strained to look around him, to find the wayward guide. Movement at the base of the crystal brought his attention back around to it, his eyes straining against the unnatural light. Boon was there, at its source, his hands cupped on the sides of the crystal, and his head thrown back. Bijan couldn't tell if he was laughing or screaming.

"We must go." Adun succeeded in turning Bijan around, his shemagh blown free and his face bared. Adun was a young man, much younger than Bijan had imagined; his diamond shaped face was smooth, save for a small moustache and chin whisker that was pitch black. His mouth was twisted now, in assertion and annoyance, a small mole dancing on his left cheek.

Bijan grabbed the young man by his shoulders and looked him in the eyes. "No." He squeezed Adun's shoulders and pushed him away. Bijan walked towards Boon, the wind blowing against him, as if to claim the large Northerner as its own. Each step was a struggle, each movement a fight. Bijan waged a war against the elements trying to reach the crystal that, only moments before, he had tried to flee from. With each strained step, his legs and back quaking with the effort, he asked himself why he was doing this for a stranger, a man he'd only known for a week. And yet Boon represented something, was a part of this fool's quest Bijan had himself been drafted into. Every muscle fibre, every instinct screamed at him to flee with the raiders, but something told him Boon was going to have a further part to play in all of this.

"Boon," Bijan yelled, only to have his breath stolen from him by the battering winds. No use, he said to himself, and pushed forward, his arm groping for the other man. As he got closer, he could hear him, hear his rough and grumbling voice as it pierced the noise that had surrounded the hill and the crystal.

"I'm here, castle," Boon yelled between laughs, "I'm finally here. Come and get me, I'm ready." Boon had taken to hitting the crystal with his closed fist, tears streaming down his face.

"Come on, you can't stay here," Bijan tried yelling one more time, on his final push towards the black marker. His hand leapt out and grasped the tattered sleeve of the larger man, grabbed it with all of his might and began to pull. He was hoping to dislodge Boon from his embrace with the crystal, but instead it only pulled himself further into the unrelenting Northerner.

Then it all stopped.

The sudden quiet was a shock to Bijan, his eyes and ears unable to understand what had just happened. He let go of Boon and stood there, blinking in the aftermath of the onslaught of wind and the beam of strange light. He turned his attention to the sky. The beam itself had disappeared, the day brightening again. Boon stared into the sky, his face a mask of disappointment and longing. He struck at the crystal marker as if, with a hard enough blow, he could make the light return.

"Where is it?" Boon said aloud, his eyes still skyward. "It must have seen that, must have known about it. It should be here, gods damn it. It should be here." He leaned his head against the flat surface of the crystal and, for a moment, Bijan thought the massive, Northern barbarian was going to weep in frustration. He thought better of it, and surveyed around them. Adun was just at the edge of the hill, his shemagh back in place now, but his eyes questioning and asking whether it was truly over or not. That same question was mirrored in all the other raiders. Though if it was from fear or from a need to be prepared, Bijan could not say.

Bijan pulled on Boon's collar, forcing his view away from the sky.

"What the hell was that?" The moment he uttered the words he regretted it. He knew what it was. It was what he had been hoping for: a signal. He wasn't sure how he expected a buried crystal to signal a flying castle, but he should have known it wouldn't have been with smoke or fire. Something with grandeur fit the situation completely, but in doing so, made it all too real. Magic existed.

Boon swatted him off and clasped his strong hands back on the crystal, his eyes squinted into the sky.

"It must be coming," he said, his fingers scratching at the surface of the crystal beneath them.

Without another word, Bijan turned from the man, content to leave him be with his crystal and castle. Adun eyed him as he approached, giving him a wide berth as he made his way past him and into the grass.

"How's the grass? Is it biting today?" Bijan turned towards the raider and tried a smirk that he knew had failed. He continued on. He would be content with digging up more of the Appolumi site until Iollan, or his master, discovered how little of use he had actually been. Perhaps Adun would help him escape. Or, maybe, it would be best to leave well enough alone and run off when they reached Haugr again. Leave the mysteries of Appolumi where they were. The important thing was that he still had options.

It was the reaction of the raiders ahead of him that made him pause. Though mostly hidden behind their shemaghs, their eyes widened as they looked to the hill behind him.

"It's coming," Boon shouted as Bijan turned, finally hearing the deep rumbling. There were uneasy groans from the raiders surrounding him, and Adun, still on the crest of the hill, seemed to waver in place. Out of the sky, the clouds, the mist, came the castle.

***

What astounded Bijan first wasn't that the castle was flying, nor was it the fact that the castle was headed directly for them, but that it carried a mass of earth underneath it in a jagged cone shape.

"It's as if the gods just plucked it from the ground and set it to the wind," he said to no one in particular. He scrambled up to Boon. "You need to move," he said weakly, pointing to the ever-nearing castle.

"Move?" Boon was incredulous. His face turned a bright red under his shaggy beard, his yellowed teeth bared. "I can't move, it's finally here." His eyes returned to the castle, a dry chuckle emanating from his throat.

"It'll be hard to lose." Bijan opened his arms to the castle, his upturned palms imploring.

"You'd be surprised," Boon said, casting a strange look at Bijan.

"Damn your stubborn, Northern hide," Bijan said and let a sigh ripple through his body. He sat on the short-cropped grass and waited with the bigger man. "I hope you're right about this," he said, his words barely audible over the grumbling of the approaching castle.

Appolumi moved slow but with purpose, never wavering from its course. It was, at the same time, the most awe inspiring and frightening thing that Bijan had ever witnessed. When he was but a boy, his father had taken him fishing on a far trek to the ocean. Bijan had little care for fishing but wanted to please his father. During their trip, his father caught a large salmon that he was quite proud of. As he was showing it to Bijan and some of his companions, Bijan sighted something approaching in the sky. He tried to point it out to his father, but his pleas were drowned out by his father's laughter. A sense of

dread fell over the young Bijan, as the large mass continued to get bigger and bigger, its path obvious, though its
intention still unclear. As his father held the salmon aloft,
a gigantic bird, an Albatross, snatched the fish from his
hand and nearly knocked him off of his feet. Bijan broke
down in tears while his father cursed, and his companions
laughed. Bijan felt that sense of dread now, though he
feared the only one laughing at the end of all this would
be Boon as he lost his mind.

Adun sat next to Bijan, his knees drawn to his chest.
"What do you think guides it?" he said without looking
at Bijan.

"I have no idea. Magic? A force of will?"

"You don't think anyone is alive there, do you?" Adun
turned to Bijan, his keen eyes narrowed.

"I should hope so. I'd rather not think of a castle being
able to move all on its own. Perhaps there is someone up
there with their hand on a rudder guiding it toward us.
Really, that would be for the best."

"How so?"

"They'd be too old to fight back." A grin broke out
over his dirty face. Adun nodded.

The castle came to a slow stop just above the black
crystal. Bijan could see small clumps of dirt fall from the
earth it carried with it, and small outshoots of roots and
twigs poked out from what remained. The castle was hardly discernible at this angle, around the mound of earth it
carried with it. Bijan and Adun looked on as it swayed
over the crystal, unsteady in its place, as if it wanted to be
carried off by the wind; a flower in the breeze.

Boon continued to stare up at the castle, his eyes transfixed, but his face had grown calm, pensive. His mouth
was a tight line under his beard, and his thick brows were

furrowed in concentration. He let go of the crystal.

A low grinding noise erupted above them that sounded to Bijan like large chains moving against one another. The speed of the sound increased and multiplied and with a loud thoom that made Adun and Bijan jump, something flew from the castle and crashed into the tall grass just beyond the hill they stood upon. From what Bijan could tell it was some sort of metal object that stood embedded in the ground, a large chain with giant links ran from the object back into the castle. Another loud thoom sounded, followed by another and another. More metal objects slammed into the ground around the large hill, digging into the soft earth and holding the castle steady in position. The world fell quiet again.

Adun was lying face first on the low hill, his hands covering his head, when Bijan returned to him.

"Get up," Bijan hissed. "Where are your men?" His voice broke the unearthly silence that had held court over the land since the chains had fallen. The constant hum of bugs, the tittering of birds, the sniffing of rodents, and the growls of foxes and wolves all went silent. Nature was waiting, staring out at the unnatural sight before it.

Adun raised his head and looked around him. He gave a small shrug that made Bijan sigh and curse.

"Someone, or something, may be coming for that marker. We'll need someone to hold it off until we can get onboard."

Again, a shrug, as Adun dusted himself off.

"Damn it," Bijan said and rubbed at his temples.

There was a rustling behind them, the soft sound of boots on grass. Boon had darted out from the hole made around the marker and launched himself at one of the big chains. He crawled up it as naturally as Bijan breathed air.

"Damn it!" Bijan said, in a run to the chain Boon was scaling. The metal, the chain links, must have been ancient, though Bijan couldn't tell by the look of them. There was no rust or wear anywhere on them, just some small sigils carved into their surface. Adun was behind him, anxious to move forward and up the chain, and Boon was already halfway up, making it look easy. Bijan's thoughts went back to Boon's earlier transformation and shuddered.

"Damn it." Bijan rubbed his hands together and began his own ascent, the chain cold on his hands, and slippery underfoot. Adun remained close behind as they made their way up the chain and after Boon.

Unbeknownst to them, an arrow whistled through the air and plunged into the ground just under the castle's stone walls. The rope it carried was sturdy, but thin, and would make easy work for anyone adept at climbing. One man started up it now, his body weighed down with larger ropes and hooks. His compatriots looked on, waiting their turn to scale the mythical flying castle.

***

Bijan landed with a grunt, narrowly missing the gaping Boon.

Appolumi.

The castle.

It was real. The cobblestones of its walkways hard under his feet, the stone walls solid and unmovable, the same as they had been for hundreds — thousands — of years.

Boon grabbed a handful of Bijan's cloak and tunic, pulling him around. The large man carried stars in his eyes, his bearded face that of a child presented with a new toy.

"I'm here," he said, his voice a whisper. "I'm finally here." Bijan patted his ham-sized hand and returned a jubilant smile. They had arrived.

"This is amazing," Bijan said, looking around him in an extended double-take, reviewing his surroundings and taking in the reality that was the castle. He shook off Boon's hand and crept further into the corridor they had found themselves in. He bent as he walked, cringing as his steps echoed along the walls that were empty, save for the creeping vines that outlined the uppermost bricks and stone. He knelt and ran his fingers through the crease between the floor and wall, his finger came away wet, mud-streaked.

A thud filled the space behind him. Bijan flinched to standing only to see Adun straighten and dust himself off, his own head swivelling to take in the castle. Bijan gave the young raider a nod and wiped his hand on his pants. He started down the corridor once more.

The steps of Boon followed him now, each of his booming footfalls causing a shudder to run through Bijan's shoulders. "Nervous?" Adun said, catching up.

"Of course not." Bijan could see a knowing smile grow under the young man's shemagh as he moved ahead and left Bijan to curse to himself. He was nervous, more than he had ever been on any previous dig or heist. That's only natural, he told himself. After all, he had never been involved in anything quite like this. Yes, he sought the rare and the antique, had handled the cursed and damned, but finding a *myth* real and intact was on a new level completely. Still, whether justified or not, his nerves were there. Bijan took a deep breath and tried to steady himself as he moved to follow Adun.

The corridor sprawled before them, rolled out like a carpet into the darkness that soon overtook the hall. They walked on in silence, no other sounds save their own breathing and footfalls. Boon had gone quiet himself, staying to the centre of the walkway, reverent and amazed of his surroundings. From time to time he would reach out his long arms, his fingers nearly touching the cold wall. Each time he'd stop just short of it, dropping his hand to his side, tentative and disappointed.

Growing in the distance was a stairwell; at its sight all three men slowed their pace and made themselves be quiet. Adun took out his scimitar and held it underhand, the blunt, curved end resting along his forearm. Bijan shot the raider a strange look.

"Now who's nervous?" he said, but the mockery fell flat in the stillness of the corridor and the approaching stairs.

Boon was first to reach the stairwell. He peered up into the darkness that was just out of reach of its cousin inhabiting the hallway.

"Nothing," he said, disappointed, over his broad shoulder.

Bijan reached out to touch the stonework of the curving stairs, to rub his hands over the walls that lay on either side. It was smooth with age and craftsmanship, but not from ill-use or disrepair. He looked back the way he had come, sizing up their path, their surroundings.

"Wait," he said, holding up a hand to freeze his companions in their places. "Something isn't right."

Bijan walked back along the hallway, aware of the questioning looks that passed between Boon and Adun. He knelt to the floor again, ran his hands along the creases, and looked at them.

"There's barely any dust," he said into his hand. "There doesn't seem to be any damage or neglect."

"And what does that mean?" Adun said, dropping his blade to his side.

"I... I don't know." Bijan stood and examined the structure again. "If I didn't know any better," he said, afraid to utter the next words, "I'd say that someone still roamed these halls."

Adun stared at him and readied his sword once more.

"Come on," Boon said, impatience straining his voice, and they continued up the stone steps. The stairs curled around a column of brick that even Boon had to grope as they climbed the darkened stairwell, their echoing foot-falls sounding like that of ten men, not three.

"Is it possible," Adun said in a whisper, just ahead of Bijan on the stairs. "Could there still be people living in Appolumi?"

Bijan stared into the darkness before him, at the subtle highlights of his companion he could barely make out in the gloom.

"I wouldn't have thought so," he said, curling his beard, "but the castle seems to be sustained by magic, perhaps the occupants are as well."

Silence was Adun's response, an increased speed in his step; Bijan struggled to catch up.

They exited the stairwell into a torch-lit hallway. At either end of the hall were wooden doors, spruce by the look of it, well maintained in their rich brown lacquer. Boon hesitated with the choice of direction so Adun took the lead, heading to the right-hand door. He put his ear to the door, sniffed the air, and seemed to look around the creases. He stood back, taking quick breaths, and rushed forward. He pushed open the door, rolled to the side and came up on his knees, poised like a lion ready to strike.

Adun had rolled out of the castle and into an open courtyard, with a lush, green garden that sprouted trees and seemed to have crops growing in the distance. No one blocked their path. The garden remained silent, save for the wind as the castle floated through the moonlit sky.

The castle walls extended in a circle around the garden; doors and windows were scattered about looking out into the courtyard, out at the newcomers.

Boon moved out into the garden, running his hands over the trunk of a tall oak tree that grew in its centre.

"This is old," he said, looking up at the high branches. "It may be as old as this castle. Older."

Bijan didn't stop to ask him how he knew that, he believed him. While he was within the walls of the castle, he could believe just about anything.

It was the harsh pealing of a shrill bell that drew Bijan out of the doorway and into the garden with his companions. They all covered their ears in fright and surprise at the sudden change in volume of their surroundings. Bijan looked to Adun, hoping to find solace in the young man's confidence. He found none. They had come out of hiding.

Heavily armoured men descended upon them, swords and spears in their hands. Three men had piled onto Adun alone, forcing him to the ground under their large shields. Four more surrounded them. Bijan found three other soldiers closing in on him, their faces covered in strange, masked helms. They held their weapons to his back and neck and guided him to his knees.

Bijan tried to stretch his neck to see what had become of Boon but couldn't move without a sharp point digging into his flesh.

As the bell tolled, they had been captured.

CHAPTER TWENTY-THREE

"Please, princess," Calix hissed through his teeth. He had one hand clamped around her thin arm and dragged her through the castle, toward her room. "It's for your protection."

Leandra fought against his grip, pummeling his muscled shoulder with her fists, but his hand never faltered. "Tell me what's happening," she growled, restarting her assault. The alarm bells had only just stopped, but they still echoed in the halls and in her head.

"Princess," Alethea gasped and tried to put herself between Leandra's fists and Calix. When the alarm bells had fist gone off, Alethea had appeared out of nowhere. Her strong hands pulled Leandra away from the confusion and fear that was growing in the crowded great hall like an infection. Calix had been struck dumbfounded, but by the mere act of Alethea doing so stirred Calix into action.

With a shout and some indiscernible hand signals, Calix had the guards move into place to help escort the princess and any nobles from the room. As Leandra was pulled away, first by Alethea, and then by the iron-gripped Calix, she saw the militiamen strong arm and club their way to the main entrance to lead the nobles away. Commoners were met by cudgels and fists.

Calix pushed open her bedroom door and threw her into the room, his blue eyes cold and piercing. Despite herself, Leandra fell to the ground in a lump of knees and skirts. Heat rose on her cheeks and she fought against her dress to rise, her hands clenched into tight balls.

"Keep her here," Calix said to Alethea, loosening the collar of his shirt. "I'll send guards to keep watch until this is all sorted."

"Yes, my lord." Alethea bowed her head and closed the door as he ran back along the corridor.

"Where's he going?" Leandra snarled, gathering her skirts around her legs to stand. "Just wait until my father hears of this."

Leandra made for the door, her teeth clenched, and her chin jutting out before her, leading the way. Calix suddenly appeared to her as the thin and arrogant boy that she'd been annoyed by all those years before, the boy that would run off the instant he was faced with any kind of opposition.

Alethea stood in her path.

"Out of the way, 'Lethe." Leandra made to move past her handmaiden, but the elder woman moved with her.

"I'm sorry, princess, I cannot," Alethea said, her watery eyes turned to the floor.

Leandra stared her old handmaiden down, anger brimming over in her mind so that words struggled to escape her clenched jaw.

"You heard Master Calix, this is for your safety, princess." Alethea chanced a quick glance at Leandra. "We don't know what's happening yet, do we? I've never heard them bells in a long, long time."

"Alethea, you can't be serious… I'm the princess!" Leandra's hands turned into claws and the urge to grip her handmaiden and shake some sense into the old woman almost overtook her.

Instead, Leandra staggered backwards and fell onto her bed. She hugged herself in a tight embrace and her eyes felt heavy and tired.

"Princess, you know that I only do what is best for you. This is the best. Master Calix will see that you are safe..."

Alethea's desperate ramblings slid into the background of Leandra's own thoughts. A prisoner. That's what Leandra had become. A prisoner in her own gilded cage, in spite of her own intentions. A slave, cared for, pampered, but a slave all the same. A slave to the expectations of Appolumi and its noble caste. A society that was so bent on its own history and traditions that it turned inward.

"You understand I want what's best for you, don't you, princess?" Alethea's voice broke through Leandra's thoughts. The sound of shuffling feet outside the door surely meant Calix's guards had arrived.

"Of course, 'Lethe. Of course, I understand." Leandra sighed, and watched a shadow lift from her old handmaiden's face. A smile now hesitant at the corners of her mouth.

"You know, Alethea, this all reminds me of a story Obelius told me once. It was a fable about a snake."

"Really, princess, I'm not sure..."

"As the tale went, the snake, who was a champion hunter and a skilled killer, had become so proficient that it needed to put forward little effort to get its meals. It seemed, to those around the snake, that all it needed was to wake from its slumber and its prey would just stumble into the snake's gullet. That made the other animals fear and hate the snake, and it made the snake arrogant." Leandra gave the door a knowing glance.

"In the snake's arrogance, it took for granted that its prey would always be available to it. That it would always be within reach. It didn't think that its prey had its own thoughts on the subject. That the prey, those animals that feared and hated it so, would decide to move further and further away from it. So, in its arrogance, the snake left itself open to starvation.

"The snake's skills had declined over those long years using little effort to find food, and it had grown fat with the inactivity. When its prey left, the snake struggled to move on and find new hunting grounds. It became hungry. So hungry that its stomach rumbled and ached, and the snake felt a terrible, continuous pain." A knock came on the door and a guard stuck in one helmeted head. He was a young man with a few days' stubble on his cheeks. Leandra didn't recognize him, and she waved him away before he could introduce himself.

"Perhaps I should go see what he —"

"One day, as the snake slithered slowly and painfully through the tall grass, it sensed something. Something familiar. Something that rekindled its dulled hunting instincts. A slight movement at its rear. The movement of prey in awe and terror of the great hunting snake. A satisfied smile came over its face then and it bared its fangs.

"'Caution,' it said to itself. 'Slowly now. Don't spook it away.'

"And the snake did move slowly, making a wide curve of its body so that it would come up behind the nervous prey. It moved so slow and so methodical it thought it might go insane. It feared that the rumbling in its stomach may alert the prey, that the dripping of its saliva and venom from bared fangs may give away its presence.

"'Slow," it said, 'slow.'

"Then it saw it. Small and brown and wiggling in the grass. No doubt frozen in place by the fear of the snake's presence. Snap," Leandra said and clapped her hands together. Alethea jumped in her seat. "The snake's old hunting instincts kicked in. No longer cautious, no longer slow or methodical, the snake had struck. It struck as quick as lightning and it was just as devastating. But something was wrong. Pain shot up its length. The prey must be fighting back, the snake thought, but it knew it wasn't. Not really. Still, it chomped down harder, just to be sure the prey was dead.

"More pain.

"In its hunger and exhaustion, the snake had bitten its own tail. The snake realized it soon enough, but its hunger remained, and it was its hunger that wouldn't allow it to let go. The snake stayed that way, forever feasting on itself. Never letting go, never sating its own hunger, but always chomping, always swallowing, getting nowhere."

"Well, princess, that was certainly a story. And Obelius told you that? That man should be ashamed of himself. Really, telling a young girl those sorts of things," Alethea said, her eyebrows furrowed in concern and worry, the same as she had shown for Leandra most of her life.

"Please leave me now, Alethea. I am suddenly very tired," Leandra said and lay on her bed, turning away from the older woman.

"Very well, dear. I'll check on you in a little while. Perhaps I'll bring some tea."

"Yes, that'd be fine," Leandra said, and clutched her pillow until the door closed and Alethea had exited the room.

Leandra closed her eyes. Her breath was still coming

in ragged breaths, a rage at Calix and Obelius, Alethea and her father. She forced herself to take a deep breath, to think of anything other than the loss of freedom. Edric came to her mind, as he was as a boy when they ran through the halls. She thought of him as he was when their lives were easier, when they didn't have to think about marriage or the Trials or leaving the castle. When the castle was their freedom.

***

Leandra woke to a dark room, a cool cup of tea resting on the table next to her bed. She stretched and rubbed at her eyes. It was still night beyond her window, but that told her very little.

Getting up from the bed, Leandra crept toward her door to listen to any of the noises coming from the other side. Footsteps, nervous coughs, hushed conversations, but nothing that would give her an indication of what was happening in the rest of the castle.

Appolumi wasn't her home anymore, and if the freedom she needed to escape wouldn't be given to her freely, she'd take it. She pushed her bed across the door, hoping that it would delay her detection some, and she changed into her trousers and tunic. She packed her bag quickly with some clothes, slung it over her back, and crawled out her window.

Leandra took one last look at the room she'd grown up in. A pang of nostalgia flitted through her stomach, but it did little to deter her. The castle, that room, was no longer where she belonged. As she made the familiar crawl along the castle walls, she made up her mind. She'd make an effort to see her father one last time. Then it was on to Edric and their escape.

PART FOUR
CHAPTER TWENTY-FOUR

"Now, this is something." Edric leaned in closer to the Proteus Stone, his fingers working to clear any dust or debris that may be left in the crevices of the etchings. It was a symbol, a character in a sequence with those that surrounded it, but this one was different. It was familiar.

It had been more than an hour since Hesperos had left, much to Edric's surprise. He had expected his master's sickly yellow eye to peer in from the doorway at any moment. Edric had played with the notion of sitting there and doing nothing. He thought of ignoring the Trials and Hesperos, just to see what would happen next, to see what more the old wizard could do to him. He wanted to test Hesperos' own theories. The more Edric thought about that course of action, the more he realized it was the ploy of a petulant child, and he had no desire to let Hesperos have the satisfaction of him living up to that name. Besides, his curiosity got the better of him.

"Where do I know you from?" He ran his palm over his chin and let his finger trace the symbol again and again. If only he had a point of reference, a beginning in which to work out the language.

"What would you have done?" Edric said to the swaying effigy of what was once Magus Claes. "I suppose you would have had some predisposed knowledge about this sort of thing. It was probably your native tongue, eh?" Edric leaned in closer to the stone, not sure what it would accomplish, but hoped it would help him remember the symbol he was preoccupied with.

"What would you have done if you didn't know it though?" Edric cast a quick glance at the Magus from behind the stone.

"Books," he said between lips that made a thin smile. He used the flat top of the stone to push himself up, but stopped as he approached the door. He could only imagine the outrage Hesperos would unfurl if he returned and did not find him there.

Perhaps he would be pleased. After all, Edric thought, he was only leaving to pick up research materials, starting with the books Hesperos had given him. With those he could complete the Trial even faster. At the same time, he found it hard to believe Hesperos would find anything he did at the moment pleasing. His shoulders slumped as he stood before the door; uncertain.

He looked back on the room, on Magus Claes and Magus Vitalis, and the surging blue light in the crystals extending from their hands. Their pale skin was so thin that Edric could see blue veins, which, as he stared closer, seemed to be pulsating with the crystal's blue light. A shiver crawled up his spine and settled his dilemma. He left the room and headed towards his own quarters.

The castle was quiet. He wasn't sure how much time had passed since he had been sequestered in the crystal room with The Circle, but night had come on. It made him feel weary. Tired. He hadn't slept well since the Trials had started, and it was starting to catch up with him. He rubbed his eyes and stifled a yawn. He just needed to get his books.

He climbed the ladder to his room on watery legs. The muscles pained him some now, and he went to work rubbing his thighs after falling onto his bed. The books were there somewhere, the books Hesperos had told him to study. Surely that's where he recognized the symbol from. He tried to work it through his mind once more, trying to remember which volume he had recognized it from, but had no luck. He would have to take some of his own books, journals, scrolls, with him as well. If he could find them. A yawn rose in his chest, his eyes felt heavy. He closed them for a moment to think about the books he wanted to bring back to The Circle with him.

His dreams were muddled and hard to follow. He moved between rooms, perhaps worlds, but could never focus on anything long enough to discern exactly where he was. He ran after something, or away from something, his lungs burning in his chest, his breathing ragged. The symbol lay before him, giant and made of flame. He tried to reach out to it, to grasp it, but when he got close it would burn his fingers, his hands. It tried to take them for its own. Finally, with a rush of will he grabbed it. The feeling was intense in both pain and satisfaction. It became so much that he heard a horrible ringing in his ears. A trilling, metallic sound that shook him with each reverberation.

Edric fell from his bed, his hands clutching the stone floor as if he might fall again. The alarm bells, had they really sounded again? He turned his ear toward the rest of the castle. Silence.

A sigh fell from his chest, and he began to gather the books he needed. Something nagged at him, tugged at his mind and thoughts. Edric shook his head. Wasn't he supposed to do something? The Trials, of course. Decipher the Proteus Stone. No, that wasn't it. There was something else.

The dungeon. His eyes went wide with the thought. The alarm bells, the prisoner, a means to escape. Leandra.

He dropped the books and descended into Appolumi proper. The castle was still relatively quiet, though men he knew to be lesser nobles passed by in their militia armour. The militia had been retained in the castle on a purely traditional level for many, many years. Edric always thought of it, and Hesperos alluded to it as such, as a distraction for the young bucks, unsettled and bored in the castle. Had they been on the ground they could have made their own way, could have explored past the confines of the castle. Appolumi could not accommodate that. Instead they were allowed to play at war games, take part in exhibitions and duels. In some ways the knowledge of war was older than all the learning gathered in all of Hesperos' books, and yet it had become much less dangerous by the passage of time without true practice. And still, it was alarming to see the impulsive noblemen wielding armour and weapons. A guard had been established, patrols. What had happened in the castle?

***

Edric stood still as the guards moved on, his heart returning to its normal rhythm with their departure. When they were out of sight, and their conversation unheard, he continued on his path. As Edric got closer he could see the orange fingers of torchlight splay themselves across the stone floor and walls, and it cheered him.

It had been easier than he had expected, delving further into the dungeons. The old fears of his youth crept up on him as he descended — the fear of a sudden breath on his neck, a drip of blood-soaked saliva on his shoulder — but he forced himself on, his shield spell made ready. Aside from some of the noble militia, he found that his fears were unwarranted. Still, he remained on guard, his nerves feeling as though they were standing on end; frayed.

The torchlight Edric followed led him to a heavy oaken door, its edges framed by a black metal that was bolted in place. In the middle of the door was a small window adorned with bars of the same black metal. The torch stood just to the side of the door, which stood ajar just a crack. The opening was too small for Edric to get a sense of the layout of the next room. With a sigh, he removed the torch and extinguished it on the stone floor. With a nod to himself, Edric then pushed the door open slowly.

As the room widened in front of him, he could tell it was merely a waiting area, perhaps a guard station. There were chairs scattered about, a table off to one side, and some spare pieces of uniform and armour laid about.

At least one guard occupied the room, judging by the low humming Edric could hear. Crouched by the wall, Edric couldn't see the source of the thrum, but knew that it was close enough that he would risk discovery by moving the door any further. He crept closer to the door and peered into the remainder of the room. An older man stood on the far side of the room; his heavy white moustache hung over his lips as he hummed a tune that was unfamiliar to Edric. As Edric watched, the guard placed one foot on a low bench before him and began to tie the long brown boot, his humming continued.

Renewing his grip on the torch handle, Edric crept

into the room from the older man's blindside. He was low to the ground in a scuttling crouch that made his legs burn as he triggered unused muscles. Still, he went about as quietly as he could manage. Now that he was inside the room, Edric could finally appreciate how small it actually was. Cluttered with tables and chairs, there was hardly room for the burly guardsmen that were meant to people the space, not including any criminals that may need to pass through. Edric saw what he was looking for on the far side of the old man tying his boot: an open door that led to another hallway. Edric could see the iron bars of a holding cell just beyond the door, but as he was about to make his move the guard grunted, adjusted his boot, and switched feet on the low bench. Edric froze in place, his heart pounding and head throbbing.

Without thinking, Edric stood, raised the torch above his head with both hands, and ran at the guard. The old man moved quickly for his age, and though surprised by the sudden attack, was able to turn into Edric and catch his arms as they plunged toward him.

"What the hell…" the guard said through a grunt of surprise and effort. Edric was thinking the same, but there was no turning back now. The two men wrestled with the torch, but it became obvious that, though Edric was the younger of the two, he was certainly not the stronger. The guard bit down and clenched his teeth, his moustache bristled, and he started to move Edric's arms to the side.

Panic set in. Edric tried to regain an advantage over the guard, but he'd lost that when the surprise had faded. With no other option, he let the torch clatter to the floor. The guard's eyes widened for a moment and he pushed Edric away from him to reach for the makeshift cudgel. Conscious thought left Edric's mind and he pushed his left hand forward. He could feel the force of will that surged first through his arm and then out towards the guard. A low thud could be heard as the older man flew through the air and slammed into the wall behind him. He slid to the floor unconscious.

Edric stared at his open palm, the power still surging in his veins and muscles. He had never used his magic on a person before. He had never even thought it an option. Even in his practice sessions with Hesperos, the old wizard had defences in place to dissipate the power of the spell. The guard had taken it at full power and the effect was evident — his pain was evident. Edric could sense it all through his open hand, where a tingling of pins and needles on the border of numbness crawled. He clenched his fist to subdue the feeling and stood. He hadn't the time to process what had just happened; he moved toward the open door in search of the prisoner that might lead to his own escape.

CHAPTER TWENTY-FIVE

"You know," Bijan said through swollen lips, a dribble of blood and spit crawling from the side of his mouth. "You know, you are supposed to be extinct." His laugh was mirthless, forced, but it allowed him to slump his head to his chest.

"Is that right?" The man that paced before him wouldn't look him in the eye, instead he pushed his shining blond hair back from his face and looked at the walls around them. "And why would you think that?" His voice was deep, clear, and smooth, and yet it was strange. It had an edge of formality to it; his accent was old and was rarely used anymore.

"Yeah, that's right. This was supposed to be an empty castle." Another laugh. Bijan looked for Adun, who was somewhere to his left. "You're all ghosts."

The pacing man gave a little flick of his wrist and a stocky young man with a short-cropped beard stepped forward. Bijan braced himself for the blow, but couldn't stop himself from falling to his side, more blood leaking from his nose. There was a blackness at the edge of his vision, and he had to force his eyes to re-open, but he was still conscious. He laughed again. "Angry ghosts."

"Get him up," the blond said, and a pair of large,

rough hands grabbed the front of his shirt and dragged him to his knees again. "Now, tell me how you did it. Tell me how you found the castle."

Bijan gave the man an unsteady gaze, could feel blood or sweat run down the side of his head, and spit a thick wad of blood and phlegm. A look of disgust came over the blond's face and he covered his mouth with a gloved hand.

"I... *we* tracked you from your former home below." Bijan nodded toward the floor. "After that, all we needed was to find one of your blasted crystals."

"How, how did you do it?" A new voice broke in, accompanied by some hushed conversation of the guards that surrounded him. The voice was old, there was a rasp to it that only the elderly were able to attain, but there was also a harshness to it. Even in its burst of excitement it was cold.

Bijan shrugged. "It was easy enough. The bastards of Haugr didn't want us to find it, but it wasn't hard if you knew where to look..."

"No, no. Not that," the voice came again. The blond looked to Bijan's left, stretching his neck to see over the others that were gathered. Bijan tried to follow his gaze but saw nothing but bodies. "How did you activate it? How did you call the castle?" The voice's impatience was palpable; there was a scuffling of feet all around him, and some whispered cursing.

"I... well, I don't know." Bijan looked around him. "Boon, he'd know."

"Where's the other one?" The blond pointed to someone else in the room. "Fetch him for me."

"Calix, are we done with this one?" The gravelly voice of the stocky man that had been disfiguring Bijan's face said. The blond, Calix, merely waved his hand and walked toward the other questioner. A delighted grunt came from the stocky young man as he moved in on Bijan once more. His thick, rough hands wrapped tight in Bijan's shirt and pulled him off the ground. A flash of light glimmered off Calix's hair as he exited the room, and it was the last Bijan would remember of his first encounter with the men of Appolumi.

***

He woke up behind the black, iron bars of a small cell. The stone floors were bare of anything but his blood and sweat, and what little light there was cast everything in silhouette. Sitting up was a chore. His body was covered in bruises, but it was his face that hurt the most. His head ached, and he couldn't close his mouth around his swollen lips. The taste of iron stung his mouth. Bijan groaned and gripped the cold bars to help him to his knees. He leaned his head against them, letting the cold soothe his sore face.

A shuffle behind him turned him in place, the instant reaction jarred his sore bones and drew wracks of pain from his misused flesh. In the dim light Bijan could just make out a shadowy mass, its slight movements seemed unnatural and foreign. Bijan moved with caution, his aching body keeping him slow. He scanned the dark floor for anything that he could use as a weapon but found little besides pebbles.

Adun lay on the floor, his head and neck at an awkward angle, in the corner of the cell. His young face was barely recognizable under bruises and swelling, his eyes worse of all as they were completely swollen shut. His shemagh was nowhere to be found, and his long black hair lay in blood-encrusted knots about his head. Bijan laid one hand on the young man's chest and could feel the shallow, uneven breaths rise and fall. From time to time the boy twitched, his arms and legs shaking in weak spasms. In the low light, Bijan could see a black liquid run from Adun's ears.

"What happened?" Boon's voice was a whisper. He stood at the bars of the cell, his wild hair and beard out-lined in the light of the single torch, his face in shadow save for a slight glistening of his eyes.

Bijan wanted to be angry. He wanted to be outraged, to rage against the bars of his cell and curse down the large man that had deserted him to capture and torture. He wanted to do all of that, but his body wouldn't let him. He was too tired, too worn down.

"Where the hell were you?" It was all he could manage.

"I hid in the tree," Boon said and shrugged. "Is that the boy?"

Bijan nodded. "I think he's dying." He looked on the broken form of Adun, the small spasms even weaker now. "Bastards."

Boon grunted.

"He was a good man, he deserved better than this."

Boon shrugged again. "He was a mercenary, a thief, and likely a spy. This was the life he had chosen."

Rage surged through Bijan's aching veins; he clenched his fist and moved toward the door.

"You cold-hearted bastard. He was a good man, a friend." Bijan's anger spewed forth, he could feel it radiating from him. Boon took a step back.

"I'm sorry. He seemed better than most of the raiders, but it was who he was. Iollan and his master are nothing if not careful, tedious, and unscrupulous. The boy there was just a pawn to them. A way to keep an eye on you," he turned his head to look over his shoulder, "and me."

Bijan tried to find Boon's eyes in the gloom, but the shadows were too thick around his face. He seemed completely delusional, but only a few days ago Bijan had thought the flying castle of Appolumi was myth and legend. Stranger things had happened.

"Get me out of here," he said, drawing Boon's attention back to him.

"I can't."

"What do you mean, you 'can't?'"

Boon's silhouette waved its arms around. "What can I do? I don't have the key, and I can't very well tear solid iron doors off their hinges."

"Listen, I know there is something different about you. Now you use that to get me out of here. Turn into a bear, get angry at grass, whatever it takes."

"It doesn't work that way," Boon said as he made to leave.

Bijan grabbed the man's huge wrist through the bars. "What are you doing? You can't leave me." He could feel the panic in his strained voice, the fear.

"I'll do what I can." Boon freed himself of Bijan's grip and disappeared into the shadows without a sound.

Bijan slid down the cool bars to sit facing Adun. The boy was no longer moving.

***

Bijan was in and out of consciousness for the next few hours until guards came to take Adun's body away. There were three of them, one to place the pointed end of a sword at Bijan's throat and two others to drag the body out by the ankles. Bijan seethed. He screamed and cursed on them until he felt the sharp end of the sword pierce his flesh, and he forced himself to be quiet. He watched them manhandle the boy as though he were an animal. He watched them toss him around as though he were a piece of garbage fit to be thrown away. He watched them and he etched their faces on his mind.

Bijan had little belief in his upbringing in the Southern deserts with wayward travellers. His mother had taken him and escaped his father's reach with that wandering band of misfits, and, for that, he would always be grateful to them. Bijan's interests led him away from their religions, however, and he didn't see much benefit in learning about their particular type of mysticism. In one belief did both Bijan and the travellers share: vengeance. His mother's people believed that if you did them wrong, revenge would be the only recourse. Swift and brutal, slow and painful, it didn't matter. For Adun, Bijan would see vengeance done.

The guards were gone in a few minutes, dragging Adun with them. His handler stayed behind just a moment longer to share a mocking sneer with him before leaving the cage and locking it behind him. He was again left alone, truly alone now. There was no Adun, and there was no Boon.

It wasn't the first time that Bijan had found himself in a prison cell. Most times he got himself arrested on purpose and in order to complete a plan, a job. Often it was a very complicated affair with bribed guards, bribed prisoners, hidden tools and weapons. He had an escape route, some assurances, but there was always a chance that he would end up dead or in a situation very much like the one he found himself in on the castle of Appolumi. There was a chance, but it never happened. He was too good at what he did. Or so he thought, until now.

'Of all the times to screw up, you managed to do it on a magical floating castle,' he thought.

"Actually, that's not bad. Not bad at all." He chuckled to himself, rubbed at his throat, and explored the small confines of his cell. It was old, but sturdy enough. The bars showed no sign of wear, no sign of rust or ill-use. It was just like the remainder of the castle: frozen in time, as if the castle had taken to the sky just the day before. He sat in the middle of the cell, his eyes on the door, his mind running over the details of his tormentors' faces.

The sound of scuffling feet and hushed words brought Bijan around. He pulled himself into a crouched position, his eyes on the door. There were sounds of a fight: the clatter of something to the floor, quick breaths, cursing. Bijan readied himself, waiting with his fists clenched. A loud crash made him jump, followed by a low groan and a sudden silence. Bijan backed himself into the cell, letting the shadows engulf him. Whatever was about to come, he'd be ready. He was going to escape.

CHAPTER TWENTY-SIX

Leandra stole across the outer wall. Her fingers found the old handholds with ease, they felt warm and smooth to the touch, and a broad smile broke across her face. The moon lit her way, high and bright, its pale rays dispelled many of the shadows that would have complicated her path.

Her path was complicated though, she thought. Since the bells had tolled, the militia had been out in force. Leandra had peeked through windows and saw the nervous-eyed glares of the young nobles who traded their silken tunics for leather armour, and their cups of wine for swords and knives. At some other time, Leandra may have found their reactions humorous, but there was something off about the whole situation. There was tension in the air, a feeling of dread that hung precariously over the entire castle. Leandra could feel it with each breath and see it in the faces of the militiamen fumbling over their weapons.

She paused; a vague sense of movement came from the courtyard below, as if a shimmer in the corner of her eye. Nothing seemed to move in the lush garden, save the elder tree as it swayed with the breeze. Leandra pressed close to the cool brick and listened; nothing. She sighed a breath of relief and let herself relax once more. The thought of being caught now, being dragged back to her room and locked away once more, frightened her. And what's more, it made her angry. It would take a lot more than Calix's firm grip to restrain her now.

Still, she thought, ducking in through a window, better safe than sorry. Leandra had been accustomed to traversing the wall only from her window to Edric's during their childhood; rarely would she even gaze into the other windows that stood in her way, for fear of discovery. And yet, she now found herself in a small room, dark save for the light that followed her in through the window. Leandra crouched low and stayed close to the wall.

The room was empty, save for a small sitting table and some chairs. Books were scattered about, and sheets of paper lined the table. It was a solar, though Leandra couldn't tell whose, nor did she care. Perhaps one of the noble houses employed it, allowing their members to take some solitude from the hustle and bustle of the castle. She wondered, as she approached the door, if her forefathers had thought of that before taking the castle to the skies. Had they thought of the constant closeness of the people of Appolumi, commoners and otherwise? As big as the castle was, it was nearly impossible for paths to not cross and cross again. Solitude was an answer, but Leandra had more than her fair share of that and it still didn't satisfy her need to get away; her need to escape.

"He's dead?" A familiar voice sounded from the other side of the door. Calix's voice froze Leandra in place, her eye looking through the small crack in the door she had just pulled ajar. "And the other one?"

"The lippy one?" A second, duller voice that Leandra didn't recognize thudded through the door. "He's a little pissed off, but he'll live." A low chuckle came from the second man and vibrated through the walls like a clap of thunder.

"Good. We may need him," Calix said. The subtle sounds of his footsteps whispered in the hallway. Leandra saw his legs pass by the door a moment later, followed closely by the plodding and thick legs of whomever he'd been speaking with.

What the hell was Calix speaking about? Who was dead, and what would they have needed him for? Leandra fought the urge to reveal herself and demand Calix tell her exactly what he meant. It was a foolish impulse that would get her no closer to her goal. She swallowed it back down and, when she was sure no one was close by, she scuttled into the corridor, hoping to pick her way toward her father's chambers.

***

Leandra bounded into an empty corridor just as guards turned a corner. The shadows welcomed her; the hall's sconces stood empty of their torches. Still, Leandra pulled herself close to the cool wall and prepared for the worst. The castle had become treacherous; the militia were on patrol, scouring every corner of Appolumi. They'd even enlisted some of the common folk to aid them. She'd seen a servant by the name of Gregory plodding around in the leather armour of the militia, looking uncomfortable as it barely fit his broad shoulders and chest. She'd met him before, as children, through Edric — the only time that she had been able to evade Obelius and Alethea long enough to make it to the Quarter. He'd always been large, even as a child, but he had grown into a burly man with thick fists. His face was soft though, his mouth surrounded by lines that came from laughter, and eyes that belayed kindness. He had no weapons with him, save a small hammer that he may have borrowed from a blacksmith, that bounced in one large fist. Even in an emergency, the nobles would not offer up weapons to those they deemed beneath them.

Guards ran past her, holding fast to their dangling weapons and helmets, their breath coming heavy as fresh curses streamed from their mouths. They hadn't seen her, but Leandra waited until she heard the distant echo of their footsteps before she allowed herself a quiet sigh of relief. She forced herself to wait another five minutes, listening to the echoing silence of the castle, before she started her trek once more. It was slow going. More than anything, Leandra wished for the days when she was small and lithe on her feet, invisible in even the most outlandish situations. Now, grown to womanhood, she couldn't even take to the solace of crawling across the outer walls for fear that someone may catch a glimpse of her. She cursed. If she had been able to continue outside, her journey would have been little more than half an hour. As it was, she was forced to walk slow, precise steps through the inner workings of Appolumi, trying not to draw attention to herself. It was safer, but much more tedious.

Stooped low, Leandra kept a keen eye on her surroundings in hopes that she wouldn't be surprised by a suddenly opened door, or militiamen barging through the corridors. She'd been lucky — so far.

"What's this?" she whispered and ran a gloved hand over the surface of stone to her right. A small symbol had been carved there, about hip height if she were to stand at her full stature. A crescent moon and a five-pointed star. Leandra allowed herself a smile. It was one of the sigils she and Edric had created together and used to mark safe passageways for their adventures and games. They'd thought they were quite mature creating the etchings. Thought that they were very responsible, even grown-up. After all, plans to keep you safe were good plans indeed. Unfortunately, Obelius, Hesperos, and her father gained no such joy in those activities. They'd taken one too many trips to places like the Quarter, the dungeons, and to Edric's chambers. With a lofty shake of his jowls, the king forbade her to continue these play dates with Edric, and certainly no more running about, making a mess of everything. Still, those sigils remained after all those years, guiding Leandra to safety.

"Calix wants us in the courtyard," a rusty voice said, accompanied by the familiar sound of boots slapping on stone.

They came up so quickly that they had almost overtaken Leandra as she admired the small etching. Without much thought, she swung herself out a window. Her fingers gripped the jagged stone that framed the open window, and her feet dangled in the open air. Leandra cursed as her boot tips scraped the brick for purchase.

"Why the courtyard?" A younger voice cracked, the shuffling sound of armour being shifted.

"Bandits," the first voice said, his breath wheezing.

"There are more?"

Their voices trailed off and Leandra pulled herself back into the hallway, her hands cramped and her knees scraped from flailing against the stone.

'Interlopers,' she thought, 'on the castle?' So, that was why the alarm had sounded; why Calix had run off to join the militia. Could it really be that the stories were all true? Was there an ancient enemy eager for revenge? How did they find the castle and, for that matter, how did they reach it?

Leandra's eyes widened, and she ran towards the throne room. If the enemy had ascended into the sky, had reached the castle, then they must have a way off again. She raced to her father, heedless of the noise and attention. Her mind was focused on Edric; focused on escape.

CHAPTER TWENTY-SEVEN

The guard was alive; there was no blood, or sign of any broken bones. Edric sighed; it was a small relief. The large man was breathing deeply and regularly, with no obvious ill effect of the magical attack. Yet. Edric wasn't sure if anything else would come of it; he'd only ever witnessed the aftereffects on himself or Hesperos, but magic was natural to them. There was nothing he could do for him now. Edric ensured that the guard was comfortable before he patted him down, looking for keys to the cells beyond. It took Edric only a moment to remove the key from its place, attached to the guard's belt. Key in hand, he stepped over the unconscious man, and moved into the dark hall beyond the doorway.

Shadows crawled along the ground of the long hallway. They were interrupted by the thin fingers of light cast by the torch in the guard's room. Edric walked into the gloom, his own shadow melting into the others, stamping out most of the light. He paused just next to the door and let his eyes adjust in the darkness. The hall was lined with cages, iron bars so densely layered that he couldn't see the individual cages against the slate grey stone walls and floor. He strained his eyes to see any sign of a prisoner, but nothing moved. There seemed to be no sign of life at all, anywhere. Edric cursed to himself and started to move further into the shadows.

As Edric moved down the hallway he noticed a small line of blood in one of the rays of torch light. Someone had been dragged through this hallway just a short time ago, bloody and hurt, possibly dead. A cold glacier of despair settled in his chest, the bastards had killed him already, he thought, there would be no escape from the castle, no escape from the Trials, and no escape from his fate. Edric stopped at each cage to stare into the blackness and try to discern any sort of life. He still had a vague hope that the intruder wasn't dead, and pushed on, despite the persistence of that cold, sinking feeling in his chest.

A hand shot out and grabbed his wrist as he passed the fifth cell. He jumped with fright and immediately tried to pull away, to escape. His attacker's hand was hard and strong, but lithe and agile. The grip on his wrist was like iron and it pulled him into the cold bars inches at a time.

"Let me out of here," the voice hissed, squeezing Edric's wrist tighter. The voice was strange, its smoky pitch coloured by a strange accent that further put Edric off balance. He had read of other cultures in Hesperos' library, but they were so far removed from Appolumi that he relegated them to the annals of myth and legend in his mind. Now a representative of that legend stood before him.

Edric held up his free hand and jingled the keys. "Are you from below?" His eyes tried to pierce the shadowy veil that hid the man's face.

"Below? Yes. I suppose I am. Now, free me or I'll snap your wrist." The man squeezed tighter still.

"I'll let you go," said Edric as he tried to pull his wrist free, "on one condition."

"And what's that?" the inmate said, tightening his grip once more.

"When you leave here, when you escape, take me with you."

The man stopped squeezing Edric's wrist but kept it held firmly. He moved in closer to the bars, bringing his face into the light for the first time. The dark-skinned face was swollen and bruised, with one eye much worse than the other. Blood and dust and dirt clung to the face, especially around his nose and in his short-cropped beard. His brown eyes sought Edric's gaze and he held it for a moment.

"You want to leave this place…" he said, trailing off as he broke their shared gaze.

Edric watched the man's ruminations as clearly as if he were jotting them down on paper before him. He could see the calculations that were being drawn, weighing the options that were now placed before him. His face was grim but concentrated.

"Very well," he said at last, and released Edric's arm. "My name is Bijan, and I am a dealer in rare antiquities."

***

They made their way through the catacombs that was the dungeon of Appolumi at a snail's pace. It was more out of necessity than anything else. Bijan limped along as fast as he could, but Edric could tell that the pain from his injuries were taking their toll.

"It's for the best," Edric said in a whisper as he waited for the stranger to catch up to him. "Guards will be patrolling. We're better off not drawing attention to ourselves."

Bijan nodded along to the boy's words, despite the anger that they drew out in him. He was never one for charity, nor was he accustomed to being at such a disadvantage. In all of his years, when his wits had failed him, his reflexes had come to the rescue. Now both were muddled.

Edric led them to the long dark hallway that would take them to an escape from the dungeons. Peering around the edge, he could see two guards making their way towards them, their torch casting an orange spotlight to draw his attention. The closer they came, the more convinced he was that they were the two guards he nearly encountered earlier. Nobles.

"Two guards," he said over his shoulder. He looked around, but there was nothing that would provide a good hiding spot. "Over here," Edric pointed to the other hallway and they both scurried across. Edric peered back into the darkened hallway, but it appeared that the guards had taken no notice of them.

"What if they come this way?" Bijan whispered as he tried to peek past Edric's shoulder.

"I saw them come down here earlier."

"So?"

"They won't come here again."

"That's what patrols do!" Bijan stood and leaned against the wall. "Do you have a weapon, at least?"

Edric patted his robes and frowned. His mind wandered to the burned-out torch he had dropped in the guard's room.

Bijan sighed.

"What's down this hallway?"

"I... I don't know." Edric could see the light of the guard's torch getting closer.

"Okay, we have two options," Bijan stroked his beard. "We could face two armed militiamen and take our chances that luck is on our side, or we go down this hallway. We will still be taking our chances with luck, but I'd rather those odds than my odds against sharpened steel."

Bijan raised an eyebrow at the crouching Edric, who cast a furtive glance around the corner once more. The dungeons frightened him; nightmares of being lost in the labyrinthine hallways had haunted his childhood, a fear that still shook him to his core. Now that he stood facing it, his mind started to wander, his heart sped up.

The stranger, Bijan, stood before him in a motley state. His breath wheezed from his chest and it whistled from his swollen nose. The man looked barely able to stand and still he pushed on, even without the cursory knowledge that Edric had of the castle.

It was the slap of leather boots approaching that decided it for Edric. He nodded to the ailing Bijan and they moved down the unknown hallway. It was brighter than its counterpart, torches were lit at even intervals along its length, and it seemed to be fairly well travelled judging by the wearing of the stone. Perhaps he had been wrong about the desertion of the dungeon.

There was no sign that they were being followed, and no sound of the alarm going off again to signal their escape. They were able to allow for a rest, giving Bijan the sorely needed time to catch his breath. He turned to Edric and said, between laboured breaths, "Why?"

"Why?" Edric's mind was racing with fear of discovery, capture, the Trials. He said this response in a whisper, before letting his thoughts reconnect around the word. "I need you to aid me in freedom…"

"Yes, yes. I know why you freed me," Bijan said, waving his hand dismissively, leaning his shoulder into the wall. "But why are you leaving?"

Edric's lips reduced to a thin line. "To escape death, perhaps fate."

"Fair enough. At whose hands?"

"My master's hands. Perhaps my own."

"And what did you do to earn this death sentence?" Bijan eyed the boy with keen interest.

Edric turned his full attention on Bijan, his wet, grey eyes gleaming in the torchlight.

"I lived, I learned. I have something the castle needs, and before today I barely dreamed to hope I would be able to put this plan to fruition."

Bijan grunted. "So, it's a woman?" He chuckled.

Edric could feel his cheeks flush.

"You Northerners of the castle Appolumi are as equally melodramatic as your land-bound cousins." Bijan's smile was wide and genuine.

It was Edric's turn to raise an eyebrow to his newfound companion. Bijan just waved it off with his lopsided smile.

"Come on then," Bijan said through a grimace. He rotated his shoulders and tried to stretch out his arms. "Luck has been good to us so far, but I'd rather not take it for granted." He waved them both on to continue.

Edric took the lead, more out of current physical ability than anything else. He knew nothing of this path out of the dungeons, which left him on the same level of experience with this place in the castle as the stranger. A pang of regret settled into his stomach. Had he been keener to explore the castle, had he set out on his own, or snuck out under Hesperos' gaze, he may have known more about the dungeons, about the castle. He may have been able to uncover the secrets and make his escape more attainable. Not for the first time, he cursed Hesperos' watchful eyes.

They breached the hallway into a small, dark room. It was akin to the guard's room they had left near the cells, but less cluttered, with signs of little use. On the far side of the room stood a thick oak door that they made for without hesitation. Just as Edric reached forward to grasp the handle, the door swung open and four men started to amble in. Their jovial conversation was cut short by the sight of the two fugitives, who stood frozen in their tracks.

They stood like that for mere moments, but Edric felt as though it lasted an hour. It was Bijan that ended the stalemate with a low, wet cough that broke through his blood-stained lips unhindered. As if roused from sleep, the guardsmen began to tear at the swords at their sides. Edric fell back some, but Bijan rushed forward. Heedless of the swords that were being drawn, Bijan jumped through the air and grabbed the arm of the man closest to him. Halting the man's effort to draw his sword, Bijan delivered a savage headbutt to the man's nose, sending a gush of blood to the floor. The man flailed backwards, his sword forgotten, and hindered the entrance of his fellow guards. Bijan rubbed his forehead and held up the sword he had just removed from his opponent's scabbard. A wild smirk crossed his face and he let loose a kick that sent the first guard and his retinue back through the door to fall in a tangle of limbs.

"Come on, Boy," Bijan said, his voice low and grave, before he leapt out of the room and over the men on the floor. Edric gaped for another moment before he followed, amazed at the agility of the badly wounded former prisoner.

They were off at a run, but the guardsmen were close on their heels, cursing them. Bijan moved like a jaguar, unhindered by his injuries for the moment, and a laugh escaped his lips. Edric struggled to keep up with the man, and yet he couldn't help but smile to himself. The thought of something like this happening in the castle was unheard of. That something so exciting, exhilarating, could be taking place in the very bowels of the sedentary castle he had grown up within was unbelievable. That thought split his face with a smile as he tried to catch up with the man that he had only recently rescued.

They were running through a wider hallway now that would allow three or four men to run abreast of each other. Edric was still unsure of where they were, but it seemed as though they were getting closer to a more populated area. As they moved through the castle, taking turns and adjustments solely decided by Bijan, it seemed that they were moving into a brighter area of the castle, the dungeons now firmly left behind them. The thought cheered Edric some.

"Halt," one of the guardsmen said from behind, drawing a small snicker from Bijan as he took a swift turn into the hallway on his right-hand side. But Edric could tell Bijan was slowing, the initial burst of excitement now fading away with the continued strain on his injuries. He was able to run alongside Bijan now, and he could see sweat dripping from the former prisoner's brow and a pained look crossing his face.

"Any hiding places around here?" Bijan panted.

Edric shook his head, his breath left him with a burning sensation in his lungs. He could not say.

They ran past another hallway, and Edric grabbed Bijan's arm to bring him to a stop. There was a small etching on one of the bricks leading down the separate hallway. A flower and a sun. It was something that Edric and Leandra had done when they had free reign of the castle. He looked down the hallway and he knew where they were.

"This way," he called to Bijan, and the two took up their run once more.

"I don't think I can run much further," Bijan said and stopped to lean on the wall, his body heaving for air, his face contorted with pain.

"It isn't much further," Edric said, but as he turned, he saw the four guards approach, their weapons drawn and their armour clattering as they halted a few feet from them.

Bijan turned and shrugged his shoulders. A sigh escaped him as he crouched and brought the sword up and to the ready. The four men poured in. Unhindered by a doorway, they fell into a circle around Bijan, who wasted no time. With a series of slashes, Bijan cut his way out of the circle, dancing away from the heavy blows of the guardsmen as he did. The guards were quick and efficient with their attack, but they looked amateurish compared to the injured man that slid out of the range of their sword swipes as easily as bird took to flight.

It continued as such for a few minutes more before Bijan had struck down one of the guards with a gash across his neck. The other three were undaunted by their fallen comrade and pushed in. Bijan's back was to the wall, hoping to avoid being encircled once more, but leaving him little space to dance away from their strikes.

Edric could see him tiring again; his endurance all but sapped. Stepping forward, Edric reached for the fallen man's sword, but then thought better of it. He pushed up the sleeves of his robes and began to make fleeting signs with his hands and arms. The air rippled about him; a small hint of power and force buzzed about him. Shifting his weight to his right foot, Edric pushed one hand forward. Immediately one of the guards took to the air and cried out in pain. Edric then began to close his other hand into a fist. The guard nearest him went stiff and toppled to the floor, a wild and panicked look upon his face.

Bijan had hardly noticed what had happened to the other guards, but was glad they had fallen to the wayside. He looked into the bloodied face of the man whose sword he had stolen, a hefty knife now flashing in his hand as he parried away blows from his own sword. They locked weapons and grabbed each other's arms, Bijan smiled as their faces came close. With no further hesitation, he stamped down onto his opponent's foot with his heel. The pain was all the distraction he needed to end the man's life, using both blades to tear through the man's neck. He took a moment to congratulate himself before he joined the dead man on the floor, letting the cool stones caress his aching body.

"We're close to a section of the castle I'm more familiar with. Do you know the way out of here?" Edric crouched next to Bijan, his hand on his shoulder.

"If you can get me to the courtyard, I can get us out of here," Bijan said, pushing himself to standing once more.

"The courtyard? Right." Edric paced the width of the hall. "Okay. I think I know the best way to go, and it will give me a chance to grab some of my things from the tower on the way out." He said this aloud, but Bijan knew it wasn't wholly addressed to him.

"Lead on," Bijan motioned with one open hand to the corridor before them. Edric nodded and they moved further into the castle.

***

"Hurry, this way." Edric ran through the halls of the

servant levels of the castle, Bijan following close on his heels. Those ambling through the corridors made clear of them but gave them strange looks as they passed.

"You sure you know the way?" Bijan said as he tried to keep up with the squirrelly young man. "This doesn't look like it would lead to a tower." Bijan eyed the damp walls in the low light suspiciously.

"I know a shortcut," Edric yelled over his shoulder, taking a quick turn into another hallway. He almost lost his footing as he made the corner, his shoulder striking the wall as he tried to steady himself without losing speed. It was a shortcut, that was true, but it hadn't been something he'd done since he was a child. He shuddered to think of the lost time they'd have to make up if the shortcut was no more.

Despite the pain of his injuries, Bijan kept up with the younger man with little trouble. They had been given a short rest and a slow walk through the inner workings of the castle, moving again before more guards stumbled upon them. The short rest was all Bijan needed. He often found himself much more agile than his castle guide, and at times he would have to slow himself to allow Edric to maintain the lead. Corners and turns were of no concern for him; neither were the small obstacles that Edric had somehow hit every one of as they flew through the castle. His mind began to wander once he began to catch up again, and he found himself wondering where Boon was. Had he been captured, or was he still roaming the castle, soaking in the history?

Edric seemed confident in where he was going, navigating the maze of the castle with an ease Bijan could not even begin to imagine. The younger man would take exits seemingly at random, navigate without stopping for contemplation, and kept his pace quick. Squirrelly or not, it was impressive.

"It's just up here," Edric said over his shoulder as they pushed through another doorway and into another small hallway. Bijan had given up on trying to keep track of where they were, and gave in to relying on the intuitions of a stranger.

"Just around th —," Edric said from just ahead, when he stopped short, his thin frame bouncing off nothing but the air, his body crumpling to the floor with a grunt. Bijan halted just before the boy's prone body and reached for his scimitar that wasn't there.

"I thought you'd be making for your room," a cackling voice said from the shadows. "I wasn't sure you'd come this way, but I was feeling lucky." A skeletal hand edged out of the shadows. Grey, corpse-like flesh clung to it around long, yellow fingernails. The hand moved in slow circles as it came forward, its owner coming into the light with it.

"Hesperos..." Edric groaned, rubbing his neck as he got to his knees.

The older man walked into the dim light; his skin pulled back in a grimace that was a mockery of a grin. The man continued to motion with his one outstretched arm, his other was hidden beneath his voluminous robes. Bijan at once became the focus of the man's strange eyes. Pouched in purple skin, they were colours at odds with one another. One a baleful blue fire, the other a sickly yellow.

"And with the escaped prisoner at that," Hesperos tutted, "I'm sure the king would love to hear of this special betrayal. Too bad you're already bound to The Circle. I'm sure there would be a fresh round of red delights in store for you."

"Who is this yaldson?" Bijan bent to help Edric to his feet and noticed that the young man's hand had somehow become one with the stone floor. Bijan jumped back, looking at Edric's bowed head, his blonde hair in his face.

The sound of stone on stone and a grumbling underfoot happened all at once. Bijan pulled his eyes away from Edric in time to see the stone floor before Hesperos form into a spike and fly upwards towards the ancient man. Sensing the danger, the older man pushed himself backwards, the spike of stone and dirt just catching him on the cheek. Both of his hands went to his face with a scream of pain.

"Run," Edric said, pulling his arm from the ground, "go to the end of the corridor. There should be a ladder there. My room is at the top. Grab my bag and whatever books you can find, I'll need them." He started towards the older man, testing the air before him but finding no resistance. He turned back to Bijan. "I'll be there as soon as I can."

Taking only a moment to assess the situation, Bijan ran off, keeping his distance from the ailing wizard as he left.

"I thought he'd never leave." Hesperos craned forward, leaping toward Edric, his hands moving in a blur. Lines of energy appeared before Edric and lashed themselves around his arms and legs, forcing him back to the ground.

"You are a foolish boy." Hesperos was standing over him, one hand tentatively dabbing at the large slash that had opened on his cheek and extended to over that one eye. "What did you hope to accomplish in all of this?"

"Freedom," Edric said, struggling against his bonds.

"It's freedom you want, is it? Freedom from the life

we've given you. The knowledge, the learning, the power that you've gained under the protection of this castle, under my tutelage." Hesperos put his foot on top of Edric's chest and leaned with his weight.

"What good is knowledge and power if you are just fuel? Just a catalyst, stuck in an endless nightmare." Edric heaved against his bindings, against Hesperos' foot.

"So, you want to be free of the castle and The Circle?" Hesperos turned his lizard eye on the boy, bending close enough so that Edric could see the reptilian slit that ran through it. "Well, that certainly does come with a price. If you leave the Trials unfinished, if you leave Appolumi, and you leave The Circle, you will pay with your magic, Boy. You'll just be another whiny, ungrateful man-child with no place, and no purpose. You'll be nothing."

"You're lying." Edric tried to see the truth in his master's eyes, but they were impenetrable.

"You'll never know." Hesperos gave him a cold smile. "Let's get you to The Circle and finish these Trials." With a waving of his hands, Edric began to float in Hesperos' wake; his screaming filled the corridor with his anguish.

CHAPTER TWENTY-EIGHT

He cursed himself for leaving the boy behind, but he had little choice. Gall burned at the back of his throat all the same. The boy knew his own business, and there were things to be done.

Bijan found the ladder just as the boy had said and scaled it as quickly as his injured limbs would allow him. He gave himself permission to slow a half-step now that Edric wasn't present; even so he didn't want to waste any time. The creepy old wizard would send someone for him eventually.

The trap door opened without issue and Bijan crawled into the small, round room. Bijan had been in castles before, and the turret was no place for a bedroom, though the view was amazing. He looked down on the castle grounds. The moon was cracking through the clouds, bathing Appolumi in its grace. Bijan could see the entirety of the flying kingdom, but his eyes fixed on one location: the courtyard. From Edric's room he could tell that it wasn't far. A plan formulated in his mind and he hurried to put it into motion. First, the boy's belongings.

The room was a mess. Books were piled in every corner, every free space. Where there weren't books there were clothes or scraps of paper. On a large table that was off to one side stood some glass bottles, liquids of different shades and colours were stoppered within. On another, smaller table were some strange-looking, metal crafted instruments that Bijan couldn't make heads nor tails of. On the floor next to the small cot was a satchel that Bijan grabbed up and slung about his chest. Judging by the heft of it, it was already full of books. He took two of the largest tomes he could find and piled them atop of the bag before manoeuvring his way out of the room and down the ladder.

The corridors were clear. Bijan skulked through the halls, heading in the general direction of the courtyard he had seen through the boy's window, but uncertain of which path would lead to it. With a shrug of the shoulders, he limped in what seemed to be the best direction. It was a slow go; the satchel jabbed into his ribs, causing a growing twinge and a dull pain that intensified as he walked. He cursed the boy and his books as they weighed down his sore muscles.

The thought of the old wizard and the boy worried him, though. He hadn't actually seen what had been happening when the old man confronted them, but there was a cold chill, a feeling of thickness that was heavy in the air. Magic, he opined. Of course, he thought, now he could just blame everything on magic. The sun went down and the moon came up: magic. Change in the seasons: magic. A man falls in love with a woman: magic. It was a silly thought that grew into a serious worry. Magic existed, now that was true, but what trouble did it bring with it?

It turned out to be a relatively short walk. Bijan shifted the satchel to his other shoulder and readjusted the books he was carrying as he came to a thick door that was so dark brown that it looked black. The colour, the stain, was so immaculate that he ran his free hand over it, his finger-tips dancing atop it, feeling its sturdy smoothness. Push-ing it open, he surveyed the garden of the courtyard, and a hope at escape.

***

He stole into the garden, silent in spite of his ach-ing bones. The sky was dark once again, the stars and moon unseen in the mist and fog that swirled through the gloomy courtyard. Bijan moved fox-like, timid yet bra-zen. He eased himself around bushes and trees, careful not to step on a wayward twig or loose branch. The dark-ness was waylaid some by torchlight from the windows of the castle and some standing torches that stood along the cobblestone walkway. It was these that Bijan used as his guide. Having now seen the bowels of the floating castle, Bijan began to wonder about the garden's growth. No roots could penetrate the stone below it; no cracked foundations or stones were at the mercy of the unrelent-ing growth of the vegetation before him. Magic, he cursed to himself, and moved closer to the flickering torch light.

"You might as well come out," a familiar voice said from behind him. "You're amongst friends."

Bijan stood with effort, clutching the satchel and books close to him as he faced Iollan. The leader of the raiders was leaning on a tree, his piercing blue eyes almost glow-ing in the gloom. He seemed to be by himself, but some-thing prickled the hairs at the nape of Bijan's neck, and he knew the raiders surrounded them.

"What are you doing here, Iollan?" Bijan swayed for a moment on shaking legs. "I thought you were minding the dig site, that you thought this was a fool's errand."

"Only because I sent fools," Iollan said, a smile in his

voice. "What's happened to you? Come closer, let me look at you." His eyes narrowed, "Where's Adun?"

Bijan's voice faltered, the images of young Adun's broken body dragged from the cell flashed before him. "Dead," he said, finally. "Killed by the bastards that live here."

Iollan nodded, pulled down his shemagh and stroked his chin. "It's a shame. He had promise."

"He was a good man," Bijan said, taking an unintentional step toward Iollan. "He was a friend, and he was just a boy." His voice cracked before he could contain it. He straightened himself and renewed his eye contact with his employer.

"Yes, he could have been a very useful member of our group." Iollan's eyes were distant. His tone low.

Bijan clenched his fist.

"You probably need some rest." He motioned with his hand and a tall, lithe raider detached himself from the shadows and stood next to Bijan. "Mufid will guide you back to the ground."

"I can't." Bijan dug his heels into the ground. "I'm waiting for someone."

"We'll find your friend. Bring him back with us."

"Why are you here, Iollan? Did you know people still lived in these halls, still guarded its secrets? Did you know what we were walking into?"

"Of course he did," Boon's deep voice said from above. Bijan and Iollan looked up, both men caught off guard by the intrusion. They saw the heavy form of the massive man fall from the tree and land on his feet with a thud.

"They want this all for themselves. The riches, the secrets, the notoriety, the magic. They want what they can take and then they'll crash it all into the ground." Boon hadn't finished speaking when a dozen or more raiders emerged, their short swords drawn and ready. Iollan's hand had also come to rest on the hilt of the scimitar he kept at his side, his pale blue eyes were baleful in the dim light.

Bijan wanted to cast the shaggy guide a venomous look as well, but at the moment, with raiders on all sides, he was grateful for his presence.

"We've all heard the rumours, but these ones," Boon jabbed a thumb at the raiders closing in on him, "these ones thought something was still alive here. They wanted it for their own, it's source of magic," Boon said as he began to roll up his sleeves.

The terrible peal of a bell quaked the air around them. Most of the raiders put their hands over their ears and shot glances into the shadowy corners of the courtyard. Bijan cringed at the sound of the bell, and he almost lost the books and satchel in his rush to cover his own ears, settling with covering just one. His eyes sprang around him, waiting for the guards to rush in as they had before. As the bell continued to shake the castle, doors flew open and men poured into the garden.

***

Despite the shock caused by the sudden ringing bell, Iollan and his raiders met the incoming soldiers of Appolumi without hesitation. Boon and Bijan lined up with the raiders just as quickly, an unspoken truce of convenience fallen amongst them. The garden brightened with the torches that the men of Appolumi carried, their untested faces alight in the orange glow they gave off. The two groups stood across from one another, the garden silent save for low mutterings and anticipatory breaths.

The tension in the air mixed with the mist and gloom; it permeated everything and everyone.

Bijan took the moment to hang the satchel from a low-hanging branch and place the extra books on the ground beneath it. With a nod, Iollan threw him a scimitar. Bijan readied himself. Bijan's keen eyes could see the blond hair of the man the guards had called Calix shining in the torchlight. His sour, sallow face still wearing an expression of distaste. Surrounding him were four men, their faces grim, but set in determination. He recognized them all, their faces burned into his mind. He gnashed his teeth, his debt to Adun would soon be paid.

It wasn't the roar of challenge or the bellowing of an order, but the disappearance of Iollan's raiders that began the skirmish. Having no torches of their own, the raiders were able to slink back into the shadows with little issue. Boon and Bijan hardly noticed it themselves, as they were suddenly alone before the Appolumi militia. It was fleeting, and soon the air sang with loose bolts and arrows. The men of Appolumi, torches in hand, were easy targets for the sharp-eyed raiders. The courtyard was soon filled with screams of pain and death. The men that remained after the first and only volley were those fortunate enough to have full plate armour protecting them. Bijan noted that Calix and his guards were amongst those still standing.

Then the madness began.

Still holding on to their folly, the men of Appolumi held their torches before them, until the raiders reached out of the shadows to kill the torchbearers. This subterfuge only worked for the briefest moment before the courtyard garden was echoing with the proper sounds of battle, as raiders faced militia. Bijan and Boon joined in the fray. Bijan danced through the soldiers that came before him, slicing and slashing at the weak spots in the armour, often wounding or maiming instead of killing. Boon, on the other hand, charged into battle with two hatchets. Those unfortunate enough to fall into the path of his whirlwind of violence were crushed underneath it.

The men of Appolumi played their part well and Bijan stumbled over more than one deceased raider as he pushed his way toward Calix.

As Bijan cut a man down by the knees, he came face to face with one of his torturers; the ugly man who had pummelled him into a stupor, and Adun, to his death. The brute of a man let a slow smirk cross his broad face as he met Bijan, sword to sword. He was stronger than Bijan, but overconfident and slow, especially with his heavy armour strapped around him. Bijan avoided the man's crushing blows, flicking out his sword only to deflect those powerful swings. Frustration overcame his opponent and he began to swing his sword about him with reckless abandon. Bijan took his chance and, as the larger man hefted his sword above his head for yet another strike, Bijan slid his sword through the opening of the man's armour at his armpit and the flesh that lay underneath. The torturer fell to the ground with blood gurgling in his throat.

The battle continued in much the same way: both sides fighting their hardest, but Iollan and his raiders gained the upper hand. After the drawn-out conflict, only Calix and four others remained of the short-lived Appolumi militia. Bijan was upset to see that of those that remained only one of his torturers stood amongst them. Calix remained behind the others, and they seemed to be trying to form some sort of human shield to provide him time to escape through a door they were inching towards. The raiders were laughing at their feeble attempts to keep them back, their wild slashes at their approach, and finally their cursing and challenging to a fair fight. Calix looked paler than ever, his face falling to a sickly hue as the battle swayed away from his favour. He held an ornate slashing sword limply in his hand, its blade untarnished by the efforts of the day.

Eager to see things to an end, Bijan moved forward, his eyes focused on the last of his enemies. A strong hand gripped him about the bicep and turned him around. Boon stood there, bloody and sweating, his beard a matted wreck that made it wilder than ever.

"I know where your friend is," Boon said.

"*Friend*," Bijan scoffed. "Aye, my friend is right there." He pointed his sword at Calix, an ardent smile on his face.

"The boy," Boon growled, and pulled back on Bijan's arm. "The old man has him locked up."

Bijan hadn't thought about Edric since before the battle had started, but now a sense of worry gnawed at him. "Yes, but this will only take a moment..."

"As we speak, he is being fed to this... this beast," Boon swept his arm wide.

"He's what?" Bijan pulled his gaze from Calix, who had lost the last of his defenders to the onslaught of Iollan's raiders.

"The boy: he's meant to be food for the castle. Fuel. Don't you understand? The Circle of Magi is what makes life on this flying castle possible. They aren't some wise council, or some all-powerful defenders, they are food. Its nourishment." Boon's face had moved close to Bijan's, his breath warm on Bijan's face.

"How... I don't understand."

"Your friend will be drained over years and years. All

his magical powers, his magical potential will be lost to the needs of Appolumi."

"No..." Bijan said. The boy had liberated him from jail and kept him clear of the old wizard only to fall into the old man's claws himself.

Bijan looked around him; all he saw were liars and deceivers. None would bat an eye at any misfortune he may fall into. Boon, who stood before him now, proved that when he left him locked in a cell with the dying Adun. Edric hadn't left him, though. He was nothing but a stranger and interloper to that boy, and still he helped him escape. Bijan cast a glance at the last man left whom he blamed for Adun's death. Calix slashed at the swords of the enclosing raiders, pleading with them to stay back. His eyes no longer possessed the confident, menacing air they had when he'd held a sword to Bijan's neck. Now all Bijan could see in Calix's eyes was fear and the certainty of what was coming.

"Take me to him," Bijan said.

He grabbed up the satchel and books, and followed Boon out of the garden.

CHAPTER TWENTY-NINE

There were several ways to enter the courtyard from the castle; favoured amongst them all was the entrance from the main hallway that entered into plain view of the old willow tree. It was the entrance that came out just in view of Edric's lonely bedroom window. Leandra nearly smiled at the thought.

Perhaps the least used was the entrance located closer to the royal quarters of the castle. Barred gate doors blocked the path and the militia kept a stalwart watch, if only for ceremony. This path to the courtyard came to be known as 'the old way' by the youth of the castle. It wasn't favoured and was out of use.

Unfortunately, this was the entrance that the white-clad, masked bandits stole into the castle from the courtyard and made things exceptionally more difficult for Leandra.

Her path back towards her father's chambers had been relatively easy since she'd taken refuge from the last two guards by hanging from a window ledge. The corridors had been quiet, the halls empty. Still, Leandra took the extra time to remain as inconspicuous as possible. She walked in a bowed-over flurry of small, quick footsteps that even she could hardly hear. Leandra had become so accustomed to the quiet, so expectant of the peace and ease, that the sudden peal of the alarm bells frightened her into a high-pitched scream that she cursed herself for just a moment later.

The bells ended nearly as quickly as they had begun, their echo hanging in the silence that they left in their wake only to be replaced by the raging sound of battle. Leandra had heard the scuffles of militia training exercises, had witnessed skirmishes in tournaments, and took pleasure in seeing Calix practice his swordsmanship. What she heard now was much different. There was no hint of laughter, no smile promised under a scowling exterior. Instead, anger gave way to fear, and the only smile promised at the end would be over the bodies of the dead enemy. Leandra could hear all of that in the battle being waged just beyond the walls she now scurried through.

If she'd learned anything of Obelius' history lessons, it was that battles were rarely as organized as the training procedures Calix and the militia played at. Battles, wars, were messy. Not just from the gore and death they left behind, but in that they often spilled over where they shouldn't be, where they had no intention to be.

"Like a drunkard sloshing wine," Obelius had said, "it gets everywhere."

Watching the white-clad, steely eyed representatives of the enemy as they fought the Appolumi militia, Leandra began to believe Obelius' lessons.

A curse rose to her lips and she sank as low as her hips and toes would allow her and still scurry forward. The bandits slashed at the militiamen who'd tried to meet them with equal measure and skill, but even Leandra could tell it was a matter of time before the bandits cut them down.

With little choice in the matter, Leandra pushed forward, wishing that she had some sort of blade to defend herself and the training to do something with it. Her great grandfather had been a warrior and a superb general, if the tales were to be believed. Since the castle had taken flight, however, the need for the king to wage war disappeared. Leandra's father enjoyed the spectacle of a tournament, the celebration after a battle won, but he detested the practice of war. He'd refused to allow his only born child a chance at the practice. Especially his only girl. Leandra scowled.

She moved forward, quiet and quick, her eyes focused on the floor to avoid catching sight of the inevitable bloodshed. She moved without a sound as she passed the entrance from the courtyard, her lithe body tucked tight into the opposite wall. Leandra breathed a heavy sigh of relief; she'd gone unnoticed. Whether it was the distraction of an all-out war, or if the men had actually killed one another, she cared little. She was free, and almost done with her obligations to the castle, to the kingdom.

Her mind raced through the many pleasant scenarios of life on the ground she'd dreamt of throughout her life, many of which involved Edric, but all involved the freedom to do as she pleased. And so, when a strong hand darted out of the darkness and twisted her wrist, it was only natural that she let loose a banshee's scream.

The man she faced seemed to smile. His face was still covered in cloth, but his too-dark, brown eyes showed signs of mirth without humour. Leandra shivered.

"Come, Shiraz," said the other intruder as he withdrew his sword from a dead militiaman. His voice had a strange accent, a lilt that seemed to shorten the words spoken harshly. "Iollan wants us to draw them out to the courtyard."

"Perhaps they'd come out if we dangled this succulent piece of meat in front of them," the man holding Leandra said over his shoulder. A grunt of laughter was his only answer.

Leandra's heart raced. She'd read the histories of Appolumi, had Obelius' long lessons about the atrocities of the enemy running through her head. She wouldn't let herself be spoiled. Without further thought, she lashed out at her captor and slashed his face with her nails. The surprise made the man reel, but he still held her wrist firm. When he'd recovered from the initial shock, he turned back to her, his face uncovered and his eyes blazing.

He was a young man. His bronze face was supple and free of wrinkles. He had the barest shine of a beard on his cheeks, and his nose was a crooked beak that looked out of place with the rest of his features. Red marks left by her open hand crossed his growling mouth.

"You idiot bitch," he said, returning the wrappings to his face. His compatriot laughed again, cold eyes watching Leandra as he rifled through the dead bodies before him.

He raised his free hand, open and ready to return the slap she'd just given him. His eyes boiled over with rage, a hatred that Leandra could feel in her spine.

She closed her eyes and prepared for the blow, but it didn't come. Instead she heard a low thud and a gurgling sigh. Leandra opened her eyes to see the whites of her captor's eyes as they rolled back in his head. His grip loosened on her wrist and she pulled away as he collapsed to the floor. Gregory, the servant, stood in the fallen man's wake, blacksmith hammer raised to deliver another blow, and looking about as startled and confused as Leandra felt.

"Princess?" Gregory said. His hammer-wielding hand dropped to his side and he stood straight as if he were about to bow before her.

Leandra was able to nod before she pushed him out of the way of the curved sword of the other intruder as it slashed between them. The attacker spared Leandra a quick glance filled with the heat of anger before he turned back to Gregory, his sword still dripping with blood.

Gregory met the man head-on, dropping his hammer to grip the bandit's sword arm in both hands. The bandit was more skilled, but Gregory's strength and size nullified any advantage the other man had. The bandit cursed and launched punches into Leandra's defender's side and stomach. The dull thud of the blows landing on the ill-fitting leather armour turned Leandra's stomach, but it seemed to have little effect on Gregory, whose bright eyes continued to alternate their focus between the sword and Leandra.

"Run," Gregory said through gritted teeth, at last resting weary eyes on her. His arms seemed to endure the wrestling for the sword, but the continued strikes to his body were taking a toll.

Leandra stared down at the fallen bandit — Shiraz — sprawled before her, with a sticky wet spot growing on the crown of his head. His sword was still sheathed and at his side. She could've grabbed it up and drove it into the back of the remaining bandit; he was preoccupied after all. Her fingers wound around the hilt of the sword and she dragged it loose of its scabbard. It was heavy. Heavier than she could've imagined, and it felt strange in her hand. Foreign; alien. The thought of piercing the man's back with it brought bile to the back of her throat. And what if she did it wrong? What if she missed and stabbed Gregory instead? She couldn't do that. She couldn't.

"Go," Gregory's deep voice drew her eyes again. Sweat caked his brow, but he managed a weak smile as the bandit cursed and threw more blows to his midsection. He nodded to Leandra, as if he knew she wouldn't lift the sword, as if he knew it was too much for her.

With a nod of her own, she ran towards the throne room tears blurring her vision, and the constant thud of fist on leather following in her wake.

CHAPTER THIRTY

Light flooded his vision, a piercing white that pulled an ache from his temples to his eyes. Edric sat up; his arm covered his throbbing eyes to shade them from the harsh light. It didn't help. The light pervaded from everywhere. He squinted and waited for his eyes to adjust.

Edric shook his head, imagined he could feel something roll around in there, and rubbed between his eyes to soothe the headache. Standing was a special chore that took far too long for him to accomplish with his hand otherwise preoccupied. He sighed.

"Where am I?" he said aloud, peering through slits. Nothing stood out save for the white light. It clouded everything beyond his immediate surroundings, which appeared to be nothing of substance. He took some tentative steps, felt the floor under his feet, and was comforted.

Edric took a deep breath and then he heard it. A soft sobbing penetrated the blank ambiance he roamed through.

"Hello," Edric called, his hand extended before him as he crept along. The sobbing continued, unbroken.

"Tell me where you are, I'll find you." It was a child's cry, a huffing and snivelling through snot and tears. Edric walked toward the crying, his speed increased, his steps more deliberate. The child came out of nowhere, as if he had just appeared in the blink of an eye. Edric made a last minute, jerky stop, almost falling atop of the boy.

The boy had his legs pulled to his chest, hugging his legs. His head was tucked to his knees, his dark brown hair bouncing in tune with his shuddering shoulders. His muffled sobs continued uninterrupted.

"What's wrong, child?" Edric said, dropping to one knee. The child's clothes were tattered and dirty. Grass and branches clung to his pants, which were stained and full of holes. His feet were bare, though Edric may not have noticed with the sheer amount of dirt that had accumulated on them in green and black layers. His hair was matted and greasy; it stuck off at strange angles in an unwashed mess. Edric reached out to caress the boy's arm.

"Do not touch him," a voice boomed from behind. Edric jumped, almost falling into the boy again. He turned to face the source of the voice and recoiled his hand from the boy, who's sobbing had started in earnest once more.

An azure haze rippled through the white light of the room and a man was there, looking down upon Edric and the child before him with indifferent white eyes.

"He is the end of this, but we are not done here."

Edric could feel fear wash over him as he stared at the newcomer. Fear because he knew the face, and the eyes. They were his own, what he had seen his entire life when he caught a glimpse in any reflection. He stood before himself.

And yet, it wasn't him. Not as he was anyway. The blue aura continued to ripple around his other self, sizzling with magic. Oh yes, he could tell it was magic; it gave off so much energy that Edric felt woozy in its presence. He immediately wanted to keep as far as he could from The Other. He fought the nausea and stood; the sobbing child forgotten in the wake of the interruption.

Edric made to face The Other but found him to be much taller. Frustrated, he looked the man up and down and realized that The Other was floating, ripples of power lifting him from the ground.

"What are you?" Edric said, using all of his considerable will to keep his voice steady and calm.

"I am you." The voice of The Other echoed through Edric's head and he grasped his ears, cringing with pain. "At least, a version of you."

"What is that supposed to mean?" Edric was bent forward, his hands still cupped around his ears.

The Other gave him a dry smile and moved away, the air rippling around him as he moved, an azure hint in the sea of white. "What do you think it means?" The Other crossed its arms and looked off into the vast whiteness.

"Where are we?" Edric straightened but kept his distance.

A small grin grew on The Other's face.

"I'd have thought you would have figured that out by now." He turned towards Edric. "Come, think. Where are we?" He bent towards Edric but didn't approach.

Closing his eyes, Edric tried to block out the sobbing boy, the eerie stare of The Other, and the vast whiteness that surrounded them all. It was obvious; he could feel the answer just within grasp, its edges tickling his fingertips. He opened his eyes.

"My mind. I'm inside my own mind."

The Other nodded.

"So that makes you a part of me?"

"Quite right."

"This boy then, he's..." the boy raised his head, red-rimmed eyes still overflowing with tears. He too nodded at Edric before returning to his doldrums. In that small moment, Edric recognized the child he had been. The child chained to the obelisk.

"We need to have a discussion," The Other said, drawing Edric's attention away from the crying boy.

"What about?" Edric didn't like the way The Other spoke, his air of superiority, his arrogance. He certainly didn't like his dismissal of the boy. Perhaps what Edric hated most about The Other was that they were connected. They were a part of one another. If so, it was a cold, hateful part that he could live without.

"Your life." The Other moved closer, his face set, his eyes intent. "We need to discuss the Trials. We need to discuss your recent— interesting — choices."

A flash of Hesperos' bony hands made Edric cringe. He shook his head.

"What choices?"

"To finish the Trials, to gain your full potential…"

"Or to leave," the boy's voice was pitched and uneven through his crying. "To be free."

"Yes, that." The Other gave the boy a sour look.

"There's no choice to make. I've already decided. I'm leaving the castle, and The Circle, behind."

"Don't you think that's a bit hasty?" The Other moved closer again, his presence making Edric woozy, nauseous. "Hesperos has warned you of the consequences of leaving before finishing the Trials."

Another flash of Hesperos, his laugh echoing in Edric's mind.

"He can't be right. How could he know?" Edric said, rubbing his head. "No one has ever left the Trials or rejected The Circle. It's just another of his games. He wants to scare me."

"And he did, didn't he," said The Other as the boy's wailing began anew. "You could lose all of this," The Other raised his hands and let the bluish aura expand into a shield of blue fire in a small display of magical power.

Edric nodded. "I could lose all of that," he waved his hand towards The Other, shaking his head. "But on the other hand, I would only have a mere moment to enjoy before…"

"…Before your magic would be drained to power The Circle, sustain the castle." The boy said it with perfect clarity before returning to his sobbing once more. Edric looked back at him and nodded.

"Yes, well," The Other relaxed his magical prowess, the blue flame wavering and fading. "It's all for the greater good, isn't it?" He backed off again.

"What good is that?" Edric didn't bother to hide the anger in his voice.

"The castle. It's people," The Other said, crossing his arms once more.

"But… that…" Edric said, caught off guard. The thought had crossed his mind, of course, but there was no proof it would happen. No one had left The Circle before.

"Oh, I know you've thought about it," said The Other, his strange white eyes peering within Edric. "I can follow your thoughts as easily as a hound tracking a scent. If you — if we — don't finish the Trials and take our place in The Circle, the castle with fall. Maybe not right away, surely five or six Magi could hold the castle afloat, but what happens when the next passes? And the next?" The Other took a moment to appraise Edric, the stern lines of his face weren't something Edric could remember from his reflections.

"You must be aware that more people are going to die in that crumbling wreckage than Hesperos and Leandra. A whole city full of people will die. The king, nobles, peasants, and Magi alike will all perish, and for what? Because you didn't want to be inconvenienced. Because you wanted a life away from the castle. Well, what about their lives, Edric? Perhaps you could think more on that if you'd stop being so selfish."

"Selfish," Edric said, feeling the bile crawl around his throat. "Selfish is changing the rules. It's when you're on the brink of a well-deserved destruction and you run away. Selfish is sustaining a hurtful, ancient, and outdated way of life for your own benefit. It's removing yourself from the world because you think you're right, that you're better.

"The people of Appolumi should have died thousands of years ago. Their time has passed." Edric clenched his teeth. "It's not my fault that the time they drew out with the souls of the innocent is finally up."

"Do you believe Leandra shares those thoughts?"

"L-Leandra?"

"Yes, the princess. Do you share that opinion of her? After all, she is a subject of Appolumi."

"She'll come with me. We've started to plan..."

"You're a fool," The Other said turning from Edric.

Edric rushed towards his double, paying no mind to the magical resonance attacking his senses. He grabbed The Other's arm and spun him around.

The Other stared down at him, his face battling between shock and fear. Edric breathed deeply, his eyes delivering poison and warning to The Other before him. He turned and walked back to the boy, who was suddenly silent.

Holding out his hand, Edric said, "Come on. Let's leave this place. We don't need him anymore." The boy, young Edric, rubbed at his eyes with the heels of his hands. He smiled under his dirt-ridden face and grasped the hand before him. They walked like that, hand in hand, away from The Other. There was no direction to follow but away, and maybe back.

***

Edric woke thrashing and gasping for air. Without taking in his surroundings, he backed himself into the nearest corner, cradling his knees to his chest. The bright white of the room he'd just left still stung his eyes, and he tried to blink away the black spots that were impeding his vision, but they were slow to leave. The child, his mind caught up with him, where is the child?

He stood too quickly and struck his head on the rocky outcroppings that dropped from the ceiling. He flailed his hands about him, trying to find the child that he had just escaped with, but all he found was rock and something else. The Proteus Stone, with its unnaturally smooth surface, stood before him. He crouched forward and ran his hands along the stone. The child wasn't real; he'd never actually met him, let alone escaped with him. The Proteus Stone was real though, and there was something he was supposed to do with it. There was something he was supposed to figure out.

"But what?" he said to the stone, his eyes regaining their focus. His fingers had found the lightly etched symbols that ran along the stone, the spells that would unlock its secrets.

"Here," a voice said, "perhaps these will help." Hesperos stood next to the Proteus Stone, his claw-like hand stretched out, holding two books.

Edric fell back and scurried into the corner of the room again. "Hesperos," he whispered, "leave me alone."

"Alone?" A dry smile creased the older man's face. "I am only here to help you finish the Trials." He placed the books on the flat surface of the Proteus Stone and stepped away from it. "The last time we spoke of it, you said you needed books to help decipher the spell. I brought some which may be useful." He motioned toward the stone with his hand, taking yet another step back.

"The last time we spoke you attacked me and brought me back here."

"Only so you could fulfil your destiny and join The Circle as the powerful Magus you are." His smile was frozen on his face, a reasonable facsimile of a smile.

Edric eyed the Magi that stood, swaying behind Hesperos. The dancing corpses that moved to the rhythm of the castle. Hesperos claimed they were alive, but there they stood, barely moving, barely breathing, chained to the castle and drained of their power. They were the living dead and he didn't want to be among them.

"No," he said, and stood. "I will have no part in this insanity." Edric gestured to the room, to The Circle.

"Boy, we've already talked about this..." Hesperos took a step closer and shook his hands out of his sleeves, his fingers flexing.

"Talk is all it is. It's all that it has been. It had been just another way for you to feel better about all of this. But it is doomed, it is coming to an end. Do you want to know what my dream was? The dream I had during the second Trial?"

The smile had disappeared from Hesperos' face, replaced by a venomous scowl.

"It was the demise of Appolumi. The fall of the Magi of The Circle, the fall of the floating castle, the fall of corrupt and morally devoid nobles. And here it is, coming to pass."

There was a silence filled with apprehension, the thrum of power in the room resonating within Edric's mind, intensifying the feeling.

A growl erupted from Hesperos and his old hands moved with lightning speed. Edric was thrown against the wall, a crystal outcropping jabbed into his back and side as he went past. A slash as if of blades swiped across his face and he could feel the warm rivulets of blood escape the wounds that had opened on his cheek.

"You think you can escape this, Boy?" Hesperos' teeth were bared as he spoke, rage crept out from his eyes. "Something that has been built for centuries, you are going to bring down? You are a truly delusional boy." He made a fist of his right hand and the result was instantaneous. Edric bent over in pain, gripping at his stomach as his innards felt like they were being torn asunder.

"Perhaps you have figured it out already," Hesperos continued to squeeze his hand closed, "but the Trials were more of a, well, they were really just a way to help initiates come to terms with what was about to happen to them. Oh, don't worry, I didn't lie to you, Boy. Your powers have come along nicely of late for a reason, but not because of your engagement in the Trials. It's your age, Boy. You're coming of age. No Trial is going to stop that one way or the other. Though, one has to wonder, would your magic be able to exist if not amplified by the castle?" He turned in a small circle and gestured at the crystal room around them.

"What is it you picture of the world below? Do you think it holds more adventure, more excitement? No, Boy. You would have grown up in some sleepy little village and would have taken a likewise boring job. Perhaps you'd have been a farmer, or a butcher. Magic is dead down there, Boy. The last magic in the world is gathered here, in this room. You want to leave magic behind? You are a foolish and arrogant child.

"Now, I don't need you to finish your Trials, but I do need you to read the spell." Hesperos released his fist and grabbed Edric by the bicep, dragging him forward on shaking legs. "So here," he forced Edric's hand onto the smooth top of the Proteus Stone and produced a piece of parchment. "Read this."

It was the translation of the etching from the Proteus Stone, written out plainly for him to see. A feeling of fear and anger reached up through him, and a curious sense of disappointment. Disappointment that he was unable to translate it himself.

Hesperos grabbed a handful of Edric's hair and pushed his head toward the paper. "Read."

The chiming of the bells startled them both, Hesperos looked around the room as if trying to discern where the sound was coming from. He cursed, "What is it now?"

"The demise of Appolumi," Edric said, smiling through the echoes of pain. "It has come to pass."

CHAPTER THIRTY-ONE

Boon lead Bijan through the twisting hallways of lower Appolumi in haste. The man moved swifter than his bulk conveyed, much to Bijan's chagrin; his aching limbs and muscles had finally come to their breaking point. Still, he pushed himself to limp after Boon, hoping to find Edric before it was too late.

They delved deeper and deeper into the bowels of the castle. The hallways became darker and narrower as they descended. As they moved, parts of the castle they had passed reminded Bijan of the dungeons he had so recently escaped from. They moved deeper.

Despite his focus on the task at hand, he was still amazed that they had encountered no other members of the Appolumi population. Where would they have hidden? Was the castle so immense that a battle could be waged on one side and no one would be alerted on the other? His mind was plagued with these thoughts, and others. What if they had just destroyed what remained of Appolumi's people? That question troubled Bijan the most. To defeat a people in battle was one thing, but to completely annihilate them — that was something else entirely. He shook his head. Boon had gained a lead on him and he would have to hurry to catch up. Adjusting the satchel about his chest, he made an effort at speed despite the protest of his limbs. He would return to his thoughts when he could afford to.

They came out of a stairwell into grass and dirt. The brown earth looked fertile and fresh, the grass so freshly cropped that Bijan thought it may have been moss at his first glance. The stone layered walls seemed to meld into the solid blue-grey rock that surrounded them as they moved forward, feet making no noise.

"This is it," Boon said, his voice echoing in the empty space. "This is the heart of the castle."

Bijan took a chance to rest. Rubbing his sore ribs, he said through a grimace, "What do you mean, the heart?"

"Can't you feel it?" Boon turned, his hands held out at his sides. "There's something at work here. Something that flows through the air. Lightning caught in a bottle." Boon's eyes had lost their seriousness, his face had gone blank. He stared up to the rocky ceiling.

Bijan felt a strange prickling at the nape of his neck, a lightness that relieved or distracted from his pain. His stomach was full of butterflies.

Boon had been watching him, caught him coming to his realization that something was different here. Something very strange.

"Why?" Bijan said, but didn't know why he would ask that.

"The very ground the castle was built upon had its own mystical properties. That's the secret of Appolumi, Bijan, it's not the people, it's the place."

"What of the Magi, what of The Circle? You mentioned it earlier; they're food?"

"Conduits?" Boon started to move ahead again. "Power sources, perhaps. Whatever the castle wants or needs, that is what The Circle provides. Nourishment."

"The Great Circle of Magi are just food for this...?" he waved his hands about him, unsure of what to call the castle-shaped creature.

"Well, in a way. Make no mistake, the people of Appolumi have bent and shaped the castle for their own needs as well. Gardens, vegetation, life. The castle needed little of this, and yet it has plenty. The castle had no need to rise from the ground all those years ago, and yet it did. Man and building had their own influence in this way of life."

In the silence that followed, the echo of the alarm bells reached the depths they had found in the castle. Again, Bijan's mind wandered. What if there was no one left alive to end whatever mechanism kept the bells ringing. It was a terrible sound with a more terrible meaning.

"It's not far now," Boon said and picked up his pace. It strained him, but Bijan kept up. They ran through the under garden, passing strange plant life and rocky outcroppings; none of which Bijan had seen back on the surface. It was when they came to large oak doors that Bijan knew they had arrived.

The doorway was strange in the garden landscape; alien. It was set into the rocky wall where moss, or grass, crawled about midway up the wall, and sprouted fingers that lashed their way toward the ceiling. The doors themselves were in pristine condition. Their dark surface seemed clean and polished, and had intricate markings that ran the length of them, from floor to arch.

"What do they mean?" Bijan bent toward the markings and ran his hand along them.

Boon shrugged.

Bijan tried to open one of the doors but the handle would not move. "Locked," he said to himself. He turned to Boon, his eyes questioning.

Boon shrugged with a sigh and threw a thunderous kick that would have crumbled any normal door into several pieces. In the door that stood before Boon and Bijan, the cracks and distress sounded as if it were shattered, but it still stood. Solid, clean, and polished. Boon cursed and threw another kick, but met the same result.

Placing the satchel and books aside, Bijan jammed his sword into the side of the door and used leverage to pry it open. He too failed and cracked his blade in the attempt. Boon made several attempts to batter the door open with his shoulder, his feet, and even his fists. When all of that failed, he took his hatchets to the door, a lusty smile growing under his thick beard. Though he wielded them with great skill, and his strikes were strong, the door would still not bend to his efforts.

Both men bent over in exhaustion. Boon stared at the door with a malice the likes of which Bijan had not seen before.

"Stand back," Boon said finally and stood to his full height. "Stand back and stay out of my way. I need to focus." Bijan nodded and retrieved the boy's belongings.

Unsure of what to expect, Bijan kept his eyes averted from Boon. He knew that Boon was different, had certain abilities, but wasn't sure what was needed to attain those. When he started to see the other man change, however, he couldn't avert his eyes any longer. He stared at him as the man became a beast and the bowels of the castle echoed with the roars of a bear.

CHAPTER THIRTY-TWO

Panic filled the halls. It was thrumming through the concrete and stone. Leandra dragged Alethea behind her, pushing through the screaming crush and toward the throne room.

"The castle had been called. Another apprentice," Alethea said between ragged breaths. "Agents of the enemy sent to pillage and murder."

"Come on, 'Lethe," Leandra said, pulling the older woman along. She'd found her old handmaiden wandering the halls, her skirts spattered with the blood of guardsmen, and a nasty gash on her cheek. Leandra's heart beat hard.

There were prisoners, or so it appeared. Those first bells signified their capture. Then they escaped, and everything changed. There were sightings of armed men in the courtyard. Strangers, intruders, more like those Leandra had encountered and Gregory engaged. They waged war on the courtyard that had only ever known peace and prosperity. Gregory. She had to get to her father.

People swelled against Leandra and her handmaiden. Shoulders and arms slammed into her as if they were blind to her presence. Hectic curses fled the mouths of those that passed her, their frantic eyes passing over her without seeing her. Leandra pushed through them, her face set and her mind determined.

As she dragged Alethea into the hallway around the throne room, Leandra discovered that it was mostly free of people. Even the guards had fled their usual positions on either side of the broad, solid wooden door. A door which stood open.

"Father?" Leandra ran into the room, not caring that she had left Alethea alone, leaning on a cold stone wall.

The throne room was dark. The waning light of dying candles danced at the back of the room, casting shadows in strange angles. Leandra stopped just inside the door, squinting her eyes and trying to adjust them to the dim light. She could see the outline of the throne before her, its red cushions and golden frame hidden in the dark.

"Father," Leandra said in a whisper, her voice quivering as she took another step into the room. Swallowing a deep breath, she said, "Do you know what is happening? The enemy is attacking." A small sound to her right made her jump and she fixed her eyes there. Nothing moved.

"We need to get you to safety."

"I'm afraid that there is no safety, princess. Not anymore." Obelius hissed from somewhere behind her, his hot breath on the nape of her neck. Leandra jumped and swirled, her hands lashing out, but she hit nothing.

"I regret to inform you, princess, that your father, the king, has been murdered. Agents of the enemy, no doubt."

Leandra barely registered that his voice had moved to another part of the room. All of her thoughts focused on the words that he had just uttered. A moan drained from her mouth. Her legs buckled, and her stomach rolled with the thunderous beat of her heart. Her father was dead.

Tears brimmed in her eyes, falling in hot droplets on her cheeks and hands. She fell to her knees.

"I... I don't believe you," she managed, her voice choked with the urge to scream. "Show me my father."

"Very well," there was a sharp click and then a whoosh of a torch catching fire. Leandra turned towards the sound, towards the throne. Her father, an old withered version of the man he once was. His once handsome and devilish features now marred by the scarred jowls that lay on his chest. The mouth that would whisper silly words into her ears when she was upset now stood slack on his face, a drop of blood trailing from it. Those coarse, but gentle hands that wiped away tears when she was sad were now open in his lap. Lifeless. Dead. Tears were driven from her eyes, and her screams echoed in the small room.

Obelius approached; she could feel the heat of the flame from the torch as he closed in on her. "There, there, little princess. I'm sure he didn't suffer. Look," Obelius cast the light of the flame towards the body of the king. "There is a blade in his heart. I'm sure he was only in pain... momentarily."

Leandra could see the dagger still protruding from her father's chest, its black handle still jostling back and forth as if to mock her in her grief. It wasn't the foreign agents that had killed her father.

"Why?" she said, trying to stand. She wiped tears from her eyes and studied her old tutor. She scanned his sallow face and found his humourless grin, one long-fingered hand reaching out to aid her.

Leandra slapped Obelius' hand away. She could feel her face turn hot; her head begin to ache. "Why did you kill him, Obelius? Why?"

Obelius stepped back, his face calm, and turned his

head to the side; studying her. He didn't say anything.

"You were his advisor. You were his friend; he trusted you." Leandra clenched her fists.

That same smile shadowed his face, but his eyes were dark, dangerous.

"You always were a foolish girl, princess. A foolish, reckless, and ultimately useless girl." He took one step forward, Leandra jumped back. His smile grew.

"Let me clarify this for you, princess: have you looked around? Have you seen what's happening? The end has come. Agents of our enemy have flooded the courtyard. They are slaughtering our slipshod defences. Appolumi will fall. Do you think we will be here by morning? We are at our end, girl."

Leandra scrubbed at her eyes, her face hot with rage and hate and grief. "You didn't have to kill him." Her voice was strained, a whisper in the empty room.

"I didn't," Obelius said, "but I wanted to." Obelius planted the torch into a sconce and approached the throne. With a tug, he drew the dagger from the king's chest and let it dance before him. "The very thought that someone other than me would deal the final blow to this exasperating piece of shit," he jabbed the knife into the air, "pushed my hand. So to speak." The smile was still there. No change, no emotion.

Leandra watched her father's blood, dark in the torch-light, drip from the blade of the dagger as she kept her distance from Obelius. "You... you..." she couldn't form words. Thoughts.

"I was his friend? I was his advisor? No, princess, I was his servant. His very own personal servant. I did everything for him. Every demeaning thing. Well, tonight was my chance to repay the favour."

He advanced on her, his free hand lashing out at her arm. Leandra jumped out of his reach, a scream escaping her lips. She made for the door.

Obelius let out a growl and grabbed up a handful of her raven hair. He pulled her back; Leandra's hands scratched at Obelius', but it afforded her no leniency.

"You know, Leandra, I was going to save you. Keep you as a prize. I'm sure the death of the king would have afforded me some favour," Obelius said, pulling her toward him. "But now, perhaps it'd be better if the ruling family shared the same fate as Appolumi. Yes, I think so. Rather poetic, wouldn't you say?"

Leandra could feel the tip of the dagger dig into her back, could feel Obelius twist it.

"Obelius?" Alethea stumbled through the door, her grey hair falling around her face, which was still red with exertion, blood trickling down her cheek. "What are you doing?"

Obelius tensed, his breath hissed from between his teeth. "I...I..."

Leandra drove her heel down on Obelius' foot, causing a stream of curses to fall from his mouth and release his grip on her.

"Alethea, run." Leandra grabbed her handmaiden around the bicep and pulled her through the door.

The corridors were empty; silent. The slapping of their feet echoed in their haste. Leandra had a vague thought, where did everyone go? It was only a fleeting thought cut off by the rage-filled scream of Obelius bursting forth from the throne room.

"Run," Leandra hissed through panting breaths.

PART FIVE
CHAPTER THIRTY-THREE

"Read it!" Hesperos clenched his gnarled hand closed again, and Edric screamed in agony. His stomach felt as though it were being torn to shreds; his chest felt as though a fire burned in his lungs.

"Physis..." Edric whispered, pain surging through his mind and body, weakening him.

"Louder." Hesperos held Edric's hand to the flat surface of the Proteus Stone.

"Physis," Edric said again.

"Yes, and the next." Hesperos shoved the paper in Edric's face once again.

"Morphe."

"Good..." A deafening bang and a sharp cracking sound brought both men around to look at the door. It hadn't been damaged, but something had attacked it.

"What is it now?" Hesperos said, his voice shrill. He turned back to Edric. "Keep reading, Boy."

Edric's stare fell to the door, his pain-riddled mind hoping that the door would collapse in on itself.

"Read, gods damn you!" Hesperos slapped Edric with a bony hand, drawing his attention back to the paper.

"Polis," Edric said as he massaged his reddened cheek.

Another cracking sound came from the door, but Hesperos leaned closer to Edric, his yellow teeth gnashed together as he shook the paper.

"Eidos," Edric read and cast daggers at Hesperos with his eyes. He stood and pushed the man back with his free hand.

"Physis Morphe Polis Eidos Metron..." He read; his voice faltered. The Proteus Stone was buzzing with power, the sigils carved into its side had begun to glow a faint orange, and the blue crystal that crusted the entirety of the room had begun to crawl up from its base. "What is..."

Boom. Another crash reverberated through the small room. Hesperos' face was lined with stress and anger.

"Finish it..."

Edric pushed his free hand out before him in a fist, sending Hesperos flying through the air. His shoulder struck one of the swaying Magi and both spun to the ground. Edric looked at the Proteus Stone again, watching the crystal crawl up it in jittering starts and stops, sometimes flailing like something alive. He tried to remove his hand from the stone, move it out of the path of the crystal, but it wouldn't budge. Panic raced around his mind as he knew what the spell was supposed to do. He calmed himself enough to take a closer look at his hand. Between his palm and the top of the Proteus Stone, the crystal had begun to form. It had latched onto his skin, the tiny filaments of crystal piercing his pores to hold his hand fast.

"The last word, Boy." Hesperos was gathering himself from the floor. "Say the last word. Finish the spell."

"But... but what about..."

"Think about your choices, Boy. Think of all the people that will die if you don't finish what you started. Think about your magic, about what you would be without it.

Where you would be without it." Hesperos stumbled forward; his voice was low and familiar, but not as Hesperos' voice. A voice from a dream. The voice of The Other.

Edric lifted his eyes to his former master and meant to attack him once more, but the old man clenched his fist too quickly, and it forced Edric to his knees, grasping his stomach.

"Say it, Boy." Hesperos panted as he moved toward him, bent over and holding his back. "Finish it, and all of this will stop. Hundreds, thousands of people will live and it'll be because of you."

Edric stared at the Proteus Stone, his eyes glancing at the last sigil left uncovered by the crystal. He could see The Other staring at him through azure-hued eyes, and the boy through his tear-stained eyes. Neither were moving, their faces blank and uninterested.

"Cycl..."

The snapping of wood halted him, and he looked to the destroyed door in time to see the large black snout of a giant bear tear into the small room. From its gaping jaws a guttural roar filled the room, its red eyes murderous.

Hesperos fell back, surprise and fear overtaking him so that he released his hold on Edric. The bear was shaggy and grey, its massive shoulders hardly able to fit the width of the doorway as it squirmed its over twelve-foot body into the room. Its head snapped back and forth, uttering grunts and groans at everything around it. Edric was just happy that the bear had turned its back to him.

Hesperos let out a stifled and frightened scream that brought the beast's attention to him. Around the girth of the bear Edric could see the frantic movements of his former master, could see his hands moving in small circles, his fingers flailing. The bear let out another ear-splitting roar and charged forward, only to stop, suddenly, just before Hesperos. The old wizard's face was slick with sweat, his expression that of relief. The bear, on the other hand, was enraged and lashed out at the magical force field that Hesperos had managed to protect himself with. The beast's claws tore into the invisible wall; scratches of electric blue appeared before Hesperos as if out of nowhere. The look of relief left the old wizard's face.

"Hey, kid," a voice called from the doorway. Edric turned to see the man he had rescued from the dungeon crawl through the entrance, casting nervous glances at the bear as he did. "I think you took a wrong turn getting to the courtyard." The man's smile was contagious and full of mischief, but Edric was in no mood to smile.

"I'm stuck," he said, pulling at his hand and the Proteus Stone, though he was pleased that the crystal had stopped spreading.

Bijan crept closer and examined the minute pieces of crystal embedded in Edric's palm. "Hmm. Lift your hand as high as you can," he said and produced his broken sword. "Now, hold very still." He moved the sword between hand and stone and made some small chops at the crystal. There was the sound of metal hitting rock, but nothing else. Bijan then ran the sword's edge back and forth over the crystal, hoping to saw it away, but there was no change.

"It's no use," Edric sighed. "It is a strange magic. Only magic will break the spell now."

"And you can do magic?"

"Yes, some."

"Well, why not do it? Quickly now, so we can get out of here," Bijan said as he looked over his shoulder at the bear.

"I can't. I don't know the right spell."

"Who does?"

"Him." Edric pointed at the beast, its head swinging back and forth, the lifeless corpse of Hesperos hanging in tatters from its massive jaws.

Bijan cursed. "I may know someone who can help." He stood then and began to hit his sword on the Proteus Stone, the loud clanging filling the room. "Boon," he yelled. "Boon!"

They watched as the bear dropped Hesperos' corpse from its mouth, the pieces of the old man hitting the ground with a sickening thud. The bear's red eyes now came to rest on the two men on the opposite side of the room. Its nose floundered in the air around it, taking in the scent of the room. The bear uttered a harsh grunt and snorted before it padded toward them. It stopped at each Magus as it passed them; with each stop it repeated a ritual of running its snout over the swaying men. Shaking its head, it moved closer and closer to Edric and Bijan.

"Boon," Bijan said, raising open hands to the bear. "Boon, do you understand me?"

The bear tipped its head to the side, sizing up the two men. Bijan cursed.

"We need to get Edric out of here. Is there anything you can do?" The bear's cold nose nuzzled Edric's immobilized hand. The bear growled and reared up on its hind legs, unable to stand at its full height in the small room.

"Whoa, whoa, whoa," Bijan said as he stepped between the bear and Edric. "He's a friend, Boon." The bear snorted and gave Bijan a gentle push with the back of his large paw. With Bijan out of the way, Boon sunk his large claws into the Proteus Stone in one violent motion. Immediately Edric snapped back in pain and he was back in his vision, standing at the edge of the treeline and looking at the onyx obelisk.

The bear was there, its claws tearing at the black stone, its anger and power tangible in the cold night air. Its words came to him again, echoed in his mind. "My rage is an old one. Beyond your comprehension. Should you, or anyone, stand in my way, I will raze you to your very marrow. To your very soul."

He escaped the dream, screaming as the Proteus Stone was torn asunder.

"Don't worry kid, you'll live." Bijan gave him a smile, a hearty slap on the shoulder, and moved toward the door. The bear, now sitting before him, gave him a quizzical look with a tip of its head. It held its paws before it, blood leaking from its pads where shards of stone were lodged. It grunted and moved off, favouring its right leg as it did.

Looking upon the bear now, Edric saw something strange, something he hadn't noticed before. The bear didn't have red eyes, like the monster from his nightmares, but had hazel eyes.

CHAPTER THIRTY-FOUR

"What do you mean you're not coming?" Bijan was squatting by the splintered door. He tried to ignore the strange mutterings of Edric from beside him, so he could fix Boon with a baleful stare.

The guide had changed forms again, had reverted to his human guise once more. Not for the first time did Bijan wonder how the larger man did such a thing, but found that letting his mind chase that question for too long would only lead to confusion or madness. Besides, it was the act that ultimately marvelled him. One moment he was the tall, brooding wildman, the next he was a massive beast.

"I need to see this place," he raised his bleeding hands, gesturing to the crystal room. "Take the boy and leave. I'll be just behind you." He moved toward the unsettling, swaying men that surrounded the room.

"What did you say they were?" Bijan turned his eyes to Edric. The boy was looking towards his recently freed hand. Glinting blue stones still stood out in his palm, and Bijan didn't envy the tedious plucking and prodding that he had ahead of him.

"The Circle," Edric said in a faint and far off voice. "Magi, wizards, wells of magic and knowledge. Prisoners," Edric drew his gaze from his hand long enough to look upon the closest man.

"Will they harm us?"

"No, I... I don't think so. They barely move, they rarely talk, aside from some moaning. For *his* purposes, they are vegetables." Edric pointed a jabbing finger at Boon, who stood before one of the Magi, studying the crystal that had engulfed the man's hand.

Bijan nodded and gave him another slap on the shoulder. "Thanks, kid." Then to Boon, "Don't dally. We need to get off this castle without delay. We'll see you in the courtyard when you get there."

Taking one last look beyond the door, Bijan moved out, backtracking his steps from earlier. Edric cast one last, hesitant look back at Boon, his sweeping eyes catching a glimpse of the scattered remains of his mentor, teacher, and torturer. Hesperos had seemed immortal, undying. He had never talked much about life before the castle took flight, never implied that he was present for the act itself, but Edric had a feeling he was. The man was a wealth of knowledge, a beacon of power, and perhaps the last true Magus the world would ever know. He was also a mean-spirited, sadistic bastard, who did everything in his power to make Edric's life miserable.

Perhaps he got what he deserved, Edric thought as he followed Bijan through the earthen base of the castle Appolumi. Perhaps Hesperos had been warped by the long years, by the power of The Circle, by the castle itself. Perhaps, but Edric had a hard time believing that.

He prodded at the shards of crystal that remained in his hand. Gripping the longest between finger and thumb, he pulled at it. A ripple of pain shivered up his arm and attacked his brain. He winced. Stupid, he thought, but continued to grip the shard and tug at it as Bijan brought him to the steep stairs that would bring them back towards the courtyard.

***

Bijan hadn't known the boy for long but could tell he was acting strange. It made him nervous. The kid was quiet when he wasn't sucking his teeth in pain, but he kept making eyes back towards the room he'd just escaped. He'd been motivated to leave when he had rescued Bijan from the dungeons, but now he seemed more preoccupied with what he would be leaving behind. Bijan shrugged; the boy was young and indecisive. He'd get over it, or he wouldn't. There was nothing more Bijan could do about it.

They climbed the rough steps. Bijan was in the lead and his pace was slow, precipitated by the cautious, sweeping surveys he made at every turn and corner. At times he would stop their progress entirely just to listen, his ear cocked in the silent echoes of the castle. Nothing. And yet, he didn't hear Iollan approach.

It was as if the foot had appeared out of the air, landing squarely on Bijan's chest and driving him down the stairs. Bijan wasn't caught completely unaware, his paranoia on the return to the courtyard preparing him for some sort of attack. He was almost able to land on his feet — if it weren't for the distracted Edric, whose complete surprise failed the both of them. They both fell backwards, rolling down several stairs before gaining the traction to stop themselves. Bijan's unhealed aches and pains flared once more, while Edric gathered his crystal-encrusted hand to his chest and bit his lip from uttering a scream of pain.

"Apologies," Iollan said, sitting on a step and folding

his arms over his knees. "I didn't know it was you. The day has been filled with excitement, as you know; I think I might have been carried away by the remnants of that." He raised his eyebrows upon sighting Edric, "Ah. I see you've found your friend."

Bijan groaned and pushed himself up to his knees, pain spreading through him like fire. "Yes. I've found my friend, and now it's time to leave. Care to lead the way?"

Iollan kept his eyes on the boy, "Of course." He stood, a smile rising on his uncovered face. Then he stopped, turned, and raised a hand. "Oh, but there is one thing we need to do first." He moved closer to the fallen men. "Take me to the chamber."

Bijan didn't need to look at Edric to tell that he was surprised by Iollan's assertion, he could see the triumph in Iollan's face.

"So there *is* such a place?" Iollan said, moving closer, focused only on Edric now. "Bring me to it, Boy." Iollan's palm caressed the hilt of his waiting scimitar.

"How did you... no. No, you...I can't." Edric's lip dripped dark blood and he pulled his hand closer to his chest, cringing away from the raider.

"Damn it," Bijan said and launched himself forward, tackling the leader of the raiders and shoving him into the opposite wall. Iollan reacted immediately and was able to reverse Bijan's attempt to grapple him into a tight trip over his extended leg. Bijan landed hard, his back crossing the edge of one of the stone steps, driving the air from his lungs and reminding him of the unhealed injuries he had just suffered hours before.

Iollan drew his scimitar from its scabbard.

"When did you become such a fighter, Bijan? Bijan the Burrower, Bijan the Vulture, Bijan the Bone Collector was never rumoured to be so…" Iollan studied his blade for a moment, addressing the reflection he saw in the freshly cleaned surface, "fiery. It was precisely why we hired you. We already have enough fire amongst the raiders." He laid the point of his curved sword at Bijan's throat. "Though, I'm sure if you take me to the chamber of The Circle, we could find a permanent place for you among our number, for both of you."

"You know," Bijan said with a grunt, "from here I can see your point." He looked to the confused Edric, who had taken to holding his head. "Unfortunately, Iollan, Edric here has all the magic he needs."

Edric's eyes cleared with understanding, and he raised his uninjured hand, twisting his fingers and rolling his wrist. Iollan gave the boy a strange look, but Bijan could see some strain grow across the raider leader's face, could see some of his muscles grow taught with effort. Then it stopped and Edric let out a pained groan, his eyes closed tight as he pulled his injured hand to his chest. The shards of crystal let off a faint, throbbing blue glow.

'Shit,' Bijan thought, slapping the scimitar away from his neck while Iollan was distracted with Edric. A small cut brought an instant, stinging pain to his neck and blood immediately started a slow leak. He swept Iollan's legs with his arm and sent the warrior crashing to the stone steps with him. Iollan didn't land on his back though, he landed on his side, and immediately threw his free hand in a punch toward Bijan's face.

Bijan wasn't sitting still and had begun his movement even as Iollan landed. He rolled out of the way of the wild punch, Iollan's hand crunching against the stone step. Even so, Bijan knew that the sword would be coming right behind it. He pushed himself down another four stairs, the scimitar cutting the air just above his head.

"What happened, kid?" Bijan said, getting back to his feet and facing the recovering Iollan.

Edric held out his injured hand, the shards left there were still glowing an eerie blue. "I think the crystal is draining all my magic." Edric's face was a mask of pain.

'Great,' Bijan thought, and got himself ready for Iollan's next move.

It came quick and hard. Iollan got to his feet and swiped his sword at Bijan in one swift movement. Bijan threw himself to the side, flattening himself into the wall, avoiding the blade, but Iollan followed through quickly. With a roar, the leader of the raiders hurled a kick at Bijan's exposed back, but his foot only found the stone wall as Bijan avoided him once more.

Bijan countered and attempted to grapple with Iollan again. He grabbed the other man's sword arm about the wrist and pushed it into the air above his head. Both men fell into the opposite wall in the ensuing struggle. Iollan used his free hand to land some punches into Bijan's side, ribs, and stomach, but the thief wouldn't release his grip. Iollan growled as they continued to vie for position against the wall, and finally landed some hard punches to Bijan's already ill-used face. With watering eyes, Bijan released the raider's sword arm without thought and gripped his nose. Iollan pushed him then and sent him falling down several more steps before he came to a stop at the earthen floor he and Edric had just left.

"That's enough of that," Iollan said, his words punctuated by a deep inhalation of breath and panting. He followed Bijan down the steps, shaking out his free hand with a mild grimace of pain. "I think I have taken you for granted, Bijan. You are a man of many talents. It would be a waste to kill you, but what else am I to do?" He stood over Bijan, miming thought.

"Go to hell." Bijan rubbed fresh blood from his mouth and tried to stand, but Iollan put his foot on his chest.

"I'll have to kill you, Bijan," Iollan said with finality. "There is nothing more for it. And it may entice your young friend to lead me to this chamber, unless he wants to suffer the same fate." He motioned to Edric, but his pale, blue eyes remained on Bijan. A quick twitch at the corners of Iollan's mouth was all that it took for rage to flood through Bijan. Iollan's sword was closing in on Bijan's throat once more, as if he were taking aim and preparing for the final swing.

It was just as Iollan raised his sword to the final apex that Edric acted. A groan of pain erupted from the younger man and he drove his good hand into the neck of Iollan. The raider leader's eyes bulged in surprise, but as he opened his mouth to speak, only wet, gurgling sounds fell from his mouth. Edric released him and Iollan fell to his knees before falling face first on the ground just before Bijan. From the side of his neck, a long shard of crystal extended, blood running along its edges.

Edric collapsed between Iollan and Bijan and stared up to the ceiling, his breath coming fast.

"Are you okay, kid?" Bijan had rolled himself to his stomach and was getting to his elbows. It was hard, and racks of pain screamed through him, blooms of black exploded at the edge of his vision; he'd try to get to his knees in a moment.

"He said this would happen." Edric lifted his hand that was still pierced by the tiny shards of crystal and set his eyes to it. There was still a weird blue glow emanating from his palm, now accompanied by small droplets of blood that covered several of the small segments. "He said that if I didn't finish the Trials this would happen. Said that I would lose my magic." He looked at Bijan from the corner of his eye, "I didn't really believe him. I've had magic my whole life. It's just been there, waiting for me to shape it, control it, use it. But now…." He let his hand drop back to the ground.

"I can't say I know much about that feeling," Bijan said, a grunt escaping him as he adjusted himself. "But what I do know is that a man will get used to just about anything. I've known men who have lost their hands. Chopped off at the wrist," Bijan made a slicing motion through the air with the flat of his hand. "For these men, that hand represented their livelihood, the way they fed their families. And then, that was just gone."

Edric pushed himself up on his elbows so he could see Bijan as he spoke. His eyes darting to his pin-cushioned hand randomly.

"So, I suppose you think that these men just gave up, that their families starved to death and that was the end of it? No, Edric. That's not what happened. They got on with their life; they lived. Could they do exactly the same things that they could do before? Not quite, but they found other ways. Other ways to make a living, other ways to support their loved ones." Bijan sat up with effort and rubbed at his neck where Iollan's sword had scratched it.

"Do we know if you lost your magic for sure? No. We may be able to get all of those shards out of your hand and you'll be back to your usual self. But, if that's not the case and your master was right about all of this, it'll be okay. You'll find new ways to do things; you'll make do. The point is, son, you're not losing yourself. You still got that in abundance." Bijan rose with difficulty and approached the boy. He helped Edric up from the ground and slapped him on the shoulder again. "Now, let's get off this castle."

***

Their second climb of the stairs wasn't as stealthy, but it was certainly as slow. Both Edric and Bijan held each other up as they limped up the stairs. It was just as well; as they reached the top stair and moved closer to the courtyard, they could hear the commotion. The entire castle had been steeped into a rabid confusion. There were people running through the halls, their clothes torn and shredded, and wounds apparent on their bared skin. Others were standing quite still, shaking or muttering to themselves as Edric and Bijan passed them. One former Appolumi soldier was quietly laughing to himself as he sat leaning against a wall, an ear in his open palm before him.

Bijan pulled Edric away from the carnage; they pushed through the first door they came to and it took them to the outer area of the courtyard. Bijan gave a silent prayer of thanks, guiding Edric around the outskirts of the courtyard. He marked the tree he'd seen when he first arrived and headed for it.

A rough laugh echoed through the courtyard, the sound of footsteps tromping through the centre of the yard.

"Found a live one." A forced laugh punctuated the slice of the air, a weak gurgle, and the low sigh of a man's death rattle. Bijan and Edric dropped low, trying to move slow and not draw unwanted attention. Bijan's thighs screamed a red fire as he crouched; he pushed his weight onto Edric, the young man helping him as they moved toward the exit.

"What'll I do with this one?" Another voice pierced the air, followed by the thud of a body hitting the ground.

"Leave it for now. It'll go over the side with its friends soon enough."

"Do you really think this was their king?"

Edric stiffened and he moved to get a better look. The sallow face and blond hair of Calix stared back at him. His pale blue eyes lifeless, his mouth agape, and blood stained his chin and neck. Dead.

"King? Maybe. Coward, certainly. After he led us to that old man and that pretty little thing, I don't think anyone would call him king material."

Leandra. Edric started again, he pushed against Bijan, trying to rise.

How could Calix do it? He screamed in his mind. How could he betray the king like that? How could he betray Leandra like that?

He pushed again, a low grunt echoing in his chest. It was only Bijan's dead weight that held him back, his eyes frantic, panicked.

"Be calm," Bijan hissed in his ear, "calm."

Edric turned to Bijan, ready to yell at him, ready to lash out and scream. Tears formed at the corners of his eyes. The injured face of the man who'd saved him, the man he'd saved, looked up at him. The sheer look of patience and understanding he found there defused his anger, set his sadness to rights. His dream, his vision, had come true. How could he have expected anything different?

The bandits moved off, looking for more survivors, laughing about all those they had slain already. Bijan could feel Edric tense against him once more. Could feel the heat of anger come from him, but he pointed him to the tree and they moved to it.

"There's the door I came in," Bijan said, putting his weight on the old, sturdy tree. He looked above him, "Where the hell is Boon?" They hadn't had much time to think about the man they'd left in the bowels of the castle, but Bijan was hesitant to move further without him.

"That leads to one of the walkways. It's a quiet place, good for thinking." Edric's eyes glazed some as he spoke, old memories dancing before him. "I haven't walked along that particular one in months. Years?"

Bijan gripped the young man's shoulder. "Are you sure you are ready for this, kid?" Edric's grey eyes filled with tears that threatened to spill down his face. "You're here by your own hand, you can turn back at anytime." Bijan didn't want to dissuade the boy, but he could see there was still some uncertainty in him. The time to shed it or give in to it was close at hand.

"I... I can. I need to leave. There is nothing left here for me, Appolumi's time has finally come." Edric stared at the door, digging at his eyes with the heel of his hand. Bijan nodded.

They waited in silence for some time. The courtyard was dark and quiet, and they heard little more from the patrolling groups. Whether they were raiders or Appolumi militia, it didn't matter, they didn't sweep this far into the courtyard. Judging by the shadows that were moving about, it seemed they were spending most of their time and attention near the heart of the battle that had taken place just hours before.

Boon wasn't coming. It was a realization that Bijan came upon naturally, recognizing the burly Northerner's obsession with the floating castle meant that he wouldn't

— couldn't — leave. Bijan shook his head, his eyes falling on the boy. They all had to make their own choices, but Edric and Boon were on the opposite side of each other. One boy scrambling to leave, the other raging to stay. Bijan sighed, Boon wasn't coming.

"Okay, let's go." He tested his legs without the support of the tree, stretched them out as best he could; they were okay.

"What about your friend, the bear?" Edric's voice didn't quite contain the contempt he had been building, and it brought a strange smile to Bijan's face.

"Kid, he'll have to find his own way." He patted Edric on the back and helped him up from sitting.

The tree was in the centre of the courtyard, so there wasn't any cover between it and the door they aimed for. The sky was lightening in the west, the sun spreading across the land and sky in its dress of orange, yellow, and purple; the clouds crosshatching the light as the rays spilled over the castle, casting harsh shadows in the first light's bright wake. Bijan looked to the sky and shrugged.

"Of all the times for these bloody Northern provinces to be rid of mists, they choose now." A smile rose on his face unhindered and he shook his head. "We'll have to run for it, kid. You feeling up to it?"

"Are you?" Edric gave him a slow once-over, his eyes sticking on Bijan's misused legs.

"I'm still a young man, Boy. I recover quickly." Edric raised his eyebrows and shrugged. "Don't question your elders, kid," Bijan said, pointing a finger at Edric that brought a smile to the boy's face.

'Better,' Bijan thought.

"See if you can keep up." Edric took off in his ambling

way, and Bijan almost felt sorry for him. He followed the kid in his silent, quick way, listening for any sign of pursuit. Nothing. The patrols may have been off getting drunk by this time, for all he knew. More likely they just didn't care much to patrol too far with so many dead around them. Bijan didn't care much either way, as long as they were lax enough to give him a chance to escape. That was always the hardest part, the escape.

They made it to the door at the same time, Edric with a wide smile on his face now, his breath coming hard and quick.

"Not bad for an old man."

Bijan gave him a sidelong glare and reached for the handle when the world suddenly started to quiver.

Edric and Bijan looked at each other in wide-eyed surprise, trying to steady themselves against the shaking that continued to get rougher and rougher.

"Earthquake," Bijan said, bracing himself against the wall.

"We're flying, not likely," Edric said, grabbing at his afflicted hand. "Something's happening with The Circle."

'Boon,' Bijan thought.

"C'mon." He threw open the door and pushed Edric through it. They made their way through the hall and stairway Bijan had taken just days before, though they had to fight at every step for footing and balance.

"It feels like the castle is going to keel over," Edric shouted over the rumbling noise that had grown with the shaking.

"Has this happened before?"

"Never."

Bijan and Edric moved through the stairway and finally to the walkway where Bijan had first landed on the flying castle of Appolumi.

"Here," he said, grabbing the wall he'd scaled before, and felt the brick for some sort of purchase.

"Look," Edric yelled, and pointed to the castle above them. Smoke had begun to billow from it, a thick black cloud that blotted out the light around it.

"Shit," Bijan said, and tried to find handholds once more.

"This way, quick." Edric ran further down the hallway, Bijan on his heels.

Edric pushed through a small hatch-like door, Bijan followed but halted quickly as the long drop to the ground confronted him. Edric's hand appeared before him, the boy's feet on a narrow ledge, his back leaning on the opposite side of the brick wall.

"Convenient." Bijan grabbed Edric's hand and made his way out to join him.

"Where is the rope?" Edric said as he looked over his shoulder.

Bijan pointed to the thick chain that had shot from the castle when they had first triggered the crystal below.

Edric raised his eyebrows again, opened his mouth as if to say something and closed it again. He moved to it, laying one hand on the closest chain link, Edric took a deep breath and wrapped his leg around it.

Bijan watched the boy, eager to get his own start down. The castle behind him continued to shake, the smoke plumed in a heavy dark cloud that blotted out the rising sun. At least it gave them cover, he thought. Though the people of Appolumi had more on their minds than two men escaping.

"It's my hand," Edric said, just two links from where he had started. The glittering of blue crystal was there, drawing Bijan's eye.

'Shit,' Bijan thought. He scurried down the chain, moving quick and economical, and came face to face with the boy in just a space of thought.

"My hand," Edric said, still staring into his palm, "it hurts. I can't grab anything with it, and I don't think I'm strong enough to make it down with just one arm."

The chain shook and swayed with the aftershocks of whatever was happening in the castle. They both held tight until it subsided some. Bijan was thankful for the delay, it had given him some time to think.

"Listen, kid, you want to get off this castle right?" Bijan grabbed Edric by the shoulder, drawing the boy's eyes to his own. "If you want something, you gotta earn it." Edric nodded.

"I'll move on ahead of you, but we'll go down together. We'll take it real slow." Edric nodded again, a nervous sigh cascading through his body. He was as ready as he'd ever be. Bijan dropped down another two links, looked up at Edric, and gave him a thumbs up. Edric started to move in his slow, laborious way, favouring his injured hand and keeping it close to his chest.

That's how their climb went. Bijan moving ahead two or three links, and then waiting for Edric to catch up. They'd both stop and grip the chain tight whenever a quake from the castle shivered down to them. All things considered, the boy did fairly well. He was red-faced and out of breath about halfway down the chain, but he had gotten himself into a rhythm. He continued to use his one good hand for the brunt of the work but started to trust himself enough to use his injured arm to wrap around the chain at the elbow for extra grip when needed. It was when the bodies started to fall past that Edric started to have a real challenge.

The first came and went in something like a flash. An all-white streak that just barely registered in their vision, but they knew something had fallen, or was thrown. If it hadn't been for the long-winded, constant screaming as the bodies went past, Edric and Bijan may never have known what it was until they got to the ground below.

It was impossible to tell who it was, or why they were falling. At some point Bijan could have sworn that he'd made out the garb of Iollan's raiders on several of the falling bodies, though more often than not it was just a blur of colour and sound. Some didn't scream at all, and Bijan imagined they might have been dead already, perhaps dead during battle or dead of fright from the fall. Either way, they were the quiet ones.

Edric put on a strong face, but as each body fell past, he held himself tighter to the chain, his head buried in the large metal links so that he didn't have to look at the destruction as it passed. Bijan gave him his space and moved on.

The dropping bodies stopped as soon as they had started, but the castle took on more violent movements, rocking hard, as if to tear away from the ground and run away from the attack it was evidently under. Bijan dropped to the ground from the second to last link and felt his legs twinge, a shock running through his knotted muscles. He sat on the ground and massaged his tender thighs, breath hissing through his teeth.

Edric was still five links up; he peered down upon Bijan, who beckoned him to hurry. He tried to keep up his momentum, ignoring the shooting pain now coming from his hand, but the chains rattled and shook violently. They were being drawn taut, a small but angry tug that caused the chain to vibrate and wobble in place. Edric looked up at the castle, a stray thought forming in his mind. Hesperos was doing this. He wasn't really dead, and he was trying to escape with the castle. Edric shuddered and moved down another link in the chain.

There was a loud snap that brought both Edric and Bijan's heads around. On the far side of the field one of the chains was flailing loose, broken. The castle tipped to its side, the chain becoming slack and bringing Edric close to the ground.

"Jump, kid!" Bijan was scrambling to his feet and trying to get under Edric to help cushion the boy's fall.

Edric was struck with panic. He could feel his chest tighten, could feel his heartbeat, and he could hear his own inadvertent moaning. He was hanging perpendicular to the ground, his arms and legs supporting him, and if he dropped, he would land directly on his back. He could sense Bijan somewhere below him, but fear kept him in place, trying to decide what to do.

"Quick, Boy, before the castle rights itself and you're tossed off." Bijan jumped in place to try and grab the younger man, but he was just out of reach.

Edric could feel the chains moving again, could hear the groan of the castle as it attempted to right itself. Bijan was right, if he didn't move immediately, he would be tossed likely to his death. With a deep breath to steady himself, Edric let go.

Though he braced for impact, Edric wasn't expecting Bijan to catch him and take the brunt of the fall, and yet, a few moments after letting go, he was lying atop the older man, hearing the laboured breathing of a man as if crushed. Edric rolled to his knees to check on Bijan. Despite a lack of air and a hard cough, he seemed fine, though he was wincing and rolling around on the ground. Edric was helping him sit when the chain close to them snapped, the castle having overcompensated for the initial imbalance.

Edric helped Bijan stand; the older man remained bent over, his hands on his knees for a few moments more, his breathing deep and ragged.

"You're heavier than you look," he mumbled as he stood straight and stretched his back.

The chain sliced through the air, spinning around back and forth; its counterpart on the ground had flailed briefly, but ultimately lay still in the tall grass, just beyond the small hill they now stood upon.

Both men stood watching the castle as it struggled with the chains that still held it. It wouldn't be a drawn-out battle. Edric could see the chains stretching under the strain already.

The castle would not be denied.

Edric saw the black crystal sticking out from a crudely dug hole and moved to it. It was his dream come to life. There were cracks in it now, its black and purple glow was fading, but that didn't surprise him. He knew what was coming, he had seen it all. Had seen the beginning and the end; this was all a part of it. He stretched out his ailing hand, the crystal shards there had also ceased their glow. The crystal greeted the shards eagerly, greedily. He ran his hand over the smooth surface of it, the pain in his hand ebbing some.

In the distance he heard the snapping of another chain, heard Bijan's surprised moan, and heard the air quiver with the rocking of the castle as it struggled to free itself from its last binding.

Edric took his hand away from the crystal. The shards

had disappeared, and all that was left was a strange looking circle of wounds and a trickle of blood. He turned his
gaze back to the black crystal and could see some of the
dings and cracks had healed, all of them, in fact, save for
one large piece that seemed to have been gouged out of
the centre. Edric knew that piece lay in the neck of the
man Bijan had called Iollan, dead in the bowels of the castle. Without it, the crystal before him — a signal used to
call the castle to it — would never be whole again. Edric
nodded at that.

"Look," Bijan said from the hill, his long arm pointing to the final chain that held tight. It was stretching and
twisting and, as Edric looked on, it snapped, sending the
castle higher into the air.

Appolumi had broken free.

CHAPTER THIRTY-FIVE

Obelius was right behind them, cursing and salivating as he slashed the knife through the air: the knife with the king's blood on it. Leandra pulled Alethea behind her, forcing the old woman to run on her short legs, trying to forget the pain and grief of her father's death. The outrage.

"Princess," Alethea said, panting, "Leandra, I can't... I can't...." The old woman fell to her knees, a crash that took the breath from her lungs and sent her face-first into the stone floor. Leandra gasped and turned to comfort her fallen handmaiden, but Obelius stood over her. A disconcerting smile splitting his lips.

The corridors were empty, and a strange silence pervaded them and the rest of castle. It was unnerving, unworldly. The castle wasn't supposed to be this quiet; it had never been. Leandra wished the throngs of panicked people were still pushing past them, that Calix came marching in with his troops, or that sweet Edric would arrive just in time with a flourish of his sword, just as he always did when they played as children.

Obelius crouched atop of Alethea, one hand wrapped in her hair and pulling her head back, the other placing the blade of his dagger to her throat. The handmaiden was crying.

"Enough of this, Leandra," Obelius' face was distorted with contempt. "Don't make me kill poor Alethea in your place."

Leandra clenched her fists together. "Yes, Obelius, this is quite enough. Release Alethea and drop the knife."

A moment of uncertainty crossed Obelius' face. His hand stuttered next to the older woman's throat. But then the lopsided smile returned, the same ugly smirk that had haunted her since she was a girl.

"Still have some of that royal authority running in your veins, princess?" Obelius tightened his grip on his dagger. "There's no one left to listen to your orders, Leandra." He ran his knife along Alethea's neck, blood pouring to the floor beneath her. "No one."

Leandra's hand shot to her mouth to stifle the gasp and scream that threatened to escape as Obelius dropped Alethea's head to the floor with a dreadful thump. Leandra's eyes were watering as Obelius uncoiled himself from the ground.

"Obelius... put the knife down," Leandra choked, tears running a hesitant stream over her cheeks. She took a slow step backwards.

"No, princess. I don't think I will."

Leandra turned on her heel and ran towards the door at the end of the hall. Obelius panted a hideous laugh as he followed. His old legs pumping to catch up with her.

Head down, tears drying on her cheeks, Leandra consciously avoided looking over her shoulder, afraid to see Obelius' claw-like hand reaching for her. She focused on the door. 'Just get to the door,' she thought, 'get there and worry about what's beyond after.' Leandra looked towards the door; so close. But there was something wrong;

the door wasn't empty. A shadow stood within it, hulking, unnatural, and alien. And then she froze and her mind shut down. The fear of Obelius disappeared, the grief of her father's death was pushed to the background, the horror of Alethea's murder before her now forgotten. All that remained was that shadow and whatever was creating it.

She vaguely felt Obelius grab her around the neck, his thin hands rough and eager, but her eyes didn't waver from the doorway. Leandra had a slight inclination that Obelius had started to say something, but it trailed off, as did his grip on her neck. She had no doubt that his eyes were now also on the person that stepped through the doorway.

He was an agent of the enemy, there was no other way around it. The man that moved out of the shadows was a hulking brute, with shaggy hair and a beard covering his features. Strung about his shoulders was a bear skin cloak, and his arms, which protruded from torn sleeves, were covered in tattoos that neither Leandra nor Obelius could understand. In a distant part of her mind Leandra recognized that this man, a full foot taller than the lanky Obelius, had blood dried on his hands, and that there may indeed be some staining his beard and mouth. All of that became secondary to his eyes. Harsh blue eyes that seemed to ignore the shadows and shined brightly in spite of the dark. Except that when Leandra first saw them, they appeared to be red.

"Greetings," Obelius' quivering voice came from beside her. "I offer you a gift, in exchange for safe passage away from this castle." Obelius' hand pushed Leandra forward, but kept her tight in his grasp.

"This is the Princess of Appolumi, Leandra, daughter of the King Vaselious. Last in her line and rightful heir to the throne. Such as it is."

The stranger's eyes were firmly set on Obelius until he mentioned Leandra's lineage. At that, he turned his weird eyes on her, something like surprise mirrored within them. The stare was only for a moment, but Leandra could hardly bear to be under that scrutiny for even that short of a time. She cringed away from it and Obelius had to fight to push her forward again.

The large man gripped Leandra tightly around the bicep and pulled her toward him; she refused to look him in the face. She could feel the heat coming from the stranger, could hear his heavy breathing, and feel his breath on her hair. She shivered, and though her mind and body screamed for her to fight and run, she knew it was of no use. If this man wouldn't take her, then it would be Obelius or someone else. Her life was at an end. Even if she managed to escape, her father was dead, her birthright rousted from her, and her home was in ruins. Nothing could save her from this ending, not even Edric and his childhood battle plans.

"There, now, I'm sure that the only remaining heir of Appolumi should fetch me a free —" Obelius was cut off. Leandra barely registered the stranger releasing her from his grip when the choking sounds began. Unconsciously, she turned toward them and saw Obelius raised from the ground, his face a mask of surprise and anguish.

The stranger had wrapped his ham-sized hand around Obelius' thin neck. So completely did it cover the man's throat that it looked as though the stranger was close to popping Obelius' head off rather than just choking him. The stranger didn't stop there. He continued to walk forward, a growl coming from his expansive chest and back. His arm, thickly corded with muscle, rippled as fresh pressure was applied to the former advisor's neck.

Confusion turned Leandra from the scene, her tears starting anew. She slid against the nearest wall and sat on the floor, fighting to hold back her sobs. She allowed herself only a few moments of grief, of relief, and then forced herself back to the task at hand: survival. The world as she knew it was at an end, but she had to hope there was something else out there for her. At the very least, vengeance against those that perpetrated this attack upon her kingdom; her home.

Obelius' knife lay off to the side, discarded when the large man grabbed him. Leandra picked it up by the handle between her thumb and forefinger. This was the dagger that killed her father, and then Alethea. It was charged with the blood of her loved ones. She took a better grip on it, her hand feeling its weight around the leather bound handle. Its grip was firm, but slick. She wiped it on her pants leg, the blood leaving a dark purple stain.

Leandra stood in the hope that she could make a run for it, but the stranger was back, one of his hands was clenching open and closed. She looked past him and saw the sole of one boot, its toes pointing to the air. Obelius was dead.

"Come, we must go," the stranger said in a gruff voice.

"I can't. I need to find my..."

"Everyone here is dead, girl. If you don't want to join them, you'll come with me."

Leandra blinked. Could what he was saying be true? Her father was dead, Alethea was dead, could Edric have fallen as well? "What's your name?" Leandra said, poking the air in front of her with the tip of her blade. She wasn't sure why she'd asked. It mattered little to the situation, and yet it flowed from her mouth as though it were a re-flex.

The stranger gave her a lopsided look, but the corners of his mouth tugged some at the question. "The name is Vali."

Leandra nodded and, wiping a single tear from her eye, walked towards him, her blade before her. "Lead the way."

The man, whose blue eyes now took on the excitement of a child, nodded in return and proceeded through the corridor.

Leandra followed close behind. Freedom.

CHAPTER THIRTY-SIX

It felt different, the uneven ground that Edric now stood upon. Better. The grass tickled his ankles as he moved his feet up and down, testing the earth. It was soft and welcoming, and he felt the urge to lie down and let it caress his whole body. The rich scent of soil, of flowers, that hung in the air excited and calmed him. He could feel the air enter his lungs, feel it fill them to capacity. He sighed, a smile upon his face.

"Haugr is just beyond those trees," a harried Bijan said at his side. "Careful of this grass here," he said as he stepped away from the small hill they had been standing upon.

Edric looked to the blue sky as it began to turn purple, the clouds restless. Mist swirled in the wake of castle Appolumi as it floated away, dark smoke wafting from it as it moved. Edric's chest tightened and he tried not to think about the fate of the castle. He rubbed at his eyes and made to follow Bijan to the trees. Memories rose in him as he moved. He could remember his father's eyes sparkling in the shade of those trees. His father watched him cry while he was chained to the marker that now stood to his back. The same trees where he engaged the bear in his Trial-fueled dreams: its dark and prophetic words still haunting his thoughts.

"It's strange," he said as he stepped into the tall grass, feeling the pull on his legs.

"Don't disturb the grass," Bijan said as he turned toward Edric, his eyes wide and mouth agape.

"Not the grass, the ground. It's still, solid." A broad smile grew on his face, unbidden but welcome.

"You'll get used to it," Bijan said around a small smile of his own and pointed to the trees. "Don't doddle." Bijan moved on. Edric followed in his own time.

***

"Be careful," Bijan said. They crept along the path just outside of the small town. "We didn't leave these people on the best of terms."

Edric crouched low to the ground, following Bijan's lead as best he could. He tried to remember this place. He wanted to remember it, but nothing would come. He knew he had been born in this village, that his parents likely still lived there, but he couldn't remember anything before the chains, the black crystal, and the castle.

Haugr was dark in the early evening. The lamps were turned down, the doors closed, and it was eerily quiet, aside from the squawks and groans of the animals in their pens. It seemed small. The squat, separated shacks open to the elements. Brittle, exposed.

"Let's get out of here," Edric said as he moved around Bijan, who had stopped to look in on a goat in its pen.

Bijan hurried to catch up with him. "I had a goat like that once. I named him Cans," he smiled.

Edric ignored him and pushed on through the small village.

***

They had made a small camp in a lightly wooded area off the path that had led to Haugr. Edric woke feeling both exhilaration and disappointment. What if the world was just a series of villages like Haugr? Small, backwards, inconsequential. He looked to Bijan for the answer but started to doubt there was much he could glean from him. Edric pictured the castle, its brightness. He remembered how well ordered it was, how clean, how engaging. Leaving that for Haugr was just as if he left a world of colour for one of only grey. Even the books Bijan had managed to pack for him were merely a sample of what the castle had offered.

They moved further along the path, the sky brightening despite a light cover of fog. Bijan was in good spirits and hummed a jovial tune to himself as they walked. The bag of books had become much heavier on Edric's shoulder. They hiked up a small hill; Edric found the elevated ground annoyed him more than anything else, and his calves began to ache. When they breached the top of the hill, the treeline had been pushed back, the sky was a bright blue and the sun was warm on their faces. Edric paused at what stood before him: land, trees, mountains, skies. In the distance, along the horizon, there was a hint of blue ocean. Edric dropped his bag and stared out before him.

"It's a fair sight," said Bijan as he stared back at Edric. "Now, if you want to see something magnificent, I can take you to the south. To my homeland. There we will shed this uncomfortable cold and unwavering mist to feel the sun and heat on our cheeks. I may even take you to see the Tower of Akas Mehul, though from afar, I think." Bijan continued on, his voice fading as he made his way down the other side of the hill.

Edric looked toward the widening horizon and smiled. He picked up his bag of books and walked after Bijan. He hoped their path would lead them on to the ocean.

EPILOGUE

The boy didn't have much in the way of skill anymore, thought Bijan as he scaled the craggy stone wall of the broken tower, but he was certainly able to do research. Bijan had been searching for clues about the location of the Baltus Tower for years. He had given the boy his notes and he had a location in a matter of days. If he hadn't been so happy, Bijan's pride may have felt a twinge of pain.

"You hanging in there, Boy?" Bijan called, feeling the rope tied around his waist tugging at him.

"Can... can we slow down?" Edric said, breathless, as he looked up at Bijan, who seemed tireless.

"Slow down?" Bijan stopped and turned to look at Edric the best he could. "Aren't you excited? Who knows what this tower holds? What treasures it may reveal. We can't stop now!" A sly smile crossed his face as he started up the wall once more. "Besides can't you just float up here or something?"

Edric frowned. "You know I can't do that anymore."

Bijan could tell the boy's mood was on its way to sullen. He did that from time to time, often when he thought about magic and the like. Bijan couldn't really blame him.

"Come on then, tell us a little more about the Baltus

Tower?"

"Well, in the histories you provided me, there was some mention of a curse..."

"A curse? Gods damn it! Why didn't you say something before?" Bijan slowed his ascent and swung into a large divot in the wall, where two men could fit with little comfort. Edric soon joined him.

They sat in silence for some time; Bijan mulled over the implications of the possible curse and Edric tried to regain his wind in deep, shaky breaths. Once Edric had his breathing under control, Bijan asked him to elaborate on the tower's curse.

"Well, essentially, the texts have said that anyone who enters the tower is subject to the scrutiny of Baltus. Those who are deemed unworthy will be reduced by plague to suffer an excruciating death." Edric wiped his forehead with the sleeve of his shirt.

"Sounds more like a trap than a curse." Bijan stood and regained his hand and foot holds on the wall. "And what about those deemed worthy?" Bijan raised his eyebrows, waiting.

Edric dug into his bag and pulled out a scroll, running his finger over the small words. "Well, it says here that, should one be deemed worthy," he looked over his nose at Bijan, "Baltus will bless you with the treasures of his... people? His kingdom? Something along those lines."

"Well, let's hope that whatever it is, there is a lot of it. Come along, wizard. We must be on time if we want Baltus to think we're worthy." Edric rolled his eyes and hurried to pack up his bag once more and get his own hold on the wall as the line around his waist kept getting tighter and tighter.

Bijan started to move out of the divot, dragging himself up by his arms.

"Wait," Edric said in a louder voice than he intended. "How can you be sure we won't be walking into a curse?"

"I can't," Bijan said, flashing a smile as he started his slow climb.

Edric grinned. The air was fresh, and he could feel the midday sun on his back and neck. Adventure, and the world, was ahead.

THE END

AFTERWORD

First, I'd like to thank Ashlee, Thomas, Brianna, Conan, and all my family and friends, who have provided the love and support as I continue on this writing journey.

I'd also like to thank my beta readers, Steve Power and Lauralana Dunne, who gave me some great feedback and guided me to a better story.

Thanks to Write Club, though COVID has kept us apart this last little while, I want you all to know that you are the bee's knees.

Special thanks go out to Ali House and AJ Ryan who helped edit the original mess I turned in, and Mandi Coates and Jon Mercer for awesome cover art!

Finally, thanks to Matt, Ellen, Erin, Amanda, and Matthew of Engen books for believing in this little book.

ON SALE NOW FROM ENGEN BOOKS

"Dunne breathes life into a world of magic and lore that will draw the reader in right up to the epic conclusion. Ashes is a heroic tale not to be missed."
Amanda Labonté
bestselling author of Supenatural Causes

When fifteen-year-old Phoenix loses her caregiver, everyone that she has ever known inexplicably turn their backs on her. Given the impossible burden of repaying an unknown debt, Phoenix sets out on her own with her trusty donkey, Muler, as her only companion. A chance encounter with Malcourt, a mysterious traveller, not only saves her life, but sets it on a trajectory that she would have never thought possible.

ABOUT THE AUTHOR

Jon Dobbin is an award winning author living in the St. John's, Newfoundland metro region.

He is a father of three, the husband to an amazing wife, an educator, and a tattoo and beard enthusiast.

Dobbin's work has appeared in the *Terror Nova, Chillers from the Rock, Dystopia from the Rock, Pulp Science-Fiction from the Rock, From the Rock Stars,* and, *Kit Sora: The Artobiography* collections. In 2019 he released his first novel, *The Starving.*

The Broken Spire is his second novel.